Driftwood Diary

Kate Boudreaux

Gilded Press

Boston, Massachusetts

www.gildedpressbooks.com

Driftwood Diary

Cover photography by Jurgen Lorenzen

Author photography by Esther Fuller

ISBN: 9798986466149 (hardcover)

ISBN: 9798986466132 (paperback)

ISBN: 9798986466156 (ebook)

First Edition: April 2023

For Max

"The light shines in the darkness, and the darkness can never extinguish it."

— John 1:5

Driftwood Diary

One

Galveston, Texas - 2008

"Have you made a decision about the baby?"

My gaze falls to Dr. Gregory's hands. The smooth skin. Polished nails filed square. The large diamond heavy on her left hand, spinning slightly as she turns the page of her notebook. Her honey blond hair is pulled back, revealing a graceful neck and small ears. She's put together in a way that only the rich can attain, and I can't help begrudge her obvious privilege. I bet she's never wanted for anything. Never experienced the kind of neglect she pretends to understand.

I consider the sparse room I share with nine other women. The rickety metal bed. Thin, musty mattress. Working at a shelter is much different than living at one.

When I look up, Dr. Gregory's brown eyes are warm, but

calculating. I'm a puzzle to solve. A task to complete and file in an identifiable category of crazy. But I don't fit in a neat little box. I'm not a broken toy she can patch and paint and mend. She just doesn't know it yet.

I narrow my eyes and press a hand to my stomach. "I'm keeping it," I say, unable to hide my animosity.

Dr. Gregory smiles. "Of course. We're here to support any path you choose. Miss Janie and I will have you back on your feet in no time. We have a very high success rate with helping young mothers learn the skills they need to be independent. Some even go on to attend college."

I frown, thinking the idea of college a little far-fetched for someone with a brand-new baby and a limited education. "So, you'll help me find a job?"

She picks up her pen. "We will certainly try. But we can discuss that at a later time."

"Please." I lean forward. "I'd really like to talk about it now."

"Alright. Do you have any previous work experience that may help us place you somewhere?"

I swallow hard. "I've taken care of babies."

Dr. Gregory writes something down. "Like at a daycare?"

"No ..." I twist my hands in my lap, unsure how to explain.

Her brows pinch together. "Do you have any references?"

I shake my head and stare at my lap, my hopes sinking by the minute.

She smiles. "Why don't we move on. Miss Janie told me you've been having nightmares. Can you tell me about them?"

"They're kind of hard to explain."

"Just do your best."

"Um ... I'm always alone," I say, my hair prickling on the back of my neck at the recollection. "I'm floating in the ocean, trying to keep my head above the water. But the harder I try, the farther I sink ... until I'm under the water. Except it's not water anymore. It's blood. My blood."

Dr. Gregory writes something in her notebook and taps her pen on the paper. "I think it's clear this is a side effect from your recent ordeal. With time, the dreams should become less frequent and then hopefully disappear completely. I'm going to recommend some tea to help you sleep, and we'll talk more next time I'm in the office."

My pulse pounds with anger. "But I thought you were going to help me."

She removes her glasses and places them beside her notebook with care. She's stalling. But why? I hold my breath, as she tilts her head and searches for words. "Max, you seem like a very sweet girl. A bright girl. But I think you need more time to come to terms with your experience before we can move to the next step." She indicates the gash on my head, crusty with salve and thirty-four stitches. "You need to rest and heal before we talk more."

I slap my palms on her desk. "No. I don't have time. I need someone to listen."

Her eyes widen and she extends her hands in what is meant to be a soothing gesture. "You're going to need to calm down."

Feelings of betrayal bubble to the surface. At first, all I wanted was to be free. But now I want justice. Dr. Gregory promised to help me, and I believed her. Trusted her. But she's just like everyone else. Out for herself.

My vision blurs as tears spill over, my body trembling with a need to be heard.

She folds her hands together and leans forward. "Please don't cry, Max. If you feel you're ready, then I'll hear what you have to say. But first, I want you to listen to me."

I wipe my eyes and take a calming breath. Even though I feel I'm about to explode with the desire for someone, anyone, to understand.

She opens a drawer and removes a dark green folder. A sheet of paper covered in someone's handwriting slides across the polished oak desk. "Do you know what this is?"

"No," I say, squinting at the even handwriting.

"It's the testimony you gave police the day you were admitted to the hospital."

My mind races as I try to conjure the events. Water. Blood. Salt. Bright lights. Nurses. A needle in my arm. A man in a uniform. The scratch of his pencil as I answer questions.

She flips the pages, scanning. "I've tried to make it out, but most of the story is pretty incoherent. Given your head trauma, the authorities have agreed to hold off on investigating your claims until I've had a chance to evaluate you properly."

My mouth gapes. "You think I'm lying?"

She shakes her head. "No. I don't. But your health and safety is my first priority. In order to truly help, I have to make sure you're ready." Her expression softens. "In order to bring your testimony to the authorities, I need to make sure you are of sound mind. Do you understand?"

"Yes. I understand. I promise I'm ready."

After a moment, her shoulders relax and she nods. "I'll need you to tell me your story again. I need every detail, even the things you may think are inconsequential."

"Of course. I'll tell you everything. Everything I can remember, at least."

She indicates the sofa next to her desk. "Perhaps you should make yourself more comfortable."

I lie on the blue velvet and fold my hands together.

"Now, I want you to relax. In order to capture your complete experience, I'm going to use a hypnosis technique called memory manipulation. It's nothing to be afraid of. You will simply be put into a dreamlike state. This will relax your mind and bring forth certain details that may be otherwise forgotten. But you must trust me completely. Do you trust me, Max?"

The question strikes me as funny. At this point, I'm not sure I'm even capable of trust. But she's my only chance. My only hope for justice.

"Yes," I say.

"Then let's get started."

I listen to the sound of her voice, my limbs growing heavy. As I relax, images flash, conjuring people and places like snippets of a forgotten newspaper.

Memories are strange things. Most fade in and out, slippery as an eel and hard to place. Some are gone completely, whole years vanished into darkness without my consent. Then, there are those too important to forget. Crisp and clear, like the inside of a prism, glittering and cutting a path that's strange and bright and painful. Pictures that play like a carousel. Over and over, without rest. My eyelids fall and I'm there. Where it all started. In the beginning.

Two

New Orleans, Louisiana - 1999

"Max. Wake up, bébé." Maggie gives me a gentle shake and my eyes open. The faint glow of the television illuminates her profile. The small chin, full lips, aristocratic nose.

I sit up, my cot shifting on thin aluminum legs, grinding into the faded linoleum. "Are we going trick-or-treating?"

She drops clothing into my lap. "Be a good girl and put them on. Quick now."

I blink in the dim light, a rush of excitement at the prospect of going door-to-door for candy. "Can I wear my fairy costume?"

She points to R.J. snoring in the recliner, one arm thrown over his face. His yellowed western shirt is unbuttoned, a half-empty bottle tucked in the crook of his elbow.

Confusion turns to disappointment as I realize I was wrong. There will be no costume, only a simple shirt and shorts, like every other day.

With my dreams of Halloween dashed, I want to bury my head in the safety of my blankets and go back to sleep. But all I can do is watch in silence as Maggie shoves some of our clothes into a plastic Walmart bag that dangles from her forearm. The light catches a new purple blotch on her cheek as she bends to fasten the thin straps of my pink sandals. Her hands shake as she fumbles with the clasp. I want to ask where we are going, but the threat of R.J.'s temper keeps me quiet.

She slides the deadbolt with a soft click and ushers me through the door. Washed in green flickering light, the hall outside our apartment is as hollow and unloved as the rest of the complex. Someone is yelling in 3B, followed by the sound of glass breaking.

"Where're we going?"

Maggie's voice is bright, her palm sweaty as it presses into my back. "We're going on an adventure."

I want to question her more. But I don't. I never do. I've been taught to respect my elders. To know my place. Which means no talking back, no matter how sick I am of moving from house to house. School to school. Man to man. For as long as I can remember, I've just wanted to be still. Be normal.

Canal Street feels strange in the dark, and I have to run to keep up, my feet tripping across the warm, damp pavement as Maggie pulls me along. Even in October, the weather hasn't cooled. The air is soft and heavy, like a well-worn cloak.

As we turn the corner, a nun on a bike speeds past, her habit flapping wildly behind her.

I tug on Maggie's arm at the sight, but she says it's just a costume.

"Why can't we go trick-or-treating?"

"Because we have somewhere more important to go. Besides you're getting too old for that, anyhow."

I heave a sigh, unsatisfied with her excuse. I want candy and costumes and friends. I want to skip through the Garden District, ringing doorbells and peeking through mail slots of the grand old homes. Instead, I'm on the big people's side of town. The busy French Quarter, where police sirens mingle with faint strains of jazz and Halloween is just another excuse to get drunk.

Adults in costume shuffle past, loud and stumbling. One man pauses long enough to puke onto the sidewalk, a frothy mixture that smells like stomach acid and whiskey. The same scent that lingers in the bathroom long after R.J. has left for work.

A block shy of Bourbon Street, Landry's red mustang is parked by the curb, windows down, radio blaring. Maggie opens the door and tells me to get in.

Landry flicks her cigarette onto the street, the last drag seeping from her nose to mingle with her perfume. Something sweet and fruity. Her signature scent.

She might be Maggie's first cousin, but the two look nothing alike. Landry is all legs and curves, with fair skin and red lips, while Maggie is thin and angular with dark eyes and hair, like me.

Ample cleavage strains against Landry's cheetah print dress as she tosses her head to the side. With long hair bleached white on the ends, I think she looks like a real-life Barbie, complete with a tiny waist and shiny sports car. I've made up my mind to be just like her when I grow up.

"Just look how big you are," she says into the rearview mirror. "My little sugar bee is growing up too fast."

I smile at the compliment, enjoying the look of pride on Landry's face. But it's not long before disdain clouds her beautiful blue eyes at the sight of Maggie's fresh bruises.

"I hope you've had enough of that son of a bitch, because this is the last time I'm doing this shit," Landry says with narrowed eyes. "Max deserves a better start than you and me had."

Maggie lights a cigarette and takes a long drag. "That's exactly why we're going to Texas. I'm done with everything. You may be content to spend the rest of your life on a pole at the Penthouse. But I'm not."

Landry bites her lip but doesn't respond, quieting the conversation until we reach the long, straight bridge spanning Lake Pontchartrain. Black, choppy water glistens below, stretching to an infinite horizon, and I shiver at the thought of going over the edge. Sinking into the dark violence of the waves.

Landry breaks the silence. "You're wrong about me, Maggie. I have dreams just like you."

Maggie turns to the window, staring into the pitch. "Dreams and plans are two different things."

———

The bus from Baton Rouge to Beaumont is crowded with people and the sickly sweet scent of cheap air freshener. I lean on the window, the cool glass smooth against my forehead, and my stomach rumbles.

"I'm hungry," I whisper.

Maggie pulls a bottle of water from her purse and hands it to me. "Here, bébé. This is all I have. But we're almost to Beaumont."

The woman in front of us turns around, her smile wide and coffee-stained. Short hair sticks out from her head in all directions and fuchsia cat-eye reading glasses are perched on her nose. I like the way the tiny rhinestones glitter when she bobs her head and wonder what they would look like on me.

"Would your little girl like to have this?" she asks, holding out a bar of chocolate wrapped in orange plastic. "I'm watching my cholesterol."

It feels odd for a stranger to acknowledge Maggie as my mother. Most people assume she's an older sister, or something, and she likes it that way. "You can't go around calling me 'Mama,' you hear? It's bad for business," she always says before we leave the house. The funny thing is, I don't remember ever needing the reprimand. She's been Maggie forever, even in my thoughts.

She takes the candy with a smile. "You sure?"

"Of course, bébé." Maggie's elbow digs into my ribs. "What do you say?"

"Thank you, ma'am."

"Well aren't you just a little doll," the woman says with a

wink. "Such ladylike manners. You don't hear that much these days."

Maggie's eyes sparkle at the praise, her smile lingering while I devour the candy.

"Listen, bébé," she whispers as I lick chocolate from my fingers. "I have something real important I've been waiting to tell you. We aren't going to Aunt Dorothy's."

Relief washes over me at the memory of the old woman's house in Beaumont. Garbage piled high in the garage. *Wheel of Fortune* blaring in the den. A mangy Chihuahua dragging its butt across orange shag carpet.

"But, I thought ..."

Maggie takes my hand and squeezes. "Forget all that. I couldn't tell Landry this. But I'm gonna tell you because you're getting bigger now. Eleven is almost a young lady, you know."

I smile, enjoying the idea of knowing something important.

She pulls a crumpled letter from her purse. "Do you remember Mr. Delacroix from the Y2K meetings?"

I nod, thinking of the tall, handsome man who pulled us aside after it was over.

Maggie smooths the pages in her lap. "Well, since he left New Orleans, he's been sending me letters. Secret letters all about what the government is up to. Here, you can read this last one." She hands me the paper and leans close, breathless with excitement. "There's no telling what's gonna happen come January first. I mean, the whole world could fall apart and then what? But Jude has it all figured out, and he's giving us the opportunity of a lifetime. He's invited us to live with him. It's the only way we'll be safe."

R.J. says Y2K is a crock of shit, but Maggie's fear of the clock striking midnight has become our constant companion in the past months. Ever since attending Mr. Delacroix's first lecture, to be exact. Standing room only, we squeezed into the musty back room of the florist shop on Canal Street among other wide-eyed souls mesmerized by his top-secret knowledge of governmental affairs and the fallout the year 2000 would inevitably bring. As the lecture concluded, anxiety warred with excitement, creating an intoxicating mix that left the crowd hungry for more. But only a select few were invited to stay after. Three from what I remember. All young women. All beautiful.

When I shake my head, Maggie holds up a finger.

"No. None of that," she scolds. "You haven't even heard the best part. You'll never believe where he lives."

"Where?"

"An *island*."

I gulp. Could it be possible? A real island? Like the kind in *Swiss Family Robinson*? Surely not.

"Ain't that something?" Maggie continues. "We'll have a whole new family. A whole new chance at the life we were always meant to have." She hugs my shoulders as I try to absorb the information. I want to believe her words are true, but I tamp down the hope. She lowers her voice to a whisper. "Plus, out there away from everybody, we'll be safe. Completely self-sufficient. Jude says we could all live the rest of our lives without needing anything from the outside world. It's like some kind of miracle, ain't it?"

I agree, but part of me doubts such a place really exists.

When she drops her purse in my lap and retreats into the

bathroom at the back of the bus, I study Mr. Delacroix's letter, fixating of the last sentence Maggie is instructed to memorize.

Be fruitful and multiply, and fill the earth, and subdue it; and rule over the fish of the sea and over the birds of the sky and over every living thing that moves on the earth.

After a moment, the woman in front of us turns back around. "Honey, can I borrow a pen out of your mama's purse?"

I feel a moment of panic at the request and hesitate, not sure how to answer. "I don't know if she has one," I finally say.

"Give it here, sweet pea, and I'll take a quick look. Won't take a minute. Promise."

"Um. I don't think ..."

The woman's eyes turn to slits, but her smile stays in place. "You wouldn't want me to tell your mama you're being rude, now would you?" Reaching through the seats, she clutches the strap before I can respond.

My heart beats fast as she tugs the purse from my lap. I lean forward, trying to see as she rifles through the contents. Within moments, she produces a blue ink pen and begins scribbling on a post card. I sigh in relief and settle back in my seat, content when she returns the purse to my lap a moment later.

"See now? That wasn't hard, was it?"

When I shake my head, she reaches into her own purse and pulls out a beautiful silver ring with an oval stone.

"This mood ring was my daughter's, but she outgrew it. Would you like to have it?"

"Oh, yes!" I say, allowing her to slip it onto my finger.

"Look," she says, pointing to the ring as it changes color on my finger. "Purple means you're very happy."

"What's that?" Maggie asks, sliding into the seat beside me.

The woman waves her hand in the air. "Oh, just something I had lying around in my purse. I'm glad it found a good home."

Maggie hugs my shoulders. "Well, isn't that the nicest thing."

The woman smiles. "Don't mention it."

THREE

The bus to Galveston idles by the roadside as Maggie stirs the contents of her purse.

"Ma'am?" The driver clears his throat and leans forward. "Ma'am, there are others waiting to board. If you don't have the fee, I'll have to ask you to step out of line."

People behind us shift and cough.

"No. I have it," Maggie says, her lip beaded with sweat. She pulls out several items then turns to me. "Max, have you seen my wallet?"

"No, ma'am."

"You're sure?"

I nod.

"It can't be gone," she whispers, closing her eyes.

"What's wrong?" I ask.

Collecting her things, she pulls me to a bench by the curb and speaks quietly. "Back there on the bus, did you see anyone touch my purse? Pick it up to move it or anything?" Her brows knit together. "Or when I went to the bathroom? You held it the whole time, right?"

I clutch my new ring to my chest and think of the woman with rhinestone glasses.

"Max? I asked you a question. Did anyone else touch my purse?"

My nose burns and a tear rolls down my cheek.

"Who? Tell me!" she demands, drawing looks from the crowd.

"I think it was that lady," I sob, not making eye contact. "The one who gave me this." I hold up my hand. "She wanted to borrow a pen. I ... tried to tell her no."

Maggie blinks, unable to comprehend the offense. "No. No, it couldn't have been that nice woman. It probably just fell out somehow ..." Her voice trails off.

"What'll we do now?"

She looks at the feeder road leading to the interstate. "We find another way. Nothing's impossible with the right attitude. Come on."

We head west on I-10, walking along the shoulder, ignoring the speeding cars and exhaust fumes. By the time we get to the outside of town, the sun is high and my hair is plastered to the back of my neck. Soggy rice fields stretch out in all directions, ugly and vast. It's a lonely stretch of road. A forgotten place to endure on the way to better things.

My plastic sandals pinch hot blisters with each step, and damp blotches appear on Maggie's shirt as she switches our bags from her right shoulder to her left then back again.

I stop and stare at my feet. "Can I take these off?"

She nods and waits for me to slip them off. But the pavement feels like fire, and I cry out, hopping from foot to foot.

"That won't work," she mumbles with a shake of her head.

I slide the sandals back on with a wince, but the whooshing noise of air brakes diverts my attention to an eighteen-wheeler pulling over ahead of us. A glimmer of hope, then fear, forms as a short man with a scruffy red beard climbs from the cab.

Maggie squeezes my shoulder. "Looks like it's our lucky day."

"You're not scared?" I whisper.

"Of what?"

I look at her bruised face and the optimism there is unsettling. Life has already taught me to be cautious. Judge a situation carefully. Never trust completely. But Maggie is different. Opposite of me in every way. I feel her vulnerability to my marrow with no way to make her stronger. Better. Smarter. Sometimes I hate her for it. But how can I hate the person I love most in the world? It's a question that grows and lingers in the back of my mind, a constant source of guilt.

The truck driver comes closer, removing his hat to reveal a few greasy strands stuck to a pale scalp. He stops and spits a stream of tobacco over his left shoulder. "Can I help you, ma'am? You and the kid don't need to be out here like this. Lots of bad folks passing through this strip."

Maggie takes a step forward. "We hate to be any trouble. But we would appreciate a ride. I'm Maggie Fontaine, by the way."

"Doug Adams, out of Wichita Falls."

She glances at the huge white sacks of powder in the back of his truck. "What are you hauling?"

"Catalyst. Use it inside them cat crackers over at the Marathon plant."

"Oil industry?"

"That's right."

"You headed to Galveston, by chance?"

"Texas City, but it's close enough."

When we squeeze into the passenger seat of Doug's massive truck, I stiffen, gripping Maggie's knee as he takes a case knife from his pocket and flips open the blade.

"Ouch!" Maggie says, swatting my hand away.

Trepidation turns to relief as Doug retrieves an empty Coke can from the cup holder and uses the knife to cut around the rim. He shoves a napkin into the can, followed by a long stream of tobacco juice. "Does this bother you, ma'am? Nasty habit, I know. Tried to quit a million times."

"Not at all."

He grins and holds the can up. "Y'all want one? A Coke, I mean. Got plenty right here." He points to a small cooler positioned between the front seats. "Some snacks in there too."

An hour later, we chug to a stop behind other trucks waiting for entrance into the Marathon plant.

"This is the end of the line for me," Doug says, turning in his seat. "You sure you'll be okay from here?"

Maggie opens the door and nods with her usual optimism. "Absolutely."

"Wait," he says, opening the cooler and tossing us a couple of drinks for the road. "It's still a little jag to Galveston."

With the help of a blue-haired lady in a gold Cadillac, the long walk from Texas City to Galveston is gladly avoided, even at twenty miles below the speed limit. The ride is filled with gospel music and a detailed listing of the woman's ailments dating back to her first round of chemo in 1987. But she is kind and eager to help, driving us all the way to the seawall where she parks at the curb.

"We're here," Maggie says, her eyes bright and unblinking.

I look out over the unending sea, the waves rolling and ceaseless.

The woman picks up a tiny worn book from the dash. "Here you go, sweetheart. Go on and take this with you. Goodness knows I've got my use out of it."

Maggie accepts the gift with a nervous laugh.

The woman leans forward. "Just remember, when you lose your way, there's truth in there."

Maggie thanks her for the ride, and the woman studies us a moment. "'Be not forgetful to entertain strangers: for thereby some have entertained angels unawares.'"

As she drives away, Maggie looks at the book a moment.

"What is it?" I say, unable to see the spine.

"Nothing we need," she says, tossing it into a wire trash can by the road. I watch it tumble to the bottom, landing next to a shriveled banana peel.

She turns to the ocean. "Would you just look at us?" Her eyes close, arms stretching wide. Her face is pink, seamless, glowing in the afternoon sun. For a moment, I let myself feel her happiness, bright and warm and sure.

"Race you," she challenges, tripping down the concrete steps that lead to the sand.

But my feet stay put. I look again at the small red book in the trash and impulsively lean forward. Using two fingers, I reach through the wire and clutch the soft leather. Pulling gently, I retrieve the book and close my palm over it, enjoying the feel of my new treasure. Holy Bible is printed in tiny gold letters on the spine. I flip through it quickly, squinting at the tiny print and wishing Maggie had let me bring my books from home. But in her opinion reading is a pastime designated for lonely old ladies and ugly people with no friends.

In the distance, Maggie laughs and jumps in the shallow waves, and I long to run after her. But a sense of foreboding settles around me as the sun glows hot and low. Soon it'll be dark. What then? Where will we sleep? What will we eat? How will we get to Mr. Delacroix's island? I shouldn't be worried, but I am.

After a while, Maggie tires of her game and comes back, plopping beside me with a contented sigh. "What's wrong, bébé? Ain't you gonna get in the water with me?"

I dig my toes into the cool depths of the sand and shrug.

She reaches out, stroking my dark hair. "Max, listen to me. I promise you everything is gonna be different from now on. Better. You know that, right?"

"Uh, huh," I finally say. But I don't know. Not really. I can only hope.

The first rays of light finger across the sky as waves lap the shore in steady rhythm. The sand is cold and damp, chilling me to the bone. I snuggle closer to Maggie but find little warmth. My stomach gurgles and broken seashells dig into my flesh. A scraggy bit of seaweed clings to the knots in Maggie's hair. I tap her shoulder, studying her face. Eyelids flutter but don't open. Bothered by my neediness, she rolls to her side.

I remember her promise from the night before, and the familiar swell of disappointment descends, choking the last bit of hope from my lungs until my breath comes in shallow gasps. Nothing has changed. Nothing is better or different. Everything is exactly as it has always been. An endless cycle of unknowns and false hopes. The island probably doesn't even exist.

I sit up and look around. An old woman and a dog are walking in the distance. Their silhouettes get smaller and smaller, eventually fading into the silent fog.

We are on a forgotten stretch of beach far from where we first arrived. *"Just keep walking to that lighthouse up there, bébé,"* Maggie had said last night, her face glowing in the moonlight. *"Lighthouses are for saving people, you know?"*

Reaching out, I touch the tall structure painted in horizontal bands of black and white. The iron is rough and familiar, worn by sun and storms and salt. I can't tell the age, but it looks ancient. Positioned on the opposite side of the structure, we are hidden from view of the cottage nearby. Surrounded by a tidy yard fenced with white pickets, the small home is built high on piers in typical beach house fashion. I wonder who lives inside, but a sound from the water makes me turn to the shore.

I huddle next to Maggie as a strange man pulls his boat onto the sand. With bare feet and eyes downcast, he walks the path to the lighthouse. When he nears, I notice he's not a man at all, but a boy. A tall boy with a lean build, clear blue eyes, and a solemn face. Dark waves fall over his forehead, and his arms and chest are bare. I freeze and wait for him to speak.

"That your mama?" he asks, jutting his chin toward her.

I nod, shaking her until her eyes open. She sits up, blinking.

"He wants to talk to you," I say, glancing at the boy.

"What's your name?" he asks.

"Maggie Fontaine," she sputters. "Did Jude send you?"

The boy's eyes narrow. "What's your purpose?"

Maggie turns to me and laughs, a nervous tittering sound that makes me embarrassed.

The boy crosses his arms. "I'll give you one more chance, but that's all."

She shakes her head, blinking in confusion. "Jude sent us. Jude Delacroix. We met in New Orleans at the Y2K meeting. You have to believe me."

I tug on her shirt. "Didn't Mr. Delacroix want you to memorize something from that letter?"

Her hands fly up. "Well, hell! How am I supposed to remember that whole thing?"

The boy shrugs and turns to walk away.

"Wait!" I say, racking my brain for the words in the letter. I open my mouth, willing myself to remember. "Fruit ... I mean

... be fruitful and multiply, and ... fill the earth, and ... and ..." I continue mumbling but the words are gone.

The boy considers my ramblings, a flicker of something contorting his features. Whether pity or annoyance, I can't tell. But after a long moment, he begins to speak. "Be fruitful and multiply, and fill the earth, and subdue it; and rule over the fish of the sea and over the birds of the sky and over every living thing that moves on the earth."

When he waves us forward, I grab Maggie's hand and release a breath. I can't explain my relief. As much as I fear the idea of moving to a mysterious island, at this point, the thought of being turned away seems even worse.

We follow the boy down the narrow path to the ocean, picking our way across wet sand, our prints filling with water as soon as they appear. Maggie hums a cheerful tune that causes the boy to frown as he helps us board the small vessel. I watch as he strains to push the boat out into the lapping waves where we rock violently for several moments. I clutch the edge of the boat and turn to face the wind.

The sharp breeze fills my mouth with salt and my mind with longing. I stare at the horizon as we row toward a dark line in the distance, the oars dipping in steady rhythm as the grayish green sea churns and swells, fighting our descent into the unknown.

Four

The boy's name is Lir.

Lir Delacroix.

I roll the name over, enjoying the sound of it as I sit up a little straighter, hoping he'll notice me.

He answers Maggie's questions as he rows, but his eyes rarely waver from the horizon. Whether shy or disinterested, I can't tell, but it takes a lot of coaxing from Maggie to keep him talking. Eventually, we learn he is Mr. Delacroix's son.

This surprises me and I turn to Maggie, my eyes searching for a clue, but she avoids me with practiced stealth.

Lir stops talking, content with his task. I want him to ask my name. But he doesn't. He doesn't ask us anything about ourselves, but every now and again I catch him glancing at us with a curious expression. His arms flex as he pulls the oars, the muscles lean and well-formed. I wonder how old he is. Around sixteen, I'd guess, and clearly not interested in a girl my age. I look down at my flat chest and thin limbs and wish puberty would hurry up. As the youngest in my grade, most of the other girls are already developing, but not me. I'm as skinny and unmemorable as ever.

"Look," Maggie says, pointing.

The outline of white sand becomes clear with water lapping the shore in a shade much bluer than at Galveston.

She grabs my hand. "Pretty, ain't it?"

Three large buildings come into view. Prow-shaped roofs, stacked one on top of the other, peek out of the palms and greenery like exotic teardrops extending to the sky. Lavish gardens surround the bamboo structures, with fountains and hammocks dotting the space.

Women carry baskets along the jungled paths. Others sit on an elaborately carved stone altar facing the sea, legs crossed, eyes closed, breasts bare.

I look at Maggie with wide eyes.

"It's okay, Max. Things are ... just a little different here."

I think back to her job at the Penthouse and frown. Things seem the same, so far.

When we reach shallow water, I notice a group of women mending fishing nets in the shade of a palm, their hands methodically tying knots. Faded red designs cover their arms and hands and portions of their feet. They drop the nets and stand, joining others who have walked out to greet us.

I don't see any children or men. Just women. All very beautiful and young.

When Lir jumps out to pull the boat to shore, the women surround us, smiling as they help us onto the sand.

"Welcome to Eden," one says.

"Namaste," says another.

The well-wishes come in steady rhythm.

"May your journey to freedom be swift."

"May your womb bear many gifts."

"May you come to know your purpose."

Maggie's face beams with pleasure as we are embraced, the women pressing kisses into the palms of our hands. Several take time to stroke our hair and comment on our good looks as they introduce themselves with names I've never heard before. Bastet, Qetesh, Hathor, Onuava, Hera, Turan, Shaushka.

"Come on. Sensei will want to see you," Lir says, waving us forward with no regard for the women's theatrics.

Maggie frowns. "Sensei?"

"Mr. Delacroix is known as Sensei on the island," he says, striding ahead.

With regret, we leave the flock to follow Lir across the beach and up a winding path bordered by fragrant plants.

We enter a large building and walk onto an open-air veranda with woven cushions scattered across the floor. A huge fireplace made of stone covers most of the back wall, flanked by alcoves for rolled blankets and yoga mats. Metal bowls in a variety of sizes sit on silk pillows in the corner, each holding a strange-looking wooden mallet. A band of decorative etching rims the metal bowls in patterns of vines or birds or geometrics. The largest has words inscribed, but I can't understand the meaning.

Lir motions for us to sit then disappears. Giant wooden wind chimes play a soothing rhythm as the sea breeze combines with the sound of crashing waves. I inhale deeply and close my eyes, surprised by the peace I feel. Peace I yearn for, but can't put into words.

Maggie takes my hand and squeezes, kindling a spark of hope that tells me everything will be all right.

Quiet footsteps grow closer and I recognize Mr. Delacroix's silhouette, lean and broad-shouldered, coming down the shadowed hall. When he steps into the light, I gasp at his transformation. His tailored suit has been replaced with a simple linen sarong, and his feet and chest are bare. Tanned deep bronze, his muscular body is accentuated with bold, primitive tattoos. A light green stone dangles from a leather cord around his neck, and glossy hair, black as pitch, is tied into a bun on his head.

His expression is sober as he takes a seat on a gold cushion in front of us. The scent of spices surround him, reminding me of the voodoo shops back in New Orleans.

He takes each of our hands in his own, his skin warm and dry and reassuring. His eyes are unblinking, like deep pools with no differentiation between pupil and iris.

"Welcome to Eden," he says in a voice much softer than I remember. He tucks a strand of wayward hair behind Maggie's ear. "So, you decided to join us after all, mon chéri?"

"How could we resist?" Her voice is breathless, barely above a whisper.

"My little French doll." He runs a finger lightly along her jaw. "Are you sure you're ready to begin this journey?"

She nods. "There's nothing left for us out there. Especially with everything that's about to happen."

He closes his eyes, inhaling deeply. His hands move to her shoulders, their foreheads touching. "I'm so pleased you're ready to give up your earthly shackles." He hums a low chanting sound for several moments then pulls back, staring into her eyes with unwavering earnestness. "From this moment forward, you are to leave your old life behind. All the greed and sin from the outside world will be exchanged for a higher consciousness that can only come from a purified body, mind, and spirit. You have been chosen for a specific purpose that will be guided by my hand and cultivated by my loins. Eden has always been your destiny. Freedom is your destiny. Others could never appreciate your value. But you will fulfill the prophecy wherein the last shall be first, and the first shall be last. The outside world is a treacherous place, made more uncertain by the day. You have been pulled up and given a great privilege. A chance to be part of something bigger than yourself. Bigger than all of us. Do you understand the gravity of this, Maggie?"

Her hands flutter to her chest. "Yes. Yes, I do." She gives me a hard glance. "We both do, don't we, Max?"

I frown, unsure of my exact feelings. Unsure what his words even mean.

He crouches before me and smiles, revealing straight white teeth. "I have made a very special exception in letting Maggie bring you here. But she assured me you will not be any trouble. Was I wrong in allowing you to join us?"

My heart pounds in my chest at the thought of his displeasure. I stare at him, his eyes pulling me in, forcing me to want his approval. "No, sir," I say.

He pats me on the head. "A humble servant, already." He walks to a large metal gong and within moments a tiny man with a solemn face appears. "This is Dr. Chen, our resident naturopath. Before you can become a true Sister and member of our family, you must be cleansed inside and out. It's a lengthy process, but a necessary first step in your journey to complete freedom." He waves a hand toward the stone altar by the beach. "Following detox, the Sisters will prepare you for the Sowing ceremony where you will receive your new name."

Maggie's eyes widen. "Name?"

He nods. "Of course. It has taken much meditation for your name to be revealed to me. You see, in order to become a Sister, you will take a new name honoring one of the many fertility goddesses that are to be your idols. I think you will be very pleased when my choice is announced at the Sowing."

He sounds the gong a second time and a tall woman with curly, blond hair steps out of the shadows. I wonder if she has been there all along. Her face is round and fresh, her expression euphoric as she sips a steaming cup of dark liquid. A large gold necklace glistens at her throat. When she looks at Maggie, her gaze doesn't waver.

Mr. Delacroix motions her closer. "This is my life partner, Freyja.

I study the woman's face, looking for traces of jealousy as she studies Maggie, but her expression remains serene as he continues speaking.

"Freyja's name honors the magical Norse goddess known for her practice of Seidr, an ancient form of magic that focuses on discerning and thereby altering the course of destiny. Based on Freyja's powerful prophetic visions, I came to realize she is actually the original Norse goddess, reincarnated."

Maggie blinks in surprise. "Oh. How wonderful. I don't know much about reincarnation."

"There will be time to learn. Time to be free and learn to feel." He closes his eyes and takes a moment to inhale deeply before finishing his speech. "Now, Freyja will show you around the island and get you settled. Your sessions with Dr. Chen will begin after lunch." He presses his palms together and bows. "Namaste."

We follow Freyja down the hall and into an open courtyard. Columns frame the area, with vines climbing and spreading to form a natural ceiling of greenery. A thick bed of sand covers the ground, and a large fire is ringed by smooth, white stones in the center of the yard. The fire is surrounded by small wooden seats that are carved in exaggerated shapes of women, bellies and breasts being predominate. Hammocks fill the rest of the space, hanging this way and that. I expect to see someone relaxing in one, but they are empty.

A few women carry buckets and garden tools along the paths, bare feet in steady rhythm, smiles lighting their faces as Freyja takes a sip from her cup and points to the fire. "This is where we gather to receive enlightenment when the weather is pleasant. Once you become a Sister, you and Max may join us in the evenings." She turns to the building we exited. "We go into the main house when it's raining or cold." Her voice is soft and kind. Too kind.

"What are the other buildings?" Maggie asks, looking at the two elaborate structures flanking the main house with rows of glass panels lining the roof.

Freyja's chin lifts. "One is our private residence. The other is where our resort guests stay."

She leads us around the perimeter of the courtyard and into three bamboo structures that serve as the kitchen, laundry, and healing center.

We learn Dr. Chen's sleeping quarters are attached to the back of the healing center by a long corridor made of glass. I look at our reflections as we pass, wavy caricatures that seem out of place at Eden. Like alien figures landing in another time. The future, maybe. Or even the past.

Freyja details Eden's achievements as we walk. "Our goal is to be a completely self-sustaining community. We farm our own vegetables, raise our own protein, and sell the excess to outside merchants. All organic, of course." She stops at a garden where rows of raised beds are clustered and points out the various vegetables, explaining the methods of growing and harvesting without the use of pesticides. Pens containing chickens, rabbits, and milk goats surround the gardens in a semicircle. I like the goats. They are mostly black, with tiny nubs sticking out of their heads in place of ears. "*Lamachas*," Freyja calls them. "*Originally from Africa. Best milk goats in the world.*" I wonder what the milk from a goat tastes like. Not very good, I would think.

She points to the distant beach where more can be seen moving across the sand. "We have a large herd. It's my son's job to tend them." She looks at me with raised brows. "Maybe that would be a good job for you. Would you like to help Lir with the goats?"

I think about the boy in the boat and nod.

"Good. That'll keep you out of the way."

Her tone is deceptively pleasant, but the words catch me, grounding my feet as they continue around the barn and out of sight. I don't want to be seen as a nuisance. I want to be part of a family. A family that will love and care for me, just like Maggie promised. The thought of anything else sends a pain through my chest. A sudden hollow ache that lands somewhere between sad and angry.

I force my feet to move, rounding the corner to catch up, but the sight stretching before me makes me stop. At least a hundred tents are interspersed in a copse of trees. Each is light in color with various symbols decorating the exterior.

Freyja leads Maggie into one on the far side of the cluster, and I run to close the distance, huffing as I step through the flap-covered doorway.

I can feel the air shift as Freyja looks up. "Oh. I was just showing Maggie your new home."

The space is empty except for a few sheepskins covering the floor and a half-burned log in the center.

"An Indian tipi?" I blurt.

Freyja gives me a small smile and takes a sip of her tea. "You've touched on what I was just explaining. Here at Eden, we have complete freedom to draw from the wisdom of any culture, custom, or religion we choose, as long as it is in line with Sensei's vision for our spiritual growth and prosperity." She waves a hand to the tipi. "Whether it's Native American customs, Buddhist, Christian, Egyptian or otherwise, we seek spiritual enlightenment through exploring the wisdom of all mankind. For instance, of all the shelters we could have offered, a traditional tipi is the most suitable for this region and environment, whether it is hot or cold. We also acknowledge the importance of sleeping close to the earth in order to become spiritually grounded. In this way, the tipi provides shelter for not only the body but also the soul.

"Why don't you live in one, then?" I ask.

Maggie's face turns red. "Don't be rude, Max."

Freyja turns away, ignoring my question, as she instructs us on the proper way to care for the fire. She points to the skins on the floor. "These are your beds. I'll have someone bring in fresh linens. The weather is still quite warm at night."

Maggie squats to run her fingers through the wool. "So soft. I've never slept on a sheepskin," she says with a dreamy sigh.

I look at the thin hides and try to match Maggie's enthusiasm, but her rose-colored glasses don't fit. They never have. All I see is the preserved carcass of a dead animal spread across the lumpy ground of a place I'm supposed to call home.

Freyja nods, seeming pleased with Maggie's attitude. "You'll come to find wool and linen have unparalleled health benefits," she says, motioning us to follow her outside. "A truly organic lifestyle is priceless. Eden is unique in that we strive for absolute freedom. Freedom from the selfish vices of the outside world. But to attain this freedom we must be very careful of what we put in our bodies. On our bodies. Into our minds. Do you understand?"

Maggie nods. "I've just never seen a place like this before. It's ... magical."

Freyja takes another sip from her cup and smiles. "It's Eden."

Five

We follow Dr. Chen to the healing center and into a large room with windows overlooking the courtyard. My eyes focus on the far wall where floor-to-ceiling shelves stretch the length of the room. The shelves house clear glass jars of what look like dried plants, roots, and other oddities I can't identify. In front of the shelves sits a long wooden table spread with numerous bottles and scales.

After taking our weight and drawing blood samples, Dr. Chen asks a series of general questions. Age, eating habits, medications, surgeries. His movements are sharp, without emotion. I'm not sure I like him.

He tells Maggie to stand as his eyes travel her body. He picks up a pen, talking to himself as he makes notes. "Short. Underweight. Delicate frame. Skin, moist. Ashen. Neurogenic type. Mental-Osseous. Must increase phosphorus foods, vitamins, minerals. Diet of nuts, seeds, fish, egg yolks, raw milk, and herbal tea. Plenty of sleep, outdoor exercise, and deep massage first month after detox."

Pulling out a camera, he takes photographs of her eyes and downloads them to a computer. He studies the enlarged the images with a frown. "Humoral zone. Right eye, five. Left eye, seven." He taps the screen. "When did you have an abortion?"

Maggie's head jerks back. "I don't know what you're talking about. I ..."

"You're lying," he says, holding up a hand. "I see everything here. You can hide nothing." He taps the tiny dark spots visible on the lower inside of the iris, close to the pupil. "Trauma to the uterus. Several times, I think."

When she starts to cry, his face tightens in annoyance. "I have no time for this. Stop!" he commands. "You are still fertile. Stop crying!"

She hiccups and wipes her eyes while he points to another spot in her right eye. "You also have a large blockage in the ascending colon. Nutritive zone. Requires two colonics." He continues to study the screen, scribbling on his notepad. "Ciliary zone. Right eye, two. Left eye, ten. When did you have your tonsils removed?"

Her expression turns wary. "I was seven. But how can you know that? You haven't looked in my mouth."

"Listen," he snaps. "You want to be a Sister? Then you need to learn to answer questions, not ask them. Here you play by the rules. My rules. Sensei's rules. If you don't like it, you can leave right now."

"I ... I'm sorry. I didn't mean anything by it," she babbles.

I hate how easily she bends, cowering to his temper. Fearful of offending, like always.

Dr. Chen arches a brow, a wicked gleam in his eye at finding the weakness. With slumped shoulders, she looks away.

He calls me forward, his mouth twitching in amusement at her discomfort. I stand tall and look him straight in the eye. I want him to know I'm not scared. I'm not my mother.

Taking a strand of my hair, he rubs it between his thumb and forefinger then gives it a sniff. "Nicotine residue," he spits in Maggie's direction. "Second-hand smoke is very bad for a young girl. Can cause cancer, lung disease, infertility."

Red blotches appear on her neck, and her eyes well like she might cry again.

He turns back to me, looking in my eyes, mouth, nose, and ears. He takes my arms, studying my wrists and hands. "Tall for your age. Long fingers. Strong, lean muscle." His thumb presses into the crease between my eyes. "Desmogenic type. So stern." He startles me by laughing, a short, snipped sound that makes me uncomfortable. "You have an iron will, I think." He writes something in his notepad. "Hard work will keep you busy. No time for trouble."

I bite the inside of my cheek and wonder why everyone keeps saying that. What kind of trouble do they think I'll cause? I've always been a good girl. In school. At home. Maggie has called me stubborn in the past, but never to the point of requiring punishment.

"Go now," Dr. Chen demands with a flick of his wrist. "You may not join the others yet. They will bring an evening meal to your tent. Report to me in the morning to begin detox. No breakfast."

Dusk falls as we walk the path to our tent. I'm relieved to see a tray of roasted meat, vegetables, fruit, and wooden cups of juice. Folded linens and pillows are stacked in the corner, and two wooden stools have been placed by the blazing fire.

As we share the simple meal, Maggie seems to have little appetite.

"What's wrong?" I ask.

She shakes her head and plasters a smile on her face. "Nothing. Nothing at all. Come on, let's get to bed."

The warm glow of the fire, along with my full belly, lull me into a drowsy trance. I snuggle into the soft wool and watch the smoke sifting through the opening overhead. As my lids fall, I feel something like contentment.

Dr. Chen is meditating when we arrive at the healing center. We wait quietly, watching. His legs are crossed, eyes closed, chest unmoving. He reminds me of a statue.

I watch his eyelids for the slight movement even sleeping people can't control and jump when they flick open, his chest heaving once, twice as he comes out of the trance.

We are instructed to go into the changing room and exchange our clothes for linen robes. My robe is too big, dragging on the ground, obviously not meant for a child. Maggie wraps the long sash around my waist, tying the ends in front.

Dr. Chen's face is expressionless when we return. Like a

snake slithering toward its prey, he approaches, his feet making no sound.

I cringe as he places sugar cubes steeped in turpentine on our tongues and tells us to swallow. As the bitterness melts, I shiver and gag, the sweetness not enough to cover the taste.

We gulp water from a shared cup then lie on tables covered with crunchy white paper. Dr. Chen inserts needles into our arms. I flinch, crying out at the sharp pinch. But the pain subsides as he tapes the IV in place. Bags containing cloudy liquid hang from a silver hook attached to the ceiling. Something he calls chelation to rid our bodies of toxins.

A roller dial opens the flow of liquid into clear tubes, and I fidget on the bed as it enters our veins. My arm feels cold, my fingers numb. Or maybe it's just my imagination. I wiggle them to see.

When Dr. Chen retreats into a back room, Maggie's eyes close, her face calm.

Time passes. I don't know how long. Long enough for me to tire of lying on my back. I sit up on my elbow, remember the IV, and lie back down.

I look at Maggie. "Is it almost done?"

She opens her eyes and smiles, but it doesn't last. The next instant, she's leaning over the side of the table, vomiting onto the floor.

I yell for Dr. Chen, who rounds the corner with a scowl. After taking in the scene, he disappears without a word. A few minutes later, he reemerges with a young woman in tow. Toci, as he calls her, is short and young with a large rounded belly.

She drags a bucket of soapy water to the mess, mopping with determined strokes.

"Is Maggie okay?" I ask in a small voice.

Dr. Chen fiddles with the IV and checks her pulse. "She's fine," he says, slipping the needle from her arm.

He does the same for me, and we are told to go to the restroom. I cling to her hand as we walk. "I don't want to do any more. Can we go back to the tipi? Please?" I squeeze her hand, hoping she'll relent and let us leave.

She stops walking and bends to cup my face in her cold hands. "You need to stop worrying," she says in a gentle voice. "Every journey has a few bumps. But this will pass. I want you to feel nothing but excitement. Nothing but joy. But first we have to go through a little discomfort." She points to my elbow. "Kind of like growing pains. Do you understand?"

I look away without answering, a small act of defiance that leaves me flushed.

"Come on. Let's see that pretty smile." When I remain silent, she sighs loudly. A signal she's disappointed in my refusal to obey, but the effort to convince me otherwise isn't worth the trouble.

I follow her back into the main room where Toci has arranged cups of juice and two bowls of seasoned rice with slices of pineapple on the side. It's plain but tasty, and my stomach growls for more.

"I'm sorry," Toci says with a sympathetic smile. "This is all you are allowed. Come on. I'll help you back to your beds."

Another IV is inserted into our right arm. Blood is extracted then passed through a machine that uses ultraviolet light to kill impurities. The blue light seeping from the edges of the device make it look magical. Like something Cinderella's fairy godmother would use if she were a doctor. I determine Dr. Chen must be really smart, despite my dislike. I wonder what a "blood impurity" even is. I suppose it's something terrible.

After a while, our blood is returned to us through the IV, and I'm allowed to get up and dress. But Maggie isn't. I watch in fascination as she spreads her legs, placing her feet in stirrups at the end of a strange-looking plastic bed. A large black pail with a pipe leading to the floor is mounted under her bottom.

My eyes bulge as Dr. Chen inserts a long rod-shaped tool into her butt, the action making her draw in a sharp breath, but she doesn't seem embarrassed. The tool is connected to a long hose with a valve in the middle. When the valve is turned, water flows down the hose and into her body. After a moment, fowl-smelling brown water gushes into a pail, flushing her intestines as Dr. Chen leans over her, massaging her stomach.

I want to look away, but I can't. I don't know why, but I need to see what happens. See if she's okay. I sit on my stool in the corner for what feels like forever and hope I'm not next.

"Does it hurt?" I ask when Dr. Chen steps out of the room.

She shakes her head, but I can tell she's relieved when he returns to stop the flow of water and remove the rod. She leans up on her elbows with an expectant look that he ignores.

When he leaves the room again, she swings her legs to the side of the table and shrugs. "Guess that's all for today," she says in a weak voice.

I nod, happy for an excuse to leave.

Walking to the bed, I take her hand, helping her stand. She

pauses to grip the railing a moment then takes a few steps. "I feel fine, really," she assures. "Just a little light-headed."

I feel her sway to the left. "Maggie?" I ask, tightening my hold.

Her face is moist and colorless. Her eyes half-closed. Lashes flutter in tandem with flaring nostrils. Then a smile spreads, even as she falls.

I stare at the empty ring in the center of our tent. The fire has died and I miss it. The flames lapping and dancing, bright and alive, mirroring Toci's enthusiasm as she spoke about her life at Eden.

"When are you due?" Maggie had asked.

Toci had rested a hand on her belly. "The end of this month. It's my first."

I look to where she sleeps on the other side of the fire, her soft breathing a contrast to her chattiness last night. After Maggie's accident, Toci was assigned to stay the night, and I enjoyed her company. The feeling of true companionship.

When the sun's first rays filter through the cracks in the tent, I feel under my pillow, my fingers brushing the soft leather of my secret treasure. I feel guilty for keeping it. I've never had a secret from Maggie. But I don't want to give it up either.

I look at her now in serene slumber and regret touching her shoulder. "Wake up. Dr. Chen is waiting."

He insisted we continue detox as planned. "She's not hurt,"

he had said after surveying her injuries. And I guess he's right. Other than a few bruises and a headache, she seems to be fine.

Her steps are steady as we follow Toci down the path to the beach. I watch to be sure, my chest growing lighter with each stride. Maggie smiles and wiggles her eyebrows when we see the tubs planted in the sand.

I dip my fingers into one, the cold sea water making me shiver. Additional water is heated in a large caldron over an open fire nearby. Two Sisters stir in spices and herbs, speaking quietly to one another as they work. Dr. Chen isn't there, but Toci has written instructions, his scrawling dictates sparse but to the point.

The bath feels nice, warm but not too hot. Bits of rosemary float on the surface, clinging to my shoulders and arms, the fragrance of ginger strong but pleasant. The sky overhead is gray, and the rush and crash of waves makes me drowsy.

It feels odd to be so comfortable lying naked in an outdoor tub as strangers hover nearby. But the lack of modesty at Eden is contagious. Everywhere I look, the Sisters are in some state of undress. Nude sunbathing, swimming, meditating—all encouraged to cultivate ultimate spiritual freedom. Or so Toci says.

I startle when she dips her fingers in my tub and adds more water until the temperature is almost unbearable. Then the Sisters wash our hair with shampoo that smells like mint, petting and cooing in a way that feels like love.

When the suds are rinsed from our hair, we are told to go cool off in the ocean. My skin turns to gooseflesh as we wade into the waves. But we don't stay long. A small hut farther up the beach awaits. Dim and hot, it smolders with the heat of a roaring fire built into the wall. Stone benches, warm to the touch, curve around the hut like a maze.

Enjoying a tray of fruit, cheese, and juice, we pop grapes into our mouths like queens at a feast.

"Well, that's done," Maggie says, reclining on a bench. "The hard part's over. They say tomorrow we start to learn meditation. Isn't that exciting? We'll be one step closer to the Sowing."

The purpose of the Sowing strikes me as something between a birthday party and a wedding. From the information Toci provided, it's a very special ceremony. A way for Maggie to become true Sister of Eden.

"Will I get a new name too?" I ask.

"No. Those are only given to the Sisters."

"Oh."

She laughs. "Don't be disappointed, Max.

"Why can't I be a Sister too?"

"Because you're too little."

"What is a Sister, anyways?"

Maggie's brows pinch together. The same look she had when I discovered her setting out my Santa gifts a few years ago.

"Well, bébé ... a Sister a very special kind of woman who seeks to live the most selfless life possible. To do good things for other people. Do you understand?"

As her words sink in, a warm feeling expands my chest. I study her glowing face and pat my own, embracing the new sensation. For the first time in my life, I feel proud.

Proud of her.

Of us.

Six

The air is thick with incense when we arrive in the main house, yoga mats spread over the floor in neat rows. The Sisters move around the space, greeting each other and speaking in hushed tones, their hands clasped together in submissive excitement. A few stretch in groups of two or three. Others lie with eyes closed, legs and arms outstretched, breathing in the essence of fragrance and salt.

My eyes scan the room hoping of seeing Lir, but he's not there. I haven't seen him since the day we arrived.

"What do we do?" I whisper to Maggie.

She leads me toward the far wall where Toci is seated, her large belly resting on her thighs.

"Are these mats taken?"

Toci pats the floor beside her. "All yours. I was hoping you'd come today. Are you familiar with dynamic meditation?"

"I don't think so."

"Oh, it's amazing." Toci flaps her hands. "A total rush."

"Will Lir be here?" I ask.

Toci seems surprised by the question and laughs a little before answering. "No. Lir has work to do."

The gong sounds, settling the group. Many sit with crossed legs, rolling their necks in exaggerated circles, the bones crunching in quiet release.

When Sensei appears in the hall, a hush falls. Everyone is still, their eyes following his path across the room. His chest is bare, his long strides elegant with purpose. A purple sarong glistens as he steps onto a small dais positioned near the railing. It's a picturesque view, the sea behind him, the sun filtering past his strong silhouette. When he speaks, his voice is deep and calm. We are safe, it says. Safe and free to become even freer through meditation.

"To truly experience this ancient practice, we must not allow our minds to interfere. We must quiet the inner voices as we reach for the fruit of the offering."

Maggie nods, her face clear and trusting.

I try to decode the meaning of Sensei's words.

Inner voices.

I stiffen at the thought and picture a woman I saw once on the street in New Orleans. Her face was painted. Hot pink lipstick smeared well outside the lines. Blotches of bright blue above her eyes. It was July, but she had on a winter coat and plastic grocery bags wrapped around her shoes. "The voices! The voices! Make them stop!" she cried as we passed. Maggie threw her a couple of dollars but told me to keep walking, that nothing could be done.

Sensei instructs us to stand and quiet our minds with a few deep, cleansing breaths. In through the nose and out through the mouth. I follow along but am wary. I don't want to end up like that woman on the street.

When we are instructed to begin breathing chaotically through the nose in deep bursts void of rhythm, I hesitate. But after a few moments of watching the others, I join in. The breathing pattern makes me feel a bit dizzy, but I'm encouraged to push through. To keep going, fast and hard, using natural movement to build my energy in an effort to become the breath.

Build. Build. Build. Don't let go.

I swing my arms and jump from side to side, frantic like the others who hop and flail around me. Then Sensei's deep voice resonates through the chaos. "Out, out," he says, over and over. "Throw everything out. Let go of the bad. Enjoy the freedom to express the now. Be real in this moment. No shame. No inhibition. Hold back nothing. Be total."

Rapid breathing is replaced with screams and shouts and even laughter as we are encouraged to let it all out. Go completely mad.

We jump, arms raised high above our heads, our feet slapping the floor as we shout the mantra: "Hoo! Hoo! Hoo!" Our group has become one, a converging of souls encouraged and exhausted with the unity of purpose.

Then Sensei snaps his fingers and the room goes quiet, the bodies around me frozen in whatever position they had been caught.

We are told to remain perfectly still as any slight movement will dissipate the energy flow and our effort will be lost.

So, we are still.

After a while, a series of bells ring indicating we may rise. "Namaste," Sensei says in a clear voice, hands pressed together as if in prayer.

"Namaste," we mimic as a group.

Then, one by one, the Sisters approach the dais to bow, their arms spread wide, heads touching the floor. "Gratitude," they say, staying in the position until he releases them to go with a ring of the bell. Occasionally, the bell is replaced with a snap of his fingers signaling they are to wait. They may not leave yet.

We are the last to approach the dais. When we bow, Sensei snaps his fingers, and we join the small, anxious group that remains. Maggie grips my hand and squeezes hard, like she does when she wants me to be good.

"Are we in trouble?" I whisper.

Her mouth presses into a tight line. "I don't know."

Sensei calls the first Sister forward. "Onuava, you may approach."

Head bowed, she kneels in front of the dais. "Yes, Sensei?"

"It has been brought to my attention that you don't care for the food you have been offered."

Onuava's head pops up, her eyes wide. "With all respect, Sensei, I do not know to what you refer."

He looks at her a moment. "It is said you refused to eat the nori portion of your lunch yesterday. Are you saying this is false?"

Onuava's face turns red. "Um ... yes, I ..."

"Yes, it's false? Or yes, it's true?"

She hesitates, her eyes bouncing around the room.

"I'm waiting," he says, studying her with a chilling calmness.

"Forgive me, Sensei. It's true. I did not eat the nori yesterday. But I promise it will never happen again."

"Oh, I know it won't," he says, signaling her to rise and walk forward. He offers his hands, and she kisses each palm.

"Thank you, Sensei," she murmurs in relief.

He steps back and tilts his head to the side. "You're welcome. But I think you are well enough acquainted with our rules to know what's expected of you."

The color drains from her face. "Yes."

He turns to address the group. "Let it be known that Onuava may only have nori and plain water for each meal until I say otherwise. This is for her own good, as we all must learn to reject aversions that stand in the way of perfect health. I correct her because I love her, just as I love you all."

As Onuava is excused to leave, bile rises in my throat at the thought of eating nothing but seaweed for every meal. I make a mental note to clean my plate of whatever I'm served in future, regardless if I like it or not. In that respect, Eden isn't much different than living with R.J. He was a tyrant when it came to meal time, expecting me to eat every bit of anything offered or face the consequences.

Turan, Shaushka, and Qetesh each step forward for similar admonishments, each with a unique punishment pronounced out of Sensei's deep love and devotion to their well-being. But the punishments don't seem fair, and I feel sorry for them.

We are the last to be called, stepping forward to take turns kissing the palms of his hands. My knees shake in fear of our unknown faults, but to my surprise, instead of a punishment, Sensei offers a compliment. "Dr. Chen tells me you did very well in detox."

Maggie blushes. "Yes. I mean, I fainted. But I'm fine now."

The corner of his mouth forms a half-smile, the kind men give when they are trying to be charming. He is charming, I guess. And certainly very handsome. But Maggie's schoolgirl reaction to his flattery makes me uncomfortable in a way I can't explain.

He extends a special invitation for her to join him that evening for a private ceremony of gratitude and enlightenment. She is told to arrive with a few fresh flowers, unbroken shells gathered from the beach, and figs from the garden.

"Did you see the way he looked at me?" Maggie says as we walk through the garden at dusk. "Like I was the most beautiful woman in the world." Her feet bounce down the path as she details Sensei's many attributes and abilities.

I bend to snip a chrysanthemum and drop it into the basket dangling from my arm, letting her talk. But I've heard it all before. Like the time a casting director from Hollywood told her she looked just like Angelina Jolie. Or how a prominent businessman once paid double for her to accompany him to a fancy party on a yacht. "Did I tell you he bought me a dress, too? I felt just like Julia Roberts, drinking champagne with all them rich people," she had bragged.

To Maggie, flattery is more valuable than money.

"Look," she squeals, running ahead to pluck a fig from a tree. She pops it into her mouth, closing her eyes with an exaggerated sigh. "That is probably the best thing I've ever tasted. Here, try one."

The dusky brown fruit is smooth and soft and still warm from the sun.

"Don't bite it. Just put the whole thing in your mouth."

The taste is sweet and mild and not unpleasant, so I pop another into my mouth as we search the tree for ripe fruit to fill the basket.

"What do you need all this for?" I ask, looking at the shells, flowers, and fruit.

She shrugs. "Guess it's a surprise. I just love surprises, don't you?"

Her excitement is contagious. Her happiness my own. And before I know it, I'm skipping behind her down the winding trail to the main house, content in the hope that things will stay this way forever.

Freyja is waiting when we arrive. Head inclined, she blinks rapidly. "Did you have a nice walk?"

"We did, thank you," Maggie replies.

Freyja claps her hands together, but the excitement doesn't reach her eyes. "Wonderful. We want you to feel very welcome here." She looks at me, her smile slipping. "Why don't you run along, Max. I'm sure Lir could use your help in the barn."

When Maggie disappears down the hall, I do as instructed. But my steps are slow, my thoughts hesitant. I wonder how my presence will be accepted by the mysterious boy. I want him to like me. But what if I screw up? Say something stupid or mess up in my efforts to help?

I enter the dim barn and find him leading a black and white goat toward a wooden contraption built about a foot off the ground.

"Can I help?" I ask in a quiet voice.

He turns and squints in a way that's hard to read. "Yeah, I guess."

I walk to the goat and reach a tentative hand toward her face.

"That's it. Let her get used to you," he says, his face still void of expression.

Her hair is course under my hand, and her head reminds me of an alien.

"What's her name?" I ask.

"Milly."

"Why doesn't she have ears?"

He laughs a little. "She does. They're called elf ears. See?" He points to the small nubs on the sides of her head.

I smile, glad I could make him laugh. "Can she hear out of them?"

"Of course she can."

Lir leads her to the stand and waits for her to jump onto it. A bowl of grain is positioned at one end, and Milly sticks her head through a wooden hole to get to the bowl. When she's in position, Lir closes the catch around her neck to hold her in place.

"Just stand right there and pet her," he instructs. "As long as she stays calm, her milk will be good."

I pet her neck as she gobbles the grain, pleased to be of use and fascinated as I watch Lir wash her bag with a cloth and squeeze long streams of milk into a metal bucket.

"Does it hurt her?" I ask, leaning over to get a better look.

He shakes his head. "Nope. The only thing that hurts is not milking her on time. Her bag will swell up, and she'll hurt real bad if that happens. Can make her sick too."

"You know a lot about goats, huh?"

He shrugs. "Don't have a choice."

I turn back to Milly and continue stroking her neck. "I think it's nice. I never had a pet."

Lir's expression hardens. "They're not pets. And don't let Sensei hear you say that, either."

"Why not?"

"We aren't to get attached to worldly things."

"Oh ..." I don't understand why loving an animal is against the rules, but based on Lir's expression, I don't question him further.

"You did pretty good," he says, releasing Milly from the stand.

My face colors at the praise. Lir is quiet, but I feel at ease around him. "Can I help you again, tomorrow?"

He looks at me a moment, indecision written on his features.

"Please? I won't get in your way. Promise."

He lets out a sigh. "Don't they have something else for you to do?"

"Freyja said my job is to help you."

"I guess it's settled, then."

SEVEN

Drums beat in rhythm, echoing through the forest of tents in steady anticipation of the Sowing.

I'm dressed in an orange silk sarong with moonstone beads at my throat, a mini version of my mother and the other Sisters. Our chests are bare, but as one of many, I've adapted to the nudity.

My dark hair is left long and loose, almost to my waist. I can't remember the last time it was cut.

"Men don't like short hair on women," Maggie would say whenever I dared to ask for another style. The air of finality surrounding the dictate always meant the discussion was over before it began. What bothered me most was the disappointment on her face. Like asking for a bob meant I possessed a serious mental flaw. An unwillingness to do whatever it took to please the opposite sex. Like she had failed as a mother, my rebelliousness the result. In her world, pleasing men equaled money, food, protection, flattery. And my desire to jeopardize this system in any way was just plain stupid.

She turns to me now and smiles, her red lips matching the henna on her hands, feet, and breasts. The Sisters spent many hours fussing over the designs. I could tell Maggie enjoyed the attention as they worked and petted her into perfection.

As we are led onto the beach, I see the altar in the distance where Sensei sits atop a huge, white sheepskin. His eyes are closed, legs folded, red henna covering parts of his face, feet, and chest. His sarong is made of the same orange silk as ours.

Flickering torches wash the area in a warm, pulsing glow of excitement that makes me feel alive as the Sisters dance around the altar in small circles of four or five. Their movements are beautifully erratic, without form or restriction, as they bend and jump and sway to the pounding of the drums.

I don't see Lir, and I miss his presence. I look forward to our time spent together tending the goats. He never talks much, but besides Toci, he's my only friend. My favorite days are when we take the herd to the other side of the island to graze. It always feels like an adventure in a world of our own making. A break from the reality and rules of Eden.

Maggie squeezes my hand before joining Sensei on the altar and Toci gives me a wooden cup of fowl-tasting brown liquid. I'm told to drink it all. Fast.

I hold my breath and guzzle quickly, but the aftertaste makes me gag. My stomach churns and my mouth feels coated with dirt. Maggie and the others take up their own cups and do the same, an official beginning to the ceremony.

Seated in the sand at the base of the altar, three Sisters take their places behind a series of four Tibetan singing bowls positioned on silk cushions. "To enhance the sacral chakra and promote fertility," Toci whispers as Sensei steps to the front of the altar, prompting the other Sisters to stop dancing and sit on the sand, an unbroken circle of crossed legs and euphoric faces around the altar.

The musicians take up wooden mallets, and the liquid in my stomach gurgles as warmth spreads throughout my body. Movement catches my eye, and I turn to see Lir has taken a seat beside me. I smile at him but he doesn't seem pleased.

Sensei asks Maggie to stand as he bows before her, putting his forehead to the stone floor where he remains for several minutes. When the Sisters do the same, Maggie's gaze travels over the crowd. I try to catch her eye, but she doesn't see me.

After a few moments, Sensei rises, stretching out his powerful arms. "From this day forward, Maggie is a new being created and set in the task of claiming her freedom. Long before her arrival at Eden, I had a vision." He closes his eyes, hands folded as if in prayer at the memory. "A vision of a woman. A dark figure floating through the mist and rain over a turbulent sea. As she came closer, her body took shape." His eyes open and he stares straight ahead. "In one hand she held the moon. And in the other, a stone wrapped in swaddling clothes. It is then I knew who she was, the ancient Greek fertility goddess, Rhea."

He pauses for effect and the Sisters murmur among themselves, nodding and smiling in approval. I turn to see Lir's reaction, but his brows are pinched together, his mouth turned down in a scowl.

Sensei reaches out, a grand gesture with his hand open and grasping. "The great goddess was so close, I could see the blush of her breasts through the sheer fabric of her peplos. I longed to take her in my arms, but I dared not. So, I sat at her feet, absorbing the wisdom and knowledge she poured into my soul concerning our new Sister." He turns to bow before Maggie a second time, then proclaims, "Just as Rhea was the mother of Zeus, may you be the mother of many worthy gifts."

When he rises, a dagger glistens in his right hand. His movements are swift as the fabric of Maggie's sarong makes a ripping sound. I sit in stunned silence as the sharp blade slices a path through the center of her garment, revealing her nakedness beneath.

My eyes widen at the sight of the knife, but my scream is stifled by Lir's hand. I struggle to escape his grip, but my arms have turned heavy, my hands useless to fight. I blink in an effort to comprehend what's happening. Understand what's wrong with me. But all I feel is the hum of the singing bowls. The sound penetrates my body, the boundaries of my skin indistinct. A series of striking notes moving to a ceaseless hum, increasing in pitch as Sensei drops his sarong to reveal himself. He is unhurried, his body graceful while on arrogant display. It's a shocking sight, but I'm too tired to react. My vision blurs and I slump to lay my head on the sand, my eyes remaining shut a little longer with each blink.

The rest of the night takes on the unfocused quality of a dream. Flesh heaving and glistening in the torch light. The Sisters humming a note to match the bowls. A moment of crescendo. And then nothing. Nothing except the distant stars and the violent silence of Savasana.

EIGHT

GALVESTON, TEXAS - 2008

Dr. Gregory snaps her fingers, bringing me out of the haze. It takes a moment to shake the memories and readjust to the reality of my surroundings. The feel of the soft velvet sofa beneath me. The click of Dr. Gregory's heels when she comes to stand beside me. The scent of her perfume, sandalwood and vanilla. I blink and focus on her outline, black against a window of gray.

She pats my arm and speaks in a quiet voice. "You're doing very well, Max. I'm so proud of your courage."

I try to sit up, but she tells me to remain where I am. "We aren't quite done yet," she explains. "While your childhood experience is very interesting, especially in understanding the dynamics of Eden, I'd like to skip ahead to the time when you knew you wanted to leave. The inciting incident, if you will. But if you need a break, I understand."

I shake my head and settle back onto the sofa a second time, listening to the soothing rhythm of her words. I'm transported back to the island, but it has changed. I've changed. I am no longer the little girl that came to Eden in search of a new life. Yet, I am still searching.

When I open my eyes, I'm back in Eden, staring at the familiar bamboo ceiling, where row after row of green and brown stalks layered with thatch extend the length of the prow-shaped roof. The structure looms over gardens of lavender and rosemary, verbena and jasmine. I take a breath, inhaling the sweet aroma of late spring as it floats over the balcony. But the scent brings no comfort.

In spite of its lush setting and extravagant decor, the main house of Sensei and Freyja is a lonely place. A showcase of items collected from around the world. A gluttony of treasures meant to impress. Tibetan rugs covering floors made of polished river rock. Hand-loomed textiles nestled in designer hanging chairs. Linen bath towels resting next to a tub hand-carved from a single volcanic boulder. Organic opulence at its finest. But the house will never be a home. It will never be the simple tent where Maggie took her final breath eight years ago. Even as she hemorrhaged blood, the smile never left her face. "If I must go, I want it to be this way," she had whispered in a weak voice.

"No!" I had screamed, tears streaming down my cheeks.

"Yes," she said, her eyes euphoric even as the blood drained from her body. "It's for the greater good. I'm at peace."

A few minutes later, Dr. Chen had wiped his hands on a cloth and stepped outside to tell the Sisters the news. "Rhea's gone," he had announced in a voice void of emotion.

But I refuse to call her Rhea, even in my mind. That was *their* name for her. A plastered label to make her feel special and coerce her into doing what they wanted. But I never got used to it. I never got used to a lot of things about Eden.

Waves crash beneath my window, the salty breeze pushing my hammock back and forth, back and forth. I pull at the cocoon of mosquito netting and look at the sea. It's gathering day and Lir is heaving a wooden fishing boat into the water.

Lir.

A man as mysterious as the sea god his name conjures. He avoids me now, refusing to meet my gaze or acknowledge my greeting. But it wasn't always this way. He used to be kind and patient as we tended the goats and explored the island together.

But that time is gone. Our stolen encounter after the last Sowing changed him. Changed me. I want more. He wants less. But perhaps his feelings will soften once he knows about my condition. I've waited as long as I can to tell him the truth. I press a hand to the slight round of my stomach and push away the dread. Maybe my situation isn't hopeless. Maybe he will know what to do.

When Lir turns to climb into his boat, his jaw is set, eyes cast down, mouth in a firm line. He's still tall and slender with strong arms from years of rowing. He could take out one of Sensei's larger boats, Bayliners with big engines and live wells and GPS navigation. But Lir has always preferred the simplicity of his small wooden vessel. The same one he used all those years ago. Back when I was still optimistic about my future here. Back when Lir was still happy. I try to remember his laugh. Or something funny he once said. I yearn for a warm memory to grasp and hold close. Something to tell me I haven't lost everyone who cares.

The warm weight on my chest wiggles, kicking his tiny legs as he nuzzles my breast. Barely a week old, the baby searches my body for food in vain.

"Hungry, little man?"

I kiss his soft, brown head and carry him to the crib where the other two infants slumber, their tiny faces serene. Twin girls, three months old, with pink cheeks and a dusting of strawberry blond hair. They'll wake soon, crying to be fed and changed and rocked, like always.

There's a certain peace inside the confines of the nursery. It's a privilege, I'm told. But I'm careful not to get too close. Care too much. These children aren't mine to love.

I cradle the baby in one arm and walk to the dresser where an African statue made of ebony sits staring. I run my finger across the smooth, cold surface. As cold and black as the ocean during a storm. My skin prickles at the thought. The unexpected velocity of the waves. The thrill of leaning over my balcony while the Sisters huddle in their tents, chanting and praying to be spared from nature's wrath. The rain spattering my face and arms as the wind picks up. Flashes of light shuttering in succession as the calm is replaced by an alternate universe that could be as loud and angry and irreverent as it wants. In that moment, anything seems possible. Even for somebody like me.

I glance toward the sea, squinting as Lir's boat gets harder to see, his face clouded by mist as he grows smaller against the horizon. I wonder what it would be like to go with him. To keep paddling until Eden's dictates and demands and rituals disappear. The things I once found enchanting about the island aren't so magical anymore. I've been here too long. Seen too much.

A sound in the garden below makes me turn. I walk to the open window and push back the sheer curtain.

I'm startled to see Aditi hiding behind a palm near the house. Her skin is sallow, her eyes wide and beseeching.

"What are you doing?" I call.

She motions for me to be quiet then glances over her shoulder. "Please," she begs, ringing her hands together. "Just one look and I'll go. I promise."

I know what she wants, but I can't give in without putting us both in danger. Aditi may not see her son. Ever. After the incident six years ago, infant care is my job and my job alone.

"This can't happen again," Sensei had whispered to Freyja on that fateful night. "We cannot jeopardize our foundation, everything we've worked for, with this kind of nonsense."

"But how?" she asked in a tight voice as Toci's cold body was pulled from the black waves.

When Sensei stared at her lifeless form, I expected to see sadness or regret. But all I saw in his cold, dark eyes was resolve. "If the Sisters can't control their attachment, I will control it for them."

I was summoned to a private ceremony the next afternoon and asked to bring the same figs, flowers, and shells I had once helped Maggie gather.

Barely fourteen, I didn't know what to expect as I followed Sensei to a small room where an altar covered in white cloth sat bathed in the dim glow of candles. Light glinted off brass objects, including a large stone statue. The statue showed a woman, naked from the waist up, with close-cropped hair and large breasts supported by her hands. Incense and a Bonsai tree sat nearby.

Sensei's warm hands cupped my shoulders. "Calm yourself. This is a ceremony of relaxation."

I hadn't realized I was trembling, afraid he would insist I follow Maggie's footsteps into the Sisterhood. I had no wish to become Sensei's new plaything. The thought of him touching me that way, ravishing me in front of everyone, made my skin crawl. So, I stood before the altar, barely paying attention, as he detailed the origins of the ancient fertility goddess, Asherah.

His arms swept wide. "In order to accept the position I will now bestow, you must learn to give honor and be present. Be total and pure. Do you know what it means to be pure?"

I looked down and nodded.

"So, you remember what happened to Hera when she lost her purity?"

"I do," I said, my throat constricting at the memory of her lifeless body displayed on the altar. Her throat slit from ear to ear by Sensei's dagger. And all for what? A few hours of pleasure with a resort guest? A man she'd never see again? Hera's actions were foolish, but I always felt her punishment was unjust. She made a mistake, but not one worthy of a death sentence.

Sensei's fingers lifted my chin. "Your new position will be a great privilege, but you will be in greater contact with our guests. I need you to promise you will not make Hera's mistake."

"No. Never."

He placed the shells, figs, and flowers in a tray on the altar, the fragrance of the flowers mixing with incense and soft light to create a soothing atmosphere. Chanting in an unfamiliar language, Sensei dipped a flower into a brass cup. He used the flower to sprinkle water onto the tray and burning incense was moved in a circle around the statue, followed by a candle in the same pattern. The chanting continued as the incense was touched to a white ball on one of the brass objects, resulting in an eruption of flame that smelled kind of like the salve Maggie used to rub on my chest when I was sick. My eyes watered as I followed the circular points of light in a drowsy dance that suspended reality. I took a deep breath in an effort to remain awake as Sensei took up the final object, his chant changing slightly. Then, it was gone. Silence filled the room as the remaining flowers were set on the tray, and he knelt before the statue. Sensei motioned for me to do the same as he repeated something over and over, but it was too quiet to make out. Each time, he said the sound a little louder until I was able to understand a word that sounded like "ahma." He indicated I was to repeat the word and keep saying it. When I began, he stopped and sat down. He told me to close my eyes as I chanted, quieter and quieter. "Now say it in your head," he said when the word became a whisper. I did as instructed, losing track of myself in the process. Time slowed and I wondered if it had stopped completely. My limbs turned to liquid, or maybe air. I wanted to stay in that place. To never leave. All my worry, stress, and grief had vanished, gone in an instant. Sensei used his power like a drug. I would have done anything to stay in that Nirvana. So, when he began telling me of his vision for my future, in that time and place, I believed him. I wanted to be the savior of the Sisters. The angel sent forth to care for the children of Eden and ensure an incident like Toci's death would never happen again.

Incidents. That was what they were always called. Never depression. Never grief. Never a Sister screaming and clawing as her infant sailed away on a yacht. Never suicide.

Aditi's cough brings me back to reality. My reality. The day in and day out of tending to other people's children for the past six years, only to hand them over to strangers and never see them again. But this is my calling. My purpose.

I study Aditi's pained expression and consider my options. Whether breaking the rules will save her from Toci's fate. My chest squeezes with pity, but I know what has to be done.

"Go away," I hiss.

She remains frozen in place, tears slipping down her cheeks as she opens her mouth in a silent scream only I can hear. I grit my teeth and turn away, hoping she'll leave, go back to her tent or beg Dr. Chen for a tonic to numb her heart in the same way I've had to numb my own on several occasions.

I place her son in the crib beside the girls and walk to the door where I wait for Freyja to hear my report.

"Good morning," I say when she rounds the corner, holding the cup she will sip until nightfall.

She stumbles a little as she approaches, already tipsy from the brew. "Anything I should know?" Her eyes are flat as she looks past me into the nursery.

"Aditi's boy is very strong. He slept most of the night."

"He's not Aditi's anything," she snaps. "He is a child of Eden. Just as they all are. That reminds me, Dr. Chen says Qetesh is slightly dilated. So, you should have a new ward soon." She waves a hand toward the twins in the crib. "Be sure they are bathed and ready for the ceremony this afternoon. Our guests seem especially anxious to be on their way."

"But they only arrived last night."

Freyja pauses, her fingers twisting the gold strands of her necklace. "Just have them ready. I ..."

Her words die as Sensei rounds the corner with the couple in tow. They are a good-looking pair, well-dressed like all of our guests.

Freyja pushes me back into the nursery, shutting the door to leave a small crack. I position myself where I can see and listen as the couple implores Sensei to let them forgo the usual ceremony in order to take the girls home immediately. He tries to dissuade them from the idea, but they are adamant.

"That's not how it's done here," Freyja interjects, her tone deceptively sweet. "The Claiming ceremony we've planned is a beautiful and very important part of this process. We will use the Anahata Chakra to unite you with the girls. In this way, their spirits will forever identify you as their true parents. It's not something that can be skipped. But as soon as the ceremony is over, you will be free to go."

My jaw tightens at Freyja's manipulative words. From what I've seen, the Claiming ceremony serves two purposes: to further indoctrinate the Sisters to believe their sacrifice is divine, and to make the adoptive parents feel less like they are paying for a child and more like they were destined to claim the infant from the beginning of time.

The woman tugs on her husband's arm. "Please, honey," she whines. "We can leave right afterward, just like she said. We'll be home in plenty of time for your thing tomorrow morning."

The man huffs and crosses his arms. "For five hundred grand, we should be able to do anything we damn well please," he drawls in a thick Texan accent.

Sensei stiffens at the insult. "Perhaps we've made a mistake. Your attitude shows you clearly don't appreciate this opportunity. Freyja, please show our guests to their boat. The deal is off. They are no longer welcome."

The couple stand in stunned silence as Sensei turns and walks away with calm grace.

"Well, I damn sure better get my money back!" the man demands.

Freyja quietly explains Eden's no refund policy. "The rules were clearly explained to you when you arrived," she says.

The man curses and yells, his eyes bulging. "Are you fucking kidding me?"

His wife collapses to the floor, sobbing hysterically. "My babies, my babies," she moans over and over. "I don't care about the money. Please, we'll give you more. Just give me my babies!"

I stiffen when the man takes an angry step toward Freyja. "You haven't seen the last of me, you uppity little bitch. You can't just take that kind of money and give us nothing in return."

Freyja remains perfectly still, her gaze direct. "Or what? You'll call the authorities?"

"You're damn straight, I will."

"And just what will you say? That you attempted to buy two infants from Eden and we didn't hold up our end of the bargain?"

His face pales at the realization.

Freyja's mouth twitches into a half-smile, like a cat cornering a mouse. She doesn't need to say more. The couple will leave empty-handed, never to return. And never to speak of the incident again.

Nine

The morning is warm, the light dim and fresh and mysterious as it filters through the mist hovering over the ocean. I stretch, enjoying the feel of the soft sheepskin beneath me and the rare quiet of an empty nursery. The twins have gone, left on a luxury yacht with a handsome Hollywood couple. Flashy men with beautiful haircuts and tailored suits. One had the most exquisite pair of red leather shoes. He noticed me staring and winked. "If you like these, I can put you in touch with the designer." I smiled politely and thanked him, unsure how else to handle the situation. In his attempt to be kind, he had unknowingly offered forbidden fruit. I would wear the clothing Sensei provided and nothing else. Nothing special. And certainly nothing designer.

Aditi's son was the last to leave with wealthy ranchers from Wyoming. They flew in by private helicopter for the occasion, an elaborate Claiming ceremony filled with music and firelight and incense. The woman cried as Freyja placed the baby boy in her arms. Great heaving sobs that made me fear she might drop him into the sacred bath that awaited his baptism. Her husband cleared his throat, overcome with emotion. "She's sure been waiting a long time for this little cowboy," he said, patting her shoulder.

But as the pair marveled over their new miracle, I thought of Aditi. Alone. Sequestered in her tent, far from the ceremony and the son she would never see. Never hold. Never know.

But that is the life she chose. Just like Maggie, Aditi knew what she was getting into before she came to Eden. She knew and she did it anyhow, drunk on Sensei's attention and overcome with the idea of living in paradise for the rest of her days.

I remember the day she arrived. "I don't mind being pregnant," she had boasted. "At least this way I get something out of it."

But, like Toci, Aditi proved unable to cope with the sadness and loss following birth. The anger and heartbreak that would swallow her whole. After the ceremony, I tiptoed through the darkness to her tent. The need to check on her more powerful than Sensei's rules. "It's like he never existed," she had whispered as the helicopter lifted into the air, taking her son to his new future. "It's like they all never existed."

The next morning at sunrise I pulled Aditi to the far end of the beach where a giant piece of hollow driftwood rested near the tree line. It was my special place, discovered right after Maggie's death when I needed a way to grieve. To remember not only the mother I lost, but the sister as well.

Aditi's eyes widened when I held out one of the giant, flat

river rocks Jude imported to line the paths of Eden. On one side, I had inscribed Aditi's name and the birthdate of her baby boy, along with any other distinguishing features that made him unique. On the other side, I put the name and location of the couple who adopted him.

"See, Aditi, he was real. They all were," I said, dropping the stone into the cavernous driftwood to take its place among the hundreds of others.

Aditi fell to her knees, staring at the stones. "How long have you been doing this?"

"Since Maggie died."

"Why?"

I shrugged, unable to verbalize the need to memorialize all the children we would never see again. Or the small poems, stories, and prayers I'd added to the collection through the years. Until that day, I'd never shown anyone my driftwood diary. Never thought anyone would care.

But Aditi nodded, understanding and gratitude shining in her eyes as she took my hand.

I flip onto my stomach and feel under the sheepskin, grasping the cool, familiar binding. Red leather, faded with use, the pages soft and pliable and fluttering in the breeze. I have no destination in mind, only the desire for hope and assurance that somewhere in the distance, things may be different. I drink in the words like a tonic. A small rebellion. My only joy.

Apart from Sensei's readings from his own holy writings, literature is forbidden, especially writings considered divine. "Not all have the gift of interpretation," he loves to say. "And what good is wisdom to a weak mind?"

I'm careful to keep my Bible hidden. I've seen firsthand what happens to those who disobey. The worst was Rosmerta. A girl I barely knew but will never forget. Picked up by Sensei on one of his trips to the mainland—Utah, I think. A shy girl, pretty and sweet, ever trusting and aiming to please. At first, Sensei told her what she wanted to hear, quoting scripture from The Book of Mormon to solidify his hold. But once she became a Sister, things changed. Sensei expected her to disavow her old religion and follow only his teachings. But she refused. Among her personal items was a devotional she liked to read in the evenings. When Sensei discovered this crime, he took the book and burned it in the fire, and Rosmerta was brought before the Sisters for questioning. But no matter what Sensei said, or how he tried to dissuade her from her beliefs, she would just smile and shake her head. "I'm sorry but I don't agree," she'd say in a soft voice. "I've done everything else you've asked, but please don't ask me to do this."

Sensei would lean in close, his expression the picture of sincerity. "You haven't been educated as I have, my dear. But it's not your fault. You are simply following the path your parents set. Just because you were taught something as a child doesn't make it true. You need to trust what I say. I've been all over the world, studied every religion in existence. I will lead you to freedom. To truth and enlightenment. To the understanding you seek. But first, you must let go of what you think you know. Quiet the voice inside and open your mind."

For hours, it continued. Sensei brought every argument he could think of, but Rosmerta continued to disagree. Eventually the Sisters started to whisper among themselves. Maybe

Rosmerta should be free to choose. What would it hurt to let her retain her beliefs?

This unrest was not lost on Sensei, and the air felt electric as he took a final stand. "Rosmerta," he said in a sad voice. "Are you certain this is how you truly feel?"

"Yes. I'm certain," she said without hesitating.

Sensei looked at her a long moment then lifted his chin. His words swift and sure as he addressed the crowd. "Rosmerta's defiance has forced me to take drastic measures. The only way we can achieve peace and harmony here at Eden is to be like-minded. To be of one accord. We cannot let one rebellious spirit bring the rest of us to ruin. Since Rosmerta will not yield, I am forced to use all means available to ensure her future obedience. Doctor Chen, please take her to the healing center. I will be there shortly."

It was several days before Rosmerta was seen again, her wheelchair being pushed by a Sister out into the courtyard for some fresh air. At first, I didn't recognize her. Her head had been shaved and partially bandaged, and her face lacked its usual cheeriness. When I spoke to her, she looked at me with a dazed expression. "Do I know you?" she had asked with childlike innocence. "Have you come to play with me?" Her behavior had frightened me, causing me to run away. It was an action I'd always regret.

After that, she stopped eating and survived only by daily IV infusions administered by Dr. Chen. "The Lobotomy was not successful. It's a shame," he had said, writing off her condition with a shrug of his shoulders. And then, before I knew it, she was gone, planted in a shallow hole behind the goat barn. Her grave marked by a single white rock. Every time I read my book, I think of her.

I finish the chapter and tuck it back under the sheepskin, rising from my bed to look out the window. Lir will be back soon with the morning catch, and I plan to meet him.

Lacing a turquoise ribbon down the length of my dark hair, I study myself in the mirror. The long face with high cheekbones. Tan skin. Eyes just like Maggie's.

I retrieve a simple linen dress from my chest and lay it on the bed, running my hand over the familiar fabric and noticing a small hole in the neck. On closer inspection, I see several holes, rips, and inconsistencies throughout. My condition isn't obvious yet, but the bodice has gotten a bit tighter around my hips and breasts, and the hem is stained and fraying. I have other dresses in the chest, but this is my favorite, soft with wear and perfect for a trek through the forest.

When I remove my nightgown, footsteps in the hall make me hurry to slip the dress over my head. I run to my door and tiptoe across the hall, the marble cold on my bare feet. But when I raise my hand to knock, my knuckles sound hollow on the thick wood of Lir's bedroom door. There are rustling sounds, but he doesn't answer. I knock again and call out his name.

"What," he says, opening the door in a great whoosh. His chest is bare and glistening with sweat.

"I ... uh ..."

"Spit it out."

"Just wanted to see if you need any help."

His head tilts to one side. "Have I ever needed your help bringing in the fish?"

"You used to let me," I offer.

He grabs a clean shirt, pulls it over his head, and brushes past. "Thanks, but I got it," he calls without a backward glance.

I watch as he descends the staircase leading to the main room. When he's out of sight, I take the back stairs leading to the hall. It's still early and no one is about, so I make my way through the quiet gardens, careful to stay hidden in the foliage. Following a thin trail through the forest, I make my way to the small inlet where Sensei's boats are lodged, one after the other, in slips.

Lir is busy unloading his catch beside the boathouse, but when I near, he doesn't look up.

"I know you can hear me."

"You're not supposed to be out here."

I cross my arms and lean against the rough wall of the boathouse. "I seem to recall a night not so long ago when you were glad for my company."

He heaves the catch onto the dock. "I'm not discussing this, Max. And you shouldn't either. We both had too much kava. It was a drunken mistake. Nothing more. I don't know what else I can say to make you see that."

I want to argue. To tell him about the baby. To scream at the top of my lungs until I'm heard. But there are risks. He could tell Sensei—my child taken and sold like the rest. Or my throat cut for losing my purity. Either way, the outlook is grim. But I have to do something soon. And I'll need Lir's help.

"Yes," I say in a calm voice. "I agree. That night was a mistake. You're not in love with me. I see that now. But I thought we could at least be friends. Back like when we were kids."

He shakes his head. "No, Max. You have your job and I have mine. Sensei's rules."

"I'm sick of Sensei's rules. I know you're taking the herd to the other side today, and I'm coming with you."

"No, you're not."

"I used to go all the time. Be practical, Lir. The herd's bigger now. You need the help."

Lir swishes his hands in the water. "Things are different now."

Disappointed anger boils in my stomach. "You're making excuses and I want to know why. You used to be on my side, remember?" I put my hand on his shoulder, but he flinches and jerks away. The action makes my throat constrict. "Why are you doing this to me? Why do you hate me so much?"

A muscle in his jaw jumps. "I don't hate you, Max."

"Then let me go with you," I beg, not caring if I sound desperate. I am desperate. Desperate to tell him the truth. Desperate to see his reaction. But our conversation isn't going as planned, and the little bit of hope I had is slipping away.

He hoists the basket of fish in his arms. "I don't have time to argue. You're not coming."

I grit my teeth in frustration. I'm not the same little girl he used to boss around, but he will never see me that way.

As Lir heads toward the kitchens, I follow at a slow pace. He assumes I'm heading back to the nursery, but I take a detour for the woods behind the barn. I'm determined and nothing will stop me.

I wait to hear the bleating of goats, their bells clanking softly as they rush from their pens to trot down the hill in organized chaos. They have been to the other side many times and look forward to feasting on the untamed parcels of fresh grass. I strain for my cue to depart, but silence meets my ears as the goats remain munching hay inside their pens. I press my back into the wall of the barn and peek around the corner.

With a leather bag of supplies strapped to his back and a second bag dangling from his hand, Lir is almost out of sight down the trail.

It's unlike him to venture to the other side with no obvious purpose. I run to catch up then follow at a slower pace, careful to remain out of sight. Off the main path, the underbrush scrapes against my legs, catching the cloth of my dress in silent opposition. But I refuse to turn back. He will hear me out, one way or another.

Soon, the forest thins and brightens, opening to reveal the peaks and dunes of the opposite shore. The landscape here is more rugged. A wild sort of beautiful that makes Sensei's expensive landscaping seem forced and overdone.

I follow Lir's footprints across the sand, eventually rounding a bend into a small cove where I crouch low in shocked fascination as he approaches a cottage I've never seen. The mysterious house is small and made of bamboo in the same style as the houses at Eden. Nestled into the cove, it remains hidden from view of the main ocean.

When Lir emerges a few moments later without his bags, I can't contain my curiosity. To my knowledge, all island inhabitants live at Eden, and I can't imagine Sensei allowing anyone to remain outside of his immediate control.

All thoughts of Lir vanish with the desire to solve the mystery. I scurry into the cover of the woods long enough for him to pass, heading back the way he came. When he's out of sight, I pick my way toward the cottage, careful to remain silent as I approach.

My breath comes in shallow gasps as I near an open window on the side of the house. The interior is dark, but I hear shuffling followed by the creaking of door hinges. I flatten myself against the wall and hold my breath. After a moment, the hinges sound again as the door shuts. I sag against the wall in relief, releasing my breath in a whoosh.

But the next instant, I'm fighting for air as sharp fingernails dig into the tender flesh of my neck. I struggle against the assault, trying in vain to loosen the grip of the calloused hand that juts from the open window.

"What do you think you're doing here?" a feminine voice growls.

I cut my eyes to the left in an effort to glimpse her face, but she remains hidden in shadows. Her grip is like iron, inhibiting my ability to answer. I make a gurgling sound, frantic for release.

She curses and slings me to the ground. I fall hard and gasp for air, stunned by the quick turn of events. In an instant, she rounds the corner and grabs my arms, dragging me into the dark house.

The cottage is small with sparse furnishings and a fireplace on the far wall. Wind chimes made of sea glass and shells hang in the windows and a bowl of dough sits abandoned on the kitchen table.

"Who are you and what the hell are you doing here?" the woman demands.

I look at her face for the first time. The silver hair. Skin tan and wrinkled. Her dark eyes hold a familiarity I can't place as she appraises me with blatant disdain.

"I'm Max ... I ..."

When I rub my tender throat, the woman's face softens. "Guess you'll want a drink," she says, handing me a cup of water from a pitcher by the sink. "But then you're gonna tell me what the hell you're doing lurking around my place. Like to scare the hell out of me." She crosses her arms. "And I know Lir didn't bring you."

"No, he didn't."

"So why're you here? You one of them brood mares Jude keeps locked away up there?"

"What? No! I mean, I'm not a Sister. I work in the nursery."

The woman crosses her arms. "That right?"

I scramble for an explanation. "I came to Eden when I was twelve. With my mother. She was a Sister. But I'm not."

"Was?"

"She died. Several years ago."

"Jude know you're here?"

"No."

Her eyes narrow, but I can feel her relief. "Be quiet," she says, walking to the door and peeking outside.

She shuts the door with a quiet click and washes her hands at the sink with agitated strokes before returning to her abandoned dough. As she kneads, she questions me further. Where I came from. How Maggie died. What my duties are in the nursery.

Eventually, I get up the nerve to ask her name, and she hesitates to study me a moment. "Don't know that I should say."

I walk to the edge of the table, the smell of yeast making my mouth water. "Why?"

"Maybe you're lying. Maybe this is just some kinda trap or something." She stops kneading and leans over, grabbing my face between her floured hands. "You swear to me what you say is true? You really didn't know I was here?"

"I swear. I just wanted to talk to Lir."

Her mouth twitches. "Don't guess it'll hurt either way. Jude don't give a shit what I do no how. I'm stuck here and he knows it. Just waiting for me to die, I expect."

"Wait, why do you say that?"

"Because I'm his mama."

The force of her words hit me like a hammer. "But why are you out here all alone? Why aren't you ..."

"At Eden? You couldn't pay me to step foot in that den of iniquity. I'm Hazel, by the way. Hazel Delacroix. Guess it's my stupidity you can thank for that little palace you're living in."

"How so?"

As the words tumble out, I get the feeling Hazel's been waiting for someone, anyone, to hear her story. "Jude always was a troubled boy. Didn't have many friends in school. Kind of a loner. See, we was just regular country people with regular ways. But he never was satisfied with that. Always wanted more. Started dressing different. Talking different. Didn't want anybody to know where he come from. And then he went off to college and got twisted up with a group who lived in some kind of commune. Weird bunch. Always gave me the willies when he'd bring them around. But eventually that petered out, and by the time he married Freyja, he'd lost touch with that group. I thought that'd be the end of it, and he'd settle down and start a family. Should've known better. Living in that commune changed him. Made him believe he could create some kind of perfect world for himself. So, when my husband died a couple years later, Jude used his part of the life insurance money I gave him as an early inheritance to buy this little island. Got it for cheap because nobody wants a place so far out with no electricity. Had big plans to create what he called a perfect society, 'independent of the world.' Problem was, he ran out of money and didn't have enough to complete his little vision." Hazel plops the dough into a pan and breathes a ragged sigh. "I should've seen it coming, but I loved my boy. Trusted him. I guess every mother just wants her kids to be happy. I wanted that so much. Of course, I was a bit skeptical of the plan, at first. But he made it sound like Eden would be some kind of a family home. Just for us. A place where I could grow old and enjoy my grandson. Guess I thought it sounded better than being put away in a home one day, so I gave in and let him have the money. But it wasn't enough. He always needed a little more. A little more. Until one day, it was all gone. My house and a hundred acres, included. I didn't much care at the time, because it was still just the four of us out here. I should've known it wouldn't stay that way."

"The Sisters?"

She nods. "Don't know where he got the idea. Probably on one of his little dope-smoking trips or something. But this place changed overnight. Turned my stomach. I told him I wanted out, but he wouldn't let me go. Afraid I'd tell and mess up his scheme."

Hazel's words sink like a stone in my stomach, validating feelings and suspicions I don't want to realize exist.

I wave my hand to the cottage. "So you came here."

"That's right. If I had to be stuck on this island, I sure as hell didn't wanna be a resident of that little Sodom and Gomorrah over there. 'Course, I had to pitch one hell of a fit to get him to build me this house over here away from everything."

"What did you say?"

"Told him I was the one brought him into this world and he better believe if he didn't do what I asked, I'd find a way to take him out of it."

My mouth falls open at the thought of someone telling Sensei what to do. Even his own mother. After years of living under his complete control, the idea is preposterous.

I walk to the window and look through the crack. Judging by the sun, it's early afternoon. "I better get back," I say with regret. "You won't tell anyone I've been here?"

"No, honey. I ain't gonna tell. But listen, you ever need anything. Anything at all. You let me know."

I nod, the sincerity of her words like a soothing balm.

"One more thing," she says before I leave. "Be careful what you tell Lir. That place is getting to him." She shakes her fist in the air. "It'll get you too, if you're not careful."

Ten

The sun dips low as I hurry through the trees, and my feet ache from the rough terrain. With Lir gone ahead, I move to the cleared path where travel is easier. No longer hindered by the underbrush, I'm able to run. I have to be back in time for the evening meal or they'll know I've been gone. I've broken small rules before but never been caught, and my stomach churns at the thought of being punished. Whipped with a cane or have my food rations taken away.

I try to pick up my pace even more, but I'm not used to running. My throat is dry and pain shoots through the side of my abdomen. Rounding a sharp corner, I stop for a moment, bending at the waist to catch my breath.

A twig snaps and my head shoots up. I remain still, waiting. My mind tells me it's just a small animal, but I can't shake the feeling I'm being watched. I stand slowly and listen, my eyes scanning the forest to my front and sides.

Nothing.

A shadow falls at my feet and I freeze, every nerve tingling with dread. I turn slowly, fearing the worst. When our eyes lock, I should feel relief, but a shiver travels my spine at the coldness in Lir's gaze.

"I was just looking for you. I was worried you weren't home yet," I say, fumbling for an excuse.

"Headed the wrong way, don't you think?"

I take a step back. "I must have got turned around."

"Drop the act, Max. I know exactly where you've been. Did you really think I didn't know you followed me?"

I grab his arm. "Please. I just wanted to talk to you."

He closes his eyes but doesn't pull away.

"Just talk to me," I beg.

"What do you want me to say?"

"Anything. I want my friend back. I need him back." I inch forward to lay my forehead on his chest. It's the closest he has let me get since our night together, and I revel in the comfort of his familiar scent, like salt and wind and sky. I'm hungry for affection. To feel like my life matters to someone. Anyone.

But after a moment, he pushes me away.

"I'm leaving, Max."

Images of Toci's lifeless body flash in my mind, making my voice shake with emotion. "What do you mean ... leaving?"

"I'm getting off this damn island. I'll go to Galveston. I'll go anywhere. But I can't stay here."

Hope bubbles in my chest at his words. "How?" I ask, barely able to contain my excitement. If he plans to leave, surely I can go with him.

"I'll take my boat. And Hazel has the rest of my stuff." He bites his lip. "I shouldn't have said that." He pulls away, squatting low as he rubs his face with both hands.

I start to go to him but stop. I need him to keep talking. To hear as many details as possible. Anything he's willing to tell.

After a moment, his laugh is harsh and mirthless. "Guess it doesn't matter, anyhow. They'll figure out I'm gone one way or another. I want my own life. I'm tired of being the unpaid help for a cause I don't believe in. Haven't believed in ... ever, I guess."

My heart hammers with newfound courage. "When will you go?"

"Tomorrow."

"Take me with you."

He looks up, his eyes cold. "Why would I do that? You'd just slow me down."

The words hit me like a hammer. I may have known he wasn't in love with me, but his unapologetic selfishness takes my breath away.

"Don't you think I deserve to get out of here too?" I say, my voice cracking with emotion.

He takes a step back and looks down. "The only way I can do this and make it work is to go alone. I can't be responsible for anybody else. For once, I have to think about me. Besides, you're fine here. It's not like you're a Sister or anything."

"I'm pregnant, Lir," I blurt, my eyes brimming with unshed tears.

His head jerks up and his nostrils flare. "What did you say?"

"I said, I'm pregnant."

He shakes his head and backs away, his eyes wild. "I don't believe you."

I rush toward him. "It's the truth. And it's your responsibility. You can't just leave me. What'll happen to the baby? Your baby? What'll happen to me? You remember what Sensei did to Hera—"

"Enough!" he yells, his face turning red. "I don't want to hear any more of your lies."

"I'm not lying," I sob.

He shakes his head and stares at me. "You know, I never thought you'd stoop this low," he scoffs. "But you really will say anything to get your way."

When he storms away, my body quivers with rage at his arrogance. To think that I'd lie about something so important is more than insulting. He should know me better than that.

By the time I make it back to Eden, the evening torches are lit and dinner is being served. The Sisters are busy eating and clapping along as Shauska plays a guitar in the center of the courtyard, but I don't hear the song. I only hear Lir's callous words. See the indifference written on his face. I glance to where he sits beside Sensei, his eyes trained on his food. I'm amazed to see his appetite remains hearty as he cleans his plate and asks for seconds.

It dawns on me that Lir truly is his father's son, caring only for himself and his own ambition. But just like my mother, I chose to ignore the warning signs and see only the good. I wanted to believe Lir was different. That I'm different. But here we are, following in the toxic footsteps of our parents.

When our eyes finally meet, his lip curls into a snarl, and he leans toward Sensei, whispering into his ear. After a moment, Sensei frowns and cuts his eyes in my direction, causing me to slide down in my seat.

"Max," he says, standing to his feet as a hush comes over the crowd.

I freeze, my blood turning to ice. "Yes, Sensei?"

He folds his arms over his chest and lifts his chin. "It has come to my attention that you left the nursery today and ventured to the other side of the island without permission. Is this true?"

I shoot Lir a pleading look, but he refuses to meet my gaze. I could lie, but given the situation, it would probably only make it worse. So, I nod and keep my eyes downcast, hoping to portray remorse for my disobedience. "Please, forgive me. I just wanted to help Lir," I say, hoping my excuse will sound innocent.

Sensei's eyes narrow. "You've followed the rules for many years, Max. Why break them now?"

I open my mouth but can't think of an appropriate answer.

Freyja's eyebrows go up as she turns to Sensei with a pointed look. "Does it matter why a rule is broken?"

He gives her a smile and shakes his head. "You're absolutely right." His eyes return to me, and he calls me forward to stand before him. Taking both my hands in his own, his voice is soft, his dark eyes penetrating. "Our rules are in place to keep you from harm. And if you choose to break those rules, there are consequences." He heaves a sigh and calls Freyja forward.

"Yes, Sensei?" she says with an innocent expression that sends shivers down my spine.

"Bring Max to the altar. You know what has to be done."

The moon is bright and round, illuminating the outside world in a way that is deceptive of the hour. It's late, well past midnight, but I can't sleep. The pain from my punishment throbs, the long marks on my back deep, biting reminders of the joy with which Freyja yields her power. Tied flat on the floor of the ceremonial altar, I endured each lash with the hope that it would be the last. But they kept coming, one after another, until I thought I might pass out. I prayed for it, even. To be taken to a place far away from the sting of Freyja's whip. When the torture finally ended, I was too weak to even cry out as I was lifted from the altar by two Sisters. As I was led away, bile rose in my throat as I caught a glimpse of Freyja's face glowing with ecstasy. And it's that look of pure evil that I see every time I try to close my eyes. So, I keep them open, focused on the distant flash of light on the dark horizon. It's the same light Maggie and I followed all those years ago. Part of me feels that if I could return to that place, to that lighthouse, maybe I could start over. Pretend like Eden never happened. Choose a brand-new path. A new life. And who's to say I can't? Lir is leaving, after all. Why should I be the one stuck here to face the consequences of our actions alone? It's not fair. Something has to give. If I want change, I have to be brave. I've seen the kind of depravity Sensei and Freyja are capable of, and I will not sit idly by while my throat is slit or my infant is ripped from my arms. I have to take action before it's too late. My future is no longer my own.

I open my door, easing it farther and farther until it's wide enough to slip into the hall. I look around to make sure no one is around, then pad softly to Lir's door where I sit and listen for sound. If he plans to escape in the middle of the night, he will have to take me with him or risk me sounding the alarm and crushing his dream.

Sensei would not take his son's deception lightly.

I lie on the floor with my ear pressed to the space beneath. I hear nothing for a long time. Too long.

Resting my hand on the knob, my heart pounds in my throat at my boldness. But when I push it open, the room is cool and dark and still. I'm too late.

Anger. Frustration. Despair. All emotions I've felt before but never with such intensity. I berate myself for not coming sooner. My chance has passed. Or has it?

Creeping back to my own room, I open my chest of clothes and pull off my nightgown, wincing at the action. Every movement still causes pain, despite being wrapped and bandaged by Dr. Chen. I carefully slip three dresses over my head, layered for easy carrying. Placing my Bible into a small pouch made of soft leather, I strap it across my chest and turn to look at the nursery. I refuse to believe this is the end. If Lir can run away, I can too.

Eleven

With the moon bright, the trail through the woods is easy to navigate. I figure I have two, maybe three hours before sun up and half a day at best before Sensei notices Lir's absence. I could've waited, but if Sensei learns of my involvement, he would put the island on lockdown and demand answers. And though I hate to admit it, I would buckle under such an interrogation. He has a way of getting in my head. A way of lulling me into a false sense of security.

And if that doesn't work, he would use force. In the end, I would tell him everything.

So, I push through the forest at breakneck speed, hoping I remember the way to Hazel's house. Hoping, by some chance of fate, she'll know what to do. Lir mentioned using Hazel's boat to escape. Maybe he's still there. Maybe I can catch him in time and demand to go along. As much as I despise him right now, I need his help to leave the island. I'm certain Hazel would take my side, especially if I tell her my secret.

I hear the waves before I see them, soft crashes in the distance. Dark dunes soft under my feet as I climb, legs burning by the time I reach the top. The sea glitters black with an energy that is felt more than seen. Like a living being, it has the power to comfort and terrify at will. I listen and try to judge its current mood. Quiet. Waiting.

After a while, the dark shape of Hazel's home stands like a boxy smudge in the distance. I run faster, unhindered except by the occasional large shell along the open shore. When I get close, my pulse pounds at the warm glow of light through the window. The signal gives me hope that I've made it in time. That it's not too late to leave this place and never look back.

I round the edge of the house and beat on the door.

Hazel jerks it open and waves me forward. "I knew you'd come."

"How?"

"Lir mentioned you might before he left."

My chest tightens at the news. "So he's gone?"

"Expect he's about half way to Galveston by now."

"Did he say what he'll do when he gets there?"

She breathes a heavy sigh. "Told him to go down to the fish market, see if he can find a job. Somewhere to sleep until he gets on his feet. We don't have no family left to help. And all my friends are either dead or in a home. Sure never thought my life would turn out like this." She plops into a chair, her elbows resting on the table, her hands cradling her head. "I've lost everything now. First Jude. Now Lir."

When she starts to cry, I stand beside her, unsure of what to do, how to comfort her when I feel just as low. Just as hopeless and scared and betrayed. I want to cry with her. Or scream and shout and roll on the floor. I think of a story from the Bible. The one where Job has lost everything. Flocks and riches and children and health. And when his friends go to comfort him, they sit on the ground beside him for seven days and seven nights without speaking a word. Some suffering is too great for words. But it's enough to simply be present. To sit in the mud with your friend.

So, I sit on the floor at Hazel's feet, wiping my own tears as she dabs at her face, blowing her nose into a dishtowel.

"I don't know what to do either," I whisper. With Lir gone, I'm out of ideas. There are no other boats that don't require keys. Keys that live inside a locked desk drawer in Sensei's office.

"What do you mean?" she asks, resting a hand on my shoulder.

I wince at the touch and pull away, my hands shaking as I touch my stomach. "I thought if I got here in time, he might take me with him."

Hazel's eyes turn to slits. "You love him?"

With my feelings so tangled, I debate what to say. How to answer. I look Hazel in the eye and reveal the only truth I'm certain of. "No, I don't love Lir. But I love his child. Our child. Even if he doesn't."

Hazel sits up straight, her eyes round. "This is bad. Real bad."

"I know."

She stands, her muscles rigid. "You gotta get out of here

before they find out. Galveston's not too far, if you just had a way ..." She paces the floor, ringing her hands together. "Wait. I just thought of something. Come on."

I run to keep up with her long strides, stopping at the small garden shed behind the house. The door creaks and a match strikes, coaxing a lantern to life. The dim glow reveals a few pots and tools and a small push mower.

"What's in here?" I ask, pushing a broken terra-cotta planter to the side with my foot.

Hazel raises the light high and points to the ceiling.

I gasp at the outline of a small vessel hanging from the rafters by a few thin ropes. Coated in cobwebs and dust, it's the most beautiful sight I've ever seen. The tiny boat represents hope. A way out.

"Where'd you get it?" I ask, climbing onto a stepladder to look over the edge. Two long oars are visible, propped on the wooden seat.

"My husband made it when he was a kid. Used to take Jude out fishing in it. It's real special to me. Guess that's why I've held onto it. But I want you to take it and get out of here."

I frown. "But I thought you said you've wanted to get away for years. Why haven't you taken it yourself?"

"Where would I go? An old woman with no friends or family. No money. If I were younger, maybe. Not now." She points to me. "But you don't have a choice. If you stay here, they'll take that baby and you'll never see it again."

"I'll never let that happen."

"Good. Come on, let's start untying these ropes. We better get a move on if you wanna beat the sun."

"Why don't you come with me?"

She shakes her head. "No. I'll stay and try to buy you a little time. You just get yourself out of this place and don't you ever look back."

I stop what I'm doing and look into her eyes. "One day, I'll come back for you. I promise. I won't leave you out here by yourself."

Hazel stares at me a moment and gives a slight nod, her eyes glistening a little brighter than before.

A gust of wind rocks the thin boat, but it's tight as a drum with no leaks or cracks in the smooth wood. It's a small miracle and one I couldn't have imagined wanting or needing just a few days ago. As swiftly as the changing tide, my life has been flipped upside down and set on an irreversible course. A course I'm not even sure I'm prepared to take. But as my arms pull the oars, I'm reminded that life doesn't wait for us to be ready. Change can happen at any moment, whether we like it or not. At least I have a plan. Hazel suggested a job at the fishing wharf to Lir. If he can find a job that easily, so can I.

I pull in the oars, check the compass Hazel gave me, and drink from the Mason jar she packed along with some fruit, nuts, and bread. My stomach recoils at the idea of eating, but I pull out a piece of bread anyhow, knowing my strength will give out if I don't. My back still hurts, but I can't let it slow me down.

As night fades to dawn, I miss the distant blink of the lighthouse. The flashing beacon of hope that drove me forward through the night. But despite my resolve, a sense of unease has me turning to look behind me, fearing Jude will appear. I'm done calling him Sensei. From now on, he is simply Jude. The name Hazel gave him, proving he's just a person, like me. He's not special. He's not and never will be a god. He brainwashes women and sells their children like cattle. It's something I've always known but never really seen. Acknowledged. Because such acknowledgment means I'm also to blame. I could have fought back. Done something. But I didn't.

My throat constricts with guilt at my cowardice even though nothing I could've done would've been enough. But maybe leaving is my way of helping. My way of breaking the chain for my own child, if nothing else.

Arms aching, blisters form on my palms, but I keep pulling the oars. I have to make it to Galveston before Jude finds me or I get caught in a storm. I shiver at the thought. What I used to find exciting is now terrifying. In this boat, a storm could be a death sentence.

I check my compass again, careful to stay in a northeast direction. I've drifted a bit off course, so I work the oars to correct the mistake. Sweat makes my hands slip and my layered dresses stick to my back.

The water around me teems with life, a whale calling in the distance, dolphins leaping and racing like rambunctious children. I find their play reassuring, like they're telling me I'm not alone.

I close my eyes, enjoying the feel of the wind, the sound of water lapping against the hull. I want to pretend I'm not on the run. That it's just another day. But a sound intrudes, quiet at first, then louder until I can no longer deny it as my imagination. I row faster, my arms burning from fatigue and fear as I spot it. A speck behind me growing larger by the minute. I could try to hide in the bottom of the boat or flip it over the edge in an attempt to conceal myself. But I know what's coming. I've been caught.

Jude usually prefers the fast yellow cigar boat. An overpriced toy to stroke his ego. But today he trolls to a stop in his white fishing boat. No need for speed today. He knows I can't get away.

By the time he kills the engine, I'm shaking so hard I have to clamp my jaw tight in an effort to keep my teeth from chattering under his cool appraisal. He's wearing dark sunglasses and a grin I'd love to smack right off his arrogant face. Especially when he removes the glasses and props his foot on the side, his mouth lifting in a grin.

Based on his expression, I'm guessing he hasn't noticed Lir's absence from Eden. Just mine. Lir was free to come and go most of the time with no one keeping tabs. But I'm different. I'm a woman.

Jude studies me, amused by my predicament. "Are you lost?" he says, his words void of the malice I'm expecting.

For a moment, I consider lying. Saying yes, I am lost. That I found the boat abandoned in the woods. That I meant to take it on a short trip around the island, but the tide took me farther. To start crying in false relief and tell him how glad I am that he's here. Pretend he's my hero.

I open my mouth, the lie on the tip of my tongue, but I

stop. I have a choice. If I give in, I'll be destined to the life I left behind. A life I can no longer accept. Or worse, no life at all.

The moment seems to last forever. I look down at the leather bag containing my Bible and remember the words written on the tiny pages. Words of strength and courage and faith in the face of fear.

I clench my fists and turn to Jude. "No," I say in a clear voice. "I'm not lost."

Twelve

Jude hauls me into his boat, my knees scraping against the hot fiberglass, the flesh blistering and burning. His hands are like steel vises, bruising my arms as he flips me over the side. I try to fight, but the effort is futile. A whimper escapes my throat as I fall to the floor with a thud.

"Be still," Jude commands, keeping a tight hold on my shoulders. "Be still, damn it. I have something to say." When I stop struggling, he towers over me, a shadow concealing his expression. "There now," he says in a softer voice.

I bristle at his tone. It's the same one he uses on the Sisters. Soft. Rational. Controlled. A deliberate means to overpower in the most agreeable way possible. His voice is rarely harsh or angry. Instead, he prefers to appear open for discussion. Ready to lend an ear in an act that simulates sincerity. Like you're really being heard. He lets you talk for as long as you like, then gently corrects your error in judgement, effectively steering you in the direction he would have you go all along.

He crouches beside me now, his face full of practiced concern as he reaches to caress my arm. When I flinch, his eyes widen in overdone shock. "Did I hurt you? If I did, please forgive me. I'm only trying to do what's best for you." He stands and indicates the seat near the back. "Come sit with me in the shade. Let's get you cooled off so we can talk."

Sucking in a shaky breath, my eyes search for a way out of my predicament. I can run for the edge and throw myself overboard. But then what? I'll never be able to outrun him in my tiny boat. I'm trapped and he knows it.

When I'm seated, he pulls a bottle of water from the cooler and hands it to me. "You must be thirsty. That's it, drink up. Let's get you back to normal."

My stomach turns at his word choice. Normal. The insinuation that only a crazy person would run away from his little paradise. It occurs to me that in his effort to make everyone else fall in line with his fabricated religion, he's come to believe it himself.

"I'm done," I say, shoving the half-empty bottle back to him.

He chuckles and takes a long drink, his eyes never leaving mine. I work to keep my expression clear. Stern. I refuse to bend, no matter what he says or promises. I will get away or die trying.

Jude clears his throat and smiles. "Now, you say you're not lost. If that's the truth, then may I ask where you're headed?"

I sit up straight and decide to be honest. No more beating

around the bush, no matter the consequences. "I'm running away."

His eyebrows lift, his head falling in a slight nod. I can't tell if he's shocked or amused or both. "Running away," he mimics. "How charming. Tell me, just where do you think you're running to?"

"Freedom."

He laughs. "Well, you certainly won't find that in the outside world. You're a smart girl, Max. Let's be rational. If it's freedom you want, then I'm sure we can work something out." He rests his hand on my thigh, his fingers drawing small circles on the fabric of my dress. "If you're tired of the nursery, I can think of another much higher calling for you. In fact, I had a vision of you just last night." He leans forward, his breath tickling my ear. "And the future looked quite fulfilling, for us both." He accentuates the final word with a wet kiss on my neck.

My heart hammers at his revolting suggestion. "No," I scream, pushing him away.

His eyes harden, the rational facade gone in an instant. "All members of Eden contribute. Haven't you learned anything, you selfish little bitch. Everything I do, every choice I make, is for the good of the community. The good of you. The least you could do is be grateful." He leans close, flecks of his saliva spattering my face. "In case you don't remember, I plucked you and your nitwit little mother from that sewer pipe of a city out of the goodness of my heart. I set you up with a life you could have never dreamed of. A life most people would kill for, and this is the thanks I get?"

I stand up, fists clenched, nails cutting into my palms. "I'm not going back," I say in an even voice. I'm proud of my resolve, my demand to be heard after years of silence.

Jude's eyes widen before he looks away. My pulse quickens at the reaction. It's only a small crack, but I can tell my strength has shaken him. Perhaps I can get away after all. Maybe, by some chance, my forthrightness has earned his respect. I take the opportunity to move a step toward the side where my boat is tied, bobbing in the water.

It takes a moment for Jude to realize my intent, that I'm serious in my endeavor to leave, no matter the consequences. But whatever weakness I saw a moment ago is gone. His eyes bore into me, nostrils flaring as he lunges. But I'm faster.

I run ahead, slipping a little on the wet floor as I get one leg over the railing. Just as I'm about to hurl myself into the water, Jude grabs a handful of my hair and jerks me to the floor. I scream and claw at his face, but he takes my hands, twisting my wrists until I fear they might snap. I cry out, my legs giving way as I try to escape the pain. When I twist to the side, he catches me under the arm and drags me toward the center of the boat.

"You're making me do this," he says, flipping open the lid of the live well full of murky water that smells like mildew and rotten fish.

"No," I manage to say just before my head is thrust into the water. I try to shake him off, but he holds me under for such a long time my body goes limp as my lungs burn for oxygen. When he finally pulls me up, I cough and gasp for air, thankful to be alive but remembering my resolve.

I look at his sweaty face, red from exertion and rage. I've

only seen him this mad once before when Rosmerta quietly defied his absolute control. Fresh rage kindles inside me at the memory, at the cold indifference for human life.

"Let me go!" I scream, fighting Jude with renewed vigor. "I'd rather die than go back!"

By the look on his face, I can tell I've rattled him and the knowledge gives me the sudden urge to laugh, a loud cackling sound that defies my situation in the most blatant way possible.

His nostrils flare and he slaps me hard, the force causing my neck to spasm and my nose to gush blood. The next instant I'm back in the live well, struggling to hold in the last bit of air from my weakened lungs. I manage to get one of my arms into the well, my hand pushing against the slimy bottom in an effort to free myself. Just when I think my lungs will burst, my fingers brush against something sharp. I grapple for the object, gripping it as Jude pulls me from the water in a rush.

I only have an instant to recognize the weapon as the broken handle of a dip net, sharp on the end that's been severed. I lunge for Jude, catching his upper arm with the blade, but not doing adequate damage to keep him away.

He glances at the scrape and laughs. "Oh, so that's how it is, then? You think you're going to cut me?" I try to get by him, but he blocks me every time, his movements too quick to process.

I stumble back, prepared to throw myself overboard if I can get close enough to the edge. But the floor is slick and causes me to slip. The next instant I'm lying flat with Jude on top of me, his weight crushing against me. Sweat drips onto my face as his hands wrap around my throat. My mouth begs for air as he slams my head into the floor over and over. I know I'm about to die. I'm on the edge of darkness, the life draining from my body with every crunch of my skull.

My light may be fading, but I'm not afraid. I've never been scared of the dark.

Thirteen

My vision is blurry, my senses numbed. The fact that I can hear Jude's motor as it fades into the distance means I'm still alive, floating in the open ocean. But the idea is still hard to comprehend. It would be so easy to close my eyes and sleep in the gentle cocoon of water. To softly surrender, content in the knowledge I did my best. Fought the good fight. But I can't stop fighting. The life within me depends on it.

I ignore the sting of salt in my wounds, the metallic taste of blood filling my mouth from my head wound. The desire to stop moving my arms is strong, to let my head slip beneath the surface and rest, just like Jude wants.

He's gone now. Back to his sanctuary of lies and the women who believe them. I wonder what kind of story he will conjure about my disappearance. That I ran away. That he couldn't find me. Or that I'm dead. To him, it's the truth. He knew what would happen when he left me, beaten and bruised, drowning in a sea of my own blood. And I know why he didn't finish the job. He wants me to suffer, my final breath filled with agony and terror.

The thought kindles fresh rage, making it easier to push through the pain throbbing in my skull. After a few tries, I manage to kick myself into a floating position on my back. Spite is a powerful motivator.

This technique requires less energy, but even so I can feel myself weakening, my breath coming in shallow gasps.

My eyes close as I force sound through my vocal cords.

"Help," I whisper.

Just one word. But it's the closest thing to a prayer I can manage.

I want to cry but my body is too exhausted for tears. Just keeping air in my lungs and blood pumping through my veins is a struggle. I wonder how far I've drifted, if I'm any closer to Galveston than before. The water is quiet. Smooth. Endless in all directions.

A dolphin jumps in the distance, followed by the cry of a seagull. If only it could stay this way, peaceful and uninterrupted. But I know what's coming. With the amount of blood in the water, it's only a matter of time before they find me. I squeeze my eyes shut, not wanting to see. But the anticipation of being eaten alive is too strong, breaking my resolve. My eyes pop back open, as if being able to see my attackers will prevent them from coming. It's a foolish notion, but I can't help scanning the water, left, right, left, right.

When I see the first fin, my stomach drops. I want to vomit or scream, but I do neither.

"Help," I whisper again. But my prayer is met with the sight of a second fin, closer this time. I tense, my hands and legs quivering as I fight a fresh wave of fear.

Maybe the sharks are my answer, a quick death versus days and days of suffering and starvation. I try to quiet my mind. Meditate. Prepare myself for the inevitable. But I can't. The fins come closer and closer and adrenaline courses through my veins like fire spreading over a parched valley.

But just as I feel my time is up, other fins appear. Different in shape and color.

Dolphins.

Beautiful, magnificent, ancient creatures circling so close I can feel their bodies occasionally slide against my own. The school is comprised of too many to count, creating a barrier of protection against the enemy.

As the sharks appear less and less, I'm overwhelmed by joy and gratitude and the feeling of what it truly means to be alive.

I am not hopeless or invisible or unloved, after all.

I'm not sure how long the dolphins circle. Minutes or hours. But the amount of blood in the water lessens, the salt closing some of my wounds. When the dolphins begin to fall away, the loss stings. With them surrounding me, I felt part of a team. Like everything would be all right. But their absence makes it clear I have survived one danger only to face another. Without any sort of floatation device, it's only a matter of time before my stamina evaporates.

My face is barely above water, my legs cramping, my hands and feet hardly able to keep up with the demand.

"Help," I try to whisper through cracked lips, the effort burning a path down my parched throat. I think of a verse I've read.

In the beginning was the Word, and the Word was with God, and the Word was God.

"Help," I say again, forcing my body to articulate my plea.

I don't want to die. Not like this. I try to keep kicking, but my legs won't move. My body feels heavy as the water tugs, calling me to the depths of a watery grave. My head slips under once. Twice. The waves grow violent, pushing and pulling as if in a storm. But the sky is clear, the sun a round orange blob that sinks lower every second.

A muffled roar fills my water-clogged ears. And then another sound, high and human.

"There! Over there! Hurry!"

The roar grows louder. A splash. Someone in the water, blurry and nearing. The feel of arms around me. Being lifted into a boat.

A woman's voice, high and shaking. "Is she dead?"

Fingers press into my throat.

"No," a man says, breathless. "Come on. Let's get her downstairs."

"Can you hear me, sugar bee?" the woman says gently.

I nod and try to open my eyes, but the light hurts. She flips a switch, dimming the glow. I crack one eyelid, then the other, and take in my lavish surroundings. I'm in the captain's quarters of what seems like a very expensive yacht. A baby bassinet filled with luxury bedding catches my eye.

When I sit up, the action reveals a dark spot on the fine linen coverlet beside my shoulder. I touch the soiled bedding, my fingers tracing a gold embroidered B on the pillowcase, now crunchy with blood and utterly ruined. "I'm sorry," I try say, but the words are garbled, unintelligible.

The woman rushes forward, a flurry of blond hair and tan lines. "Oh, honey, don't mind that. You just be still and rest." She turns her face toward the door, cupping a hand around her mouth. "Phillip! She's awake!"

A moment later, a tall man in wet clothes enters the room, carrying a tray with bottled water, crackers, and cheese. With his sandy hair and broad shoulders, he reminds me of a Ken doll. "Sorry, this is all I could find down there." He sets the tray on the bed and gives the woman a pointed look. "I told you we should've brought Marguerite along. You know I don't like traveling without staff."

"I believe we already discussed that, honey." Her tone is syrupy sweet, yet sharp as a tack. Clearly, she's the type of woman who stands her ground. She reminds me of someone but in the dim light, I can't say who.

He places the tray on the bedside table and turns to me with a frown. "Shit. She don't look good. Try to get some water in her and I'll get us turned around. Galveston should have the closest ER."

When he leaves the room, the woman opens the water

bottle and shoves a plastic straw in the top. "Here now, let's see if we can get you to drink some of this," she says, leaning over to hold the straw to my lips.

Her perfume is strong and sweet, like candy or fruit. I swallow a few sips and study her face up close. The big blue eyes, lips painted red. She looks at me and smiles, kindling the picture of someone I used to know.

"Hang on, sugar bee," she says as I close my eyes. "We'll get you some help. Just hang on."

FOURTEEN

When I wake from the trance for the second time, it's dark and I'm starving. Dr. Gregory has removed her glasses and sits hunched over her desk, massaging the bridge of her nose.

"How do you feel, Max?"

"Okay," I say, sitting up to place my feet on the floor. "A little stiff."

"You've been here for some time." She holds up a thick notebook. "We filled up three of these."

"I'm sorry. I didn't mean to go on for so long."

"No. Don't apologize. I've also recorded everything on this." She picks up a black recorder sitting on the desk. "Your story is completely fascinating. I've ... never met someone who has gone through quite the same thing. I know the police will want all this information so they can catch this man."

My body quivers with nervous excitement at the idea of vindication. "Thank you." I take a deep breath, overcome with the idea that my story is being taken seriously. That someone on the outside is willing to listen and understand. With the release comes pain, but also relief. Relief in the pain of a burden finally shared.

Dr. Gregory's brows pinch together. "Just to clarify, the man that tried to kill you is named Jude Delacroix, correct?"

"That's right."

"And you say that several other women were also held captive by him on the island."

"Are being held," I correct, my voice shaking with adrenaline. "The women. And his mother, Hazel. They're all still there. I'm the only one who got away."

When I first left Eden, the idea of justice wasn't a notion I entertained. My only thought was of protecting my child and myself. But now that it's over, I can't walk away and pretend it never happened. That Eden doesn't exist. I have to let the world know what kind of monster Jude Delacroix really is.

Dr. Gregory flips a couple of pages, her finger following a line of text. "I do have one question, though. You say here that the father of your child is Jude Delacroix's son, Lir. But later you say that Lir left the island. Did you leave together?"

"No. We left the same night. But not together."

"So, you haven't seen him since that time?"

I shake my head.

"Can you explain your relationship?"

I stare at my lap. "At first, we were just friends. But then ..."

"You had sex?"

"Yes."

"Was it consensual?"

"It was."

"That's good to know. I'm sure the police are going to want to find him and bring him in for questioning, as well. Do you think he would be willing to talk to them about Eden?"

I shrug. "I don't know. Maybe."

She checks her watch. "Charlie—I mean Chief Andrews is working late tonight, so I'll go ahead and run your testimony to the station." She drops the notebooks into a leather briefcase and places the recorder inside her desk drawer.

When she grabs her car keys from a hook by the door, I hold up my hand.

"You know him? The police chief?" I ask.

She stops, a surprised look on her face. "Oh, yes. I thought you knew. He's my father-in-law. Well, soon to be father-in-law."

Hope surges to the surface at the revelation. Her familial ties to the police force could be useful in persuading them to take action. Surely, if she believes my story, they will too.

"When are you getting married?"

"In the fall." She walks to her desk, flipping a frame around to reveal herself embracing a man. He's handsome in a very ordinary sort of way. Ruddy complexion, large build, round face, and short, dark hair.

"What's his name?"

"Kent. He works at the station too."

"Really? That's great. So you must see each other a lot."

"That's actually how we met. My work here at the shelter ensured our paths crossed and the rest was history."

"So you think they can help me? The police, I mean."

She winks. "I know they can. Now stop worrying and go have dinner. We'll talk more tomorrow."

Fifteen

Tomorrow came and went with no sign of Dr. Gregory. I even walked by her office several times to check, but the room remained empty, the light off.

"Oh, honey, she'll be back as soon as she can," Miss Janie assures, squeezing my shoulders in a gentle hug. "Dr. Gregory usually visits every few weeks, so it shouldn't be too much longer. Besides, we have plenty of things to keep you busy until then. Like our field trip today." Her head bobs up and down with enthusiasm. "I didn't see your name on the list, but it's not too late to join us. Gladys puts on the most wonderful class for beginners over at the Golden Thimble." She leans forward, her voice lowering to a whisper. "Don't tell the others, because I don't want to get their hopes up, but I think we are gonna make aprons. Doesn't that sound like fun?" She claps her hands together in delight.

I can't help but smile at Miss Janie's eagerness, but the thought of focusing on anything other than the problem at hand feels overwhelming. I know I should try to get my mind off of my troubles, but I've never been good at distracting myself. I can't count the number of times I've been told to relax and just breathe. To open my mind to gratitude. Be total. Like any of that bullshit works. In fact, it's that sort of lackadaisical attitude that lands people in bad situations. Places like Eden. Or the Penthouse. Or jail. In my opinion, going with the flow leads to nothing but destruction. If I want my life to change, I refuse to wait for the karma fairy to take care of it.

I stop in the hallway and look at my reflection. My bruises are gone and the cut on my head has healed nicely. Except for my growing stomach, I look like my old self.

When I get back to my bunk, I stretch out on top of the coverlet. Closing my eyes, I listen to the sounds of the shelter, a baby crying in another room, two women arguing over whose turn it is to clean the bathroom. Rain pelts the roof, lulling me into a light sleep until the sound of Miss Janie's voice makes me jump to my feet.

"Max, where are you?" she calls, rounding the corner with bright eyes. "Oh, there you are. We're about to go. Are you sure you don't wanna come along? We'd just love to have you."

"Yeah, I'm sure. Think I'll just stick around here if that's okay."

"All right, then. Oh, I almost forgot. Thought you'd like to know Dr. Gregory called and said she'd be here around noon today."

My chest lightens at the news. I check the clock on the wall. It reads a quarter to eleven.

When Miss Janie hurries outside, I turn to the arguing women. "I'll do it," I say, grabbing the bucket of supplies by the door.

They look at me with wide eyes. "You sure?" one of them asks, a hint of skepticism at such an offer.

I shrug. "Yeah. I need something to keep busy."

By the time I hear the click of Dr. Gregory's heels in the hall, I've scrubbed the bathroom and half of the kitchen. The work was exhausting but just what I needed to pass the time.

As I head down the hall, my pulse pumps in anticipation of what news she may bring. Her door is open, so I rap lightly on the frame.

"Hello, can I come in?"

She looks up for a brief instant. "Uh, yeah. Sure."

Her expression makes my presence feel intrusive, like I'm interrupting something important.

"Are you sure? I don't mind waiting if you're busy."

She shoves something into a desk drawer and shakes her head. "No, it's fine. What'cha got?" Her tone is casual, like she wasn't expecting me.

"Oh ... I just ... wanted to ask about my testimony. If maybe you've heard something?"

Her cheeks turn pink, but she doesn't look up from collecting papers into neat stacks on her desk. "Not yet. But you'll be the first to know when I do."

I take a few steps forward. "Do you know if they've read it yet?"

She stops shuffling papers, her body rigid. "Honestly, I really have no idea. Chief Andrews is a very busy man, Max. I'm sure he'll get to it when he can."

Strangled with disappointment, I open my mouth but can't think of anything to say.

Tears burn hot trails down my face as I walk out of her office. It's times like this that makes me wonder why I even try. What hope is there anyhow? The police probably think my story is too outlandish to be true. But who can blame them?

I glance at the television hanging on the wall of the recreation hall. The same one that broadcasts a daily dose of thinly-veiled horror known as the local news. Rapes, stabbings, robbery, assault. With such things happening every day, right in front of them, why should the police care about three notebooks filled with my ramblings? To the average person the accusations probably seem outrageous. Why should paid professionals waste time investigating what could easily be the fantasies of a teenage runaway with an overactive imagination?

I might not be educated, but I'm smart enough to know when the odds are stacked against me. I sit down on the worn, plaid sofa and pick up a throw pillow with the words "Be Patient" embroidered in green thread. I take it as a sign. Maybe I should wait. But for what? And whom? I guess I should give Dr. Gregory more time. Perhaps eventually she will have some answers. I cling to that hope. Hope is all I have.

The bell on the front door clangs, announcing Miss Janie's arrival. I rush to hold it as she struggles to close her umbrella without dropping the stack of damp mail pressed to her chest.

"Thanks, dearie. I swear all it does is rain these days. I tell you, we're due to have another hurricane. Mark my words, by the end of September, we'll have a whopper on our hands. I can always tell when it's getting time." She pulls a Kleenex from her purse and dabs at her face. "Here," she says, shoving the mail into my hands. "Can you sort that? Just stick it into the slots over there. They should all be labeled."

I take the letters and file them accordingly, enjoying the small task. But my hand stills when I come across one marked to myself from the Galveston Police Department. I hurry to file the remaining letters and run to my bunk. It's been weeks since I last spoke to Dr. Gregory, and I'm anxious for news. My hand shakes as I rip the envelope, careful not to tear the return address. The note is one page, hand written in neat cursive.

Dear Miss Fontaine,

I would like to inform you that after careful consideration of your testimony given to the office of Chief Charles Andrews of the Galveston, Texas Police Department by Sarah Gregory MD, I have decided not to pursue any further investigation into the alleged crimes of Mr. Jude Delacroix or any other named individuals. Over the past couple of weeks, our force has been in contact with Mr. Delacroix and have found no reason to believe foul play is involved. A thorough welfare check has been conducted on all individuals in question and the city of Galveston is satisfied that all persons residing on Eden Island are happy and content with their living arrangements and are in no danger, mentally, physically, or otherwise.

Mr. Delacroix also informed me that the events leading up to your recent hospital stay are the result of your decision to leave the island in favor of pursuing a life elsewhere. He says he tried to offer safe passage for you to Galveston, but that you refused, insisting on going alone in a small boat hardly suitable for such an endeavor. He wishes to extend his deepest regrets for your untimely accident and best wishes for the future.

Sincerely,
Chief Charles Andrews
Galveston Police Department

I stare at the letter a long time, rereading the words over and again. The complete incompetence of the authorities is stunning. Of course they didn't find any foul play when they went to the island! Jude always covers his tracks, coaching the Sisters on what to say, how to act, if the authorities were ever to show up. To think the police would actually believe they could just trot in and have everyone confess to a multi-million-dollar human trafficking business is beyond stupid.

I shake my head as if the action will wake me from the perpetual nightmare that is my life. To make matters worse, Jude knows I'm alive. Where I'm staying. It won't be long before he comes to finish the job and silence me forever.

One glance at the window shows the rain has stopped, dusk taking its place. With my safety in danger, I can't risk staying another night. I don't want to leave Miss Janie, but I have to get away. Go somewhere, anywhere I'm not recognized. Maybe I can find Lir, like I had once planned. I cringe at the thought of begging him for help, but I don't have a choice. I can't live on the street. Hazel mentioned a job at the fish market. Maybe he'll be there.

I pull a plastic milk crate from beneath my bed and survey the inventory. Pajamas, a T-shirt, socks, underwear, bra, and jeans held over my growing belly with the help of a hairband looped through the buttonhole. All of the clothes are hand-me-downs from the communal closet upstairs. But I decide the borrowed clothing and shoes must stay. The last thing I need is to be accused of theft on top of my other troubles.

I dig deeper and find the only four possessions I can truly call mine. One linen dress, still loose enough to fit over my tummy, a small leather bag, a bottle of prenatal vitamins given to me by the clinic, and my Bible. The dress is in pretty good shape, having been shielded by two others during my ordeal with Jude. My Bible, on the other hand, will never be the same. Stained and waterlogged, I'm amazed it's still intact. I touch the blurred ink, the clumps of pages permanently fused together. I should throw it away, but I can't. Something inside refuses to let go. To let Jude win. He tried to take everything, but he can't have this. It may not be useful in the way it once was, but it's mine. A permanent reminder of the life I left behind and the life I hope to gain by doing so.

It's long after lights-out when I creep from my bed and tiptoe down the hall to Dr. Gregory's office. I twist the knob, the quiet click of the latch sounding loud as I slip inside and fumble through the darkness. When I reach the desk, most of the drawers are locked. But I breathe a sigh of relief when my fingers find the black recorder in the only one left open. The recorder may be useless at this point, but something tells me to slip it into my pocket. It's my voice, after all, telling my story. And every word is the truth, whether or not anyone chooses to believe me.

Making sure to leave the office as I found it, I ease down the hall and toward the kitchen door. Moonlight seeps from the small squares of dirty glass, casting angular shadows over the worn linoleum floor that feels sticky under my bare feet. My hand trembles as I slide the deadbolt, cringing at the slight squeak when I pull it open an inch. I freeze, holding my breath and listening for sound, but nothing except the *tick, tick, tick* of the hall clock breaks the silence. The crack widens enough to slip outside into the moist night air. With the security light on the opposite side of the property, I'm able to stay hidden in the shadows as I slink across the backyard, past the dumpster, and onto a narrow street leading toward the center of town.

My plan is to stay out of sight, at least until I'm far away from the shelter. Leaving was easier than expected. Too easy almost. I stiffen at the thought that my exit may have been anticipated. A part of Jude's plan all along. Why else would he send a message through Chief Andrews? What if Jude wants me to run so he can pounce? As a runaway, who would notice? Sure, Miss Janie would go to the police, and they might tack up a few missing person flyers, but she would never learn the truth. No one would. I glance over my shoulder, palms slick with sweat, heart pounding in my ears at the thought of being watched. Followed. I start running. The road is rough and uneven, but I don't stop. I can't. I have to get as far away from the shelter as possible.

I run until sharp pains shoot through my ribs, forcing me to pause, my breath coming in quick gasps as I wipe sweat from my forehead with the back of my arm. When the breeze picks up, cooling my overheated skin, I turn my head, trying to figure out exactly where I am. In the distance, I hear the distinct sound of waves breaking on the beach, but I'm still disoriented. In my haste, I must've veered off course. South instead of east.

Heavy clouds cover the moon, and very few houses seem to occupy the area. With little light, attempting to correct my mistake might force me back toward the shelter. Toward danger. So, I keep walking toward the sound of the waves, eventually feeling the tall unkempt grasses of the sandy dunes that rim the beach.

When the grass thins to reveal clean, soft sand, I sigh in relief. I need to rest. To lay flat and let my body and mind recover. Out here, hidden in the darkness, I'm unlikely to be seen. I've done all I can for now. Tomorrow, I'll worry about the rest.

Sixteen

"Get up. You can't sleep there," a voice says.

I roll over, the silhouette of a man dark against the sun. By its position, I know I've overslept. I sit up, blinking to make sure I'm really awake. That the man before me isn't the product of a dream. His face is small and wrinkled, his frame thin and muscular. When he stands to his full height, I can't help staring at his legs, shown off by a pair of tight fitting denim Daisy Dukes. The tan limbs are long and graceful. The legs of a dancer, refined in a way that contrasts with the tattered marching band jacket covering his torso. Blue with gold braiding and buttons, the jacket seems both ancient and juvenile. Like the kind a high school kid would wear in a parade. He even has the matching hat, complete with a chin strap and large plume of white feathers that flutter in the breeze.

"You okay?" he asks, craning his head forward.

When I nod, he extends a twirling baton in my direction. I

stare at it a moment. The weighted rubber tips worn with age, hard and cracked with dry rot. The silver rod, long and smooth, just like the kind I used to play with back in New Orleans.

"Here," he says, shaking it.

I grip the baton, stumbling a bit as I'm jerked to my feet.

The man glances around. "You gotta get out of here before they see you."

"Before who sees me?"

"The cops."

"Oh."

"You need a place to stay?"

"I'm okay," I say with a bit of reluctance. "But thank you for the offer."

The man looks down, clearly disappointed. "Oh, okay. I see ... sorry to bother you."

When he turns to walk away, I want to stop him. To wipe the hurt from his eyes and tell him my rejection of his offer was not a rejection of his friendship.

I hold out my hand and call out the first thing that comes to mind. "Do you twirl?"

He turns, his eyes crinkling at the corners as he drops his bag on the sand. His chin lifts as he marches a few feet away. As he bows low, his expression is serious. Focused. Then his baton flashes, glinting in the sun as he bends and kicks with unexpected ease. When he throws the baton high in the air, he spins multiple times before catching it. After a few more kicks and spins, he ends the routine in an elaborate kneeling pose.

I clap my hands together, genuinely impressed. "That was amazing!"

Satisfied with my reaction, he bows low and turns to leave.

"Wait," I say, thinking of my need to find Lir. "Could you tell me where the fish market is located?"

"Which one?"

"The one most likely to hire part time labor, I guess."

He frowns. "It's a long walk."

"I'm looking for somebody. Somebody that might be there. Can you give me directions?"

I'm told to travel north until I reach Pleasure Pier. "You'll know it by all the carnival rides," he says. "Then take a left and keep walking down 25th until you can't walk no more. Take a right and it'll be a little ways down on the left. Pier 19, I think."

Then he's gone, marching away, his form growing smaller and fading into the crowd of early morning joggers filling the sidewalk above.

I climb onto the seawall and head in the opposite direction, past people walking dogs and couples on tandem bikes. The concrete feels nice under my bare feet, warm and just a bit rough. With the relaxed beach town dress code, I don't worry about anyone noticing my lack of shoes. But as the crowd thickens, my pulse jumps at the idea that Jude's lurking presence could be anywhere. I study each man's face with growing dread as my feet move faster.

A cooling breeze sweeps in from the water, pushing my hair from my shoulders. It flies in the wind. I gather it in my left hand, working my fingers through the mass to untangle the knots as I try to calm the debilitating anxiety that threatens to surface.

Lullaby music from an ice cream truck floats over the din of children splashing in the water up ahead. For a moment, my soul is soothed by the sound. As the kids abandon their sand pails and boogie boards to swarm the truck like flies, I place a hand on my stomach and imagine my own child jumping and squealing in anticipation of a treat. The image brings a smile to my face. It's nice to know that just as there will always be despair and darkness, there will also always be joy and light.

From here I can see Pleasure Pier, its large Ferris wheel jutting into the sky. Other rides and amusements crowd the long wooden plank, spinning and whirling to the screams of passengers, making me wonder what it would be like to walk the pier at night. To see it all lit up. Watch the flashing colors and feel the energy of a place built only for pleasure. I faintly remember attending a county fair long ago. The taste of cotton candy. The smell of pork kabobs and funnel cakes coated in powdered sugar. The swirling thrill of the rides.

How different my life might have been if we had stayed in New Orleans. Better? Worse? Who knows. But at least it would have been mine. I would have had choices. Or would I? Jude loved to elaborate on the great service he was doing by pulling the Sisters out of desperate situations. "Eden gives you purpose," he'd say. "You have been called to serve the greater good while living in paradise. Just as it was in the beginning with Adam and Eve."

I know his manipulative words aren't true. But as I stand penniless, pregnant, and alone, I can't help wondering if I've made a mistake thinking I could make it on my own. The world can be a cruel place for an uneducated woman. Miss Janie instilled this knowledge with every class and lecture she offered.

"You need a GED. You need a driver's license. And you will eventually need a permanent residence where you can receive mail before you apply for a job," she would say. But for me, all those things felt perpetually out of reach. It took weeks for her to even locate a copy of my birth certificate and social security card, both of which I was forced to leave behind in my haste.

I turn onto twenty-fifth, a street busy and crowded with traffic. Luckily, narrow sidewalks shaded with large oaks line each side of the street, accenting historic homes painted in shades of slate, sage, ebony, wine, ivory, dove, and buttercup. Each in a combination unique to the residence. I skip along a large hopscotch painted on the sidewalk in front of a dove gray Victorian with white trim and ebony shutters. It's a bit childish, but I can't help the urge to indulge in something frivolous. To play a game I loved as a kid. Experience a bit of normalcy that was missing from the alternate universe of Eden.

When the Galveston Channel is visible at the end of twenty-fifth, I take a right, passing old brick buildings with lovely restaurants overlooking the water. A young woman rises from one of the tables and bends to wipe ketchup from the mouth of a little girl. "Are you sure you're full?" she says, eyeing the girl's paper basket of leftover chicken strips and fries. "Just one more bite? One more bite and you can have an ice cream." When the child adamantly refuses, the woman huffs and crosses her arms. "Well, I'm not bringing that with us. So in five minutes when you decide you're hungry, you're just gonna have to stay that way until we get home."

I wait until the woman and child are out of sight before approaching the table. The crowd is thin, the lunch hour coming to a close. I glance around to make sure no one is looking and swipe the child's basket of chicken and kiddie drink from the table in a moment of desperation. Walking fast, I hold my breath and pray I haven't called attention to myself as I dart into an alley a few blocks away. Sitting on the ground behind a green dumpster, the chicken and fries are gone in an instant, washed down with what ended up being an almost full cup of apple juice. I sit for a few minutes longer, leaning back against the rough brick of the building, enjoying the feeling of semi-fullness and self-reliance. That wasn't so hard, I guess.

After a while, I ease back onto my aching feet and make my way toward Pier 19. It doesn't take long to find the gray metal building with Wharf Road Seafood written in faded black letters with huge rolling doors held open on both ends. But even with fresh air circulating through the building, the smell of fish is overwhelming.

"Can I help you?" a woman asks from behind the counter, her hair covered by a ball cap with the words Beach Hair Don't Care embroidered in hot pink letters. She waves a hand at the long trays of ice holding fresh shrimp, snapper, redfish, and grouper. "We have some nice specials today if you're interested."

I crane my neck toward the men standing around a table in the back. Clad in white rubber boots and gloves, they concentrate on sorting crabs into buckets. "Actually, I'm looking for a guy who may work here. His name is Lir. Do you know him?"

The woman whistles at one of the men, but his expression tells me he's less than thrilled to be called away from his task.

"You hire a guy named Lir?" she asks.

"Lir? You mean Leo?"

"Leo?" I repeat.

His head bobs up and down. "Tall guy. Dark hair."

"With blue eyes?"

"Yeah. Hired him a few weeks back."

Excitement swells inside my chest. "Is he here?"

"Nope."

I shake my head. "Well, can you tell me when he'll be back?"

The man takes a few steps toward the door, leaning over to spit a stream of tobacco juice into the parking lot. "Wish I could say, little lady, but he ran off about a week ago. Hated to see him go. Sure was a hard worker."

"Ran off? You mean he quit?"

The man shrugged. "It's hard to keep good help."

My stomach clenches, my high gone in an instant. "Do you have any idea where he went?"

"No, but listen I gotta get back to work. Good luck."

"Wait," I say, holding out my hand. "Since he left, are you hiring?"

He shakes his head. "Sorry, we filled his position yesterday."

When he walks away, the woman behind the counter leans forward. "You know, Leo ran with a wild bunch. I hate to say this, but maybe you should check with the police department."

I stiffen at the suggestion. Based on my recent dealings with the police, I doubt they will be any help. "Is there anywhere else I can go to get information? Public records or something?"

"You can always try the library."

Seventeen

On the way to the library, I pass an art shop with a sign out front:

~ Free Glass Fusion Class ~
~ 6pm Today Only ~
~ Complimentary Refreshments ~
~ Walk-ins Welcome ~
~ Bring a Friend ~

I linger at the window, enjoying the sight of the colorful paintings and sculptures on display. Many are related to the sea. Sunsets, sand dollars, dolphins, and sail boats.

An elegant woman with brown hair walks to the door. "Would you like to come inside?" she asks, leaning against the frame.

I jump back, nervous at the request. "Oh, I wouldn't want to impose."

She gives me a friendly smile and holds out her hand. "I'm Sloane. Now we're friends so it won't be an imposition. I'd love to have you come back for my glass fusion class at six."

"I'll think about it," I say, reading the advertisement for refreshments a second time.

As I continue on, I ponder what glass fusion involves. It sounds complicated, but I suppose I can suffer through anything if free food is involved.

The large statue of a man looms over the extravagant exterior of Rosenberg Library, and I feel very small mounting the front steps. Like I'm about to enter a fairy-tale palace or cathedral. I pause at the door, my eyes hovering on a sign reading: *No Shirt, No Shoes, No Service*. I look down at my bare feet and bite back disappointment. So much for my plan. Now what?

The bright blue donation box beside the door catches my eye, and I check to see if anyone is watching. Easing over to the box, I work quickly, rummaging through used sweaters, old stuffed animals, and mismatched socks until I find a worn pair of green flip-flops near the bottom. I hurry to slip them on and frown at the result. They are a size too big and hold the stained footprints of the previous owner, but I guess they are better than nothing.

Wiping my sweaty hands down the sides of my dress, I hope no one notices my ragged appearance as I enter the building. But as I approach the front desk, the quiet atmosphere and welcoming faces behind the counter calm my anxiety.

A young woman with pink cheeks and red hair gives me a big smile. "Can I help you find something?"

"Yes ... I'd like to do some research," I say, unsure of how to vocalize my need.

The woman introduces herself as Olivia and leads me to a computer near the front desk. "This contains a catalog of everything we offer. Do you know what the book you're looking for is called, by chance?"

"I'm not sure," I say, chewing my thumb nail to the point of pain.

Olivia repositions her black frames, the smile never leaving her face. "May I ask what subject you'd like to know more about?"

"I don't know," I say, feeling like a complete failure.

When she giggles, I get the feeling she's one of those perpetually happy people. The kind that see the glass as half full even if it's empty, or chipped, or shattered on the floor in a million pieces. She clasps her hands together, her gaze darting upward. "Okay, let's try it this way. Is it a person, place, or event?"

"Person."

"Living or deceased?"

"Living."

"Is the person famous?"

"Not that I'm aware of ..."

"Okay. Let's head on up to the computer lab. It's on the third floor."

The lab consists of about forty computers situated on long tables where people sit typing, their fingers flying across the keyboards with ease. Olivia shows me to a seat and explains how to search for keywords that bring up information about anything I'd like to learn, public records included. After seven years of darkness, I know next to nothing about the internet, but the power to easily learn about anything in the world sounds magical. I yearn to search for all kinds of frivolous things, but first I need to accomplish the task at hand.

When Olivia walks away, I type Lir's full name into the box. Nothing. I try using the alias he gave the fish market. Nothing. Then Jude's. Again nothing. Not even a photograph to show they exist. After close to an hour of searching, I've exhausted every avenue I can think of and no trace of Jude's family can be found. Not even Hazel.

I walk back downstairs and find Olivia categorizing books in the children's section. "Did you find what you needed?" she asks.

"Not quite. Maybe I'm just not understanding, but can you tell me why a person wouldn't be listed anywhere online? Even in public records?"

A wrinkle appears between her eyes. "Hmm. Honestly, I have no idea. I've heard of famous people paying to have certain personal information hidden."

"Really? They can do that?"

"I think with enough money, a person can do just about anything they want."

Her forthright manner puts me at ease. "That's kind of what I'm thinking," I whisper.

She winks and waves me forward. "Come on. Maybe I can help." She leads me to the computer in her private office and pulls an extra chair behind her desk. After several minutes of searching, she leans back in her chair and taps her chin. "You say you know this man, but you don't have an address?"

The fish market was my only clue. On an island this size, Lir could be anywhere.

"What about a place he might frequent?" she continues. "Like a bar or restaurant?"

I sit up straight, my heart beating fast as I think of Lir's young silhouette pulling his boat to shore all those years ago. "There is a place. A lighthouse ... but I don't remember the name or exactly where it's at."

"As far as I know, there're only two lighthouses on the island," she says, her fingers flying across the keyboard. "The one at Bolivar Point and another down at Jamaica Beach." She shows me a photograph of the one at Bolivar Point, a tall brown structure that doesn't look familiar. "Let's try this one," she says, clicking an article about the history of the Claiborne Lighthouse at Jamaica Beach. Olivia taps the screen and smiles. "This one's close to my house. It's really something."

The link brings up a black and white photograph of a man leaning against the exterior of a lighthouse painted with horizontal stripes. He is barefoot with loose jeans rolled high and a Newsboy cap pulled down to shade his eyes. Taken in profile, the photo shows the jut of his chin, rough hands cupping to light a cigarette.

I lean forward, squinting to get a better look as Olivia scrolls down the page. "So, the man's name was Owen Claiborne, and his family were the keepers of the Claiborne Lighthouse since it was built in the eighteen hundreds up until the nineteen eighties. Owen served as the keeper for over seventy-five years, eight of which he received the Lighthouse Efficiency Flag for best-kept station in the district." Her eyes dart down the screen. "It says the lighthouse is no longer in their care, but the Claiborne family remains a beloved fixture of the Jamaica Beach community." She turns to me with raised brows. "What do you think?"

"I feel like it's the one."

She prints out the article and grabs a notepad. "There's my number." She gives me a warm smile. "I'd really like to stay in touch. Hear how your search turns out."

"Me too," I say, taking the article and slip of paper. "Thank you so much."

She gestures to the front desk. "I think there's a brochure up there with a map that'll lead you right to it."

I twist my hands in my lap. "But what will I do once I'm there? Do you think the Claibornes would be willing to talk to me?"

She shrugs. "If I knew them personally, I'd introduce you. But it can't hurt to try. Most of the people in Jamaica Beach are pretty friendly."

"Now be sure to score the glass before trying to break it," Sloane explains, holding up a piece of crimson glass with a scratched line across the surface. There's something familiar about her that puts me at ease, but I can't say exactly what.

I do as she says, enjoying the precision of the scoring tool, the snap of the glass. Broken pieces of blue and gray lie before me, arranged into the shape of a dolphin against a clear background.

"Just do the best you can and don't worry if it's not perfect. After all, perfection is boring," she declares in a dramatic voice that prompts laughter from the class.

I'm one of six students, all middle-aged women and all more curious about my personal life than learning the art of glass fusion. I'm just here for the food, but they don't know that. And though well-meaning, the women's incessant questions feel more like an interrogation rather than polite conversation.

"Where did you say you grew up?" one asks.

"New Orleans."

"I knew I recognized that accent." She nods to a woman across the table. "Did you hear that, Dixie? New Orleans."

Dixie looks up from positioning a piece of black glass in the center of her sunflower creation. "New Orleans is one of my favorite places. The music! The beignets! I begged my son, Jonathan, to go to LSU just so I'd have a reason to go down that way every now and again, but he insisted on going to A&M instead. Broke my heart," she says, patting her chest.

Although I'm unsure of her meaning, I nod and try to pretend I'm impressed.

"Tell us more about yourself," she says. "Where did you go to school?"

"Oh, uh. I went to public school."

"No, sugar. Where did you attend college?"

Feeling my ears grow hot, I jump to my feet and make a hurried excuse about seeking the restroom where I spend more time than necessary washing and rewashing my hands. When I return, the women are deep in conversation about a local scandal. With squeals and sporadic fits of laughter, they are consumed by the gossip and blind to anything else. I hover near the refreshments table where I eat exactly eleven cookies, followed by three glasses of lemonade.

When the class comes to an end, Sloane waves me over and motions to my abandoned project. "Are you done?"

Without a tail or eyes, the dolphin hardly looks complete.

"Why don't you add the finishing touches while I clean up the studio?" she suggests.

With my stomach full, I should really be on my way. But leaving without finishing the project would look suspicious, so I nod and work as fast as I can, scoring and breaking the glass, dabbing a bit of glue on the clear glass background to hold each piece in place. Without the other women blasting me with questions, I'm done in no time.

Sloane places her broom in the corner and comes to inspect my work. "That looks wonderful! Are you sure this is your first time?"

"I've never done anything like this before. Thank you for letting me try."

"You did better than try. Just let me give it a quick coat of this and it should be good to go," she says, spraying the creation with a generous coating of Aqua Net.

"Hairspray?" I ask.

"Funny, but it does the trick. Just got to keep the pieces in place until I can stick it in the kiln. I should have this one ready to go home with you in about a week." She places the project on a wire shelf behind her desk and turns to study me. "I've been meaning to ask where you got your outfit. The dress and jewelry."

"Oh, this?" I ask, touching the shells around my neck. "I ... I made it," I admit, a bit embarrassed by the inadequacy of the ornament I assembled while living at the shelter.

"You're kidding."

I look away, regretting my honesty. "I should get going," I say, taking a step toward the door.

"No, wait. I want to show you something."

I pause to stare at my feet, despising my dirty flip-flops and chipped toenails.

"Come on," Sloane calls over her shoulder.

Not wanting to seem rude, I follow her to a side door leading into a boutique. When she flips on the light, I gasp at the rows of beautiful clothing showcased against walls made of reclaimed driftwood. Jewelry, shoes, hats, and scarves provide the occasional pop of color to the otherwise monochromatic shades of ochre, white, and nude.

"Great, isn't it?" she asks.

I run my fingers over an ivory silk scarf hanging by the door, enjoying the cool smoothness of the fabric. "It's wonderful. Are you friends with the owner?"

She smiles. "No. I am the owner."

"Oh." I notice the sign in the back bearing her name for the first time. "Sorry, I didn't realize. With the art studio and everything ..."

She flips off the light. "Fashion and art have always been my two passions. This way I get to have the best of both worlds. I try to fill the boutique with work from local artisans when I can. I'm always on the lookout for something fresh." Her eyes go to my throat. "Would you mind if I take a look at your necklace?"

"Of course," I say, my fingers fumbling to slip the tiny shell through the loop securing it behind my head.

Sloane picks up a magnifying glass and bends over the lamp at her desk. After a few moments, she straightens, cradling the necklace in her palm. "I have to say, this design is exquisite."

I flush with embarrassment. "It's not too simple?"

"The simplicity is what makes it so great. From the natural cording to the selection of shells, you've done a fabulous job. On this and your dress."

"Thank you."

"I mean it. Listen, I have a proposition for you. Would you be interested in selling me a few of your pieces to carry in the boutique?"

"Really?" I ask, confused by the sincerity I read on her face.

"Absolutely. Elegant simplicity is exactly what my customers are hungry for. They want unique designs. Things that no one else has. Things like this." She places the necklace back in my hand. "In fact, I'd be willing to buy your necklace right now for say, one-fifty?"

I look at the shells in my hand, contemplating the time and energy put into the creation. But I'd be lying if I said I know anything about the price of jewelry. And Sloane is clearly an expert. So, rather than try to haggle, I decide to accept her offer. Some money is better than none. A dollar fifty will have to do.

"Deal," I say, doing my best to smile as I place the necklace in her hand.

"Do you want cash or check?"

"Cash, please."

When she pushes a stack of bills across the counter, I feel the need to speak up. "Is this right?"

"Oh," she says, her brow furrowing. "Let me recount. Twenty, forty, sixty, eighty, one, one-twenty, one-forty, one-fifty. Looks right. Is the price still okay?"

Feeling a little light-headed, I give a quick nod and stuff the money into my bag before she has a chance to change her mind. Never could I have dreamed my little creation would bring such a price.

Sloane extends her hand. "It's been a real pleasure getting to know you, Max. I would love to take a look at anything you come up with in the future. Can I take down your information and give you a call to set something up?"

My heart races at the thought. "Um, I kind of have a lot going on right now. But maybe another time?"

Her face falls, but her voice remains bright. "Of course. Here's my card. When you get ready, be sure to let me know. I guarantee to give you a better price than anyone else in town."

As I walk down the dark sidewalk, I roll Sloane's offer over in my mind. If only I had a way to gather a few materials. Linen, scissors, needle and thread, jewelry twine, shells, stones. But with limited time and money, Sloane's offer will have to wait.

I pull out the article about the Claiborne Lighthouse and the glossy map of Galveston. Armed with this and my recent payday, I keep to the shadows, retracing my steps back to Pleasure Pier. The glowing lights are better than I imagined, twirling against the ebony night. I want to stay and watch the colors, but I need to put some miles in before daylight. With every passing hour, the folly of traipsing around the tourist attractions of Galveston is heavy. If I continue to remain so visible, I'm likely to be seen and recognized.

I head west toward Jamaica Beach, pausing only to buy two hot dogs and a Dr. Pepper from a vendor pushing his cart along the seawall. Following the shoreline, I'm busy inhaling the first hotdog when a man's voice stops me.

"Hey, you doing okay?" he asks from the shadows below the seawall.

I stop chewing and freeze. But as I peek over the steep ledge, I'm relieved to see the twirler man staring back.

"Oh, hi!" I walk down the steps leading to the sand.

"You find the fish market?"

"I did. Thank you for the directions."

He nods to my half-eaten hot dog. "See you got some food."

"Would you like one?" I say, pushing the other hot dog forward.

"I don't wanna take your supper."

I take in his thin frame, the hollows under his eyes. "How long has it been since you've eaten?"

He shrugs. "Few days, maybe."

My heart hurts at the thought of such suffering. "Here," I say, counting out sixty dollars from my payday. "Go get yourself something to eat."

His eyes widen at the offer. "You sure?"

I shove the money into his hand, giving him a wink. "Just don't spend it all in one place."

He glances around and bends to shove it into his shoe. "You

sure you don't need a place to go? Like I said before, it ain't safe sleeping out here in the open."

"Yeah, I'll be fine." I hold out my hand. "But I better get going. Good luck."

I walk until my body forces me to stop and rest on the soft sand. Huddled by the side of a large dune, I hope to remain out of sight, the twirler man's warning echoing in my head. Sleep is needed, but adrenaline only lets me doze, nodding in and out until I feel rested enough to continue. The last thing I need is to be arrested for loitering, or vagrancy, or whatever it's called. With no home, or family, or identification, I doubt the justice system would give me a fair shake. If I got one at all. I've already been labeled as crazy by the police, with three whole notebooks as proof. It's a miracle they didn't try to stick me in some institution where people tie you up and feed you pills. Places like where Dr. Chen worked before coming to Eden. He never spoke of his time working for the state, but the Sisters would often whisper about the kinds of depravity that existed in such places. I'm right to trust no one. Justice is a joke, and I was a fool for ever believing in it. Telling my story only served to put me in danger all over again. Jude wants me dead, and he always gets what he wants.

Crawling back onto my tired feet, I'm determined to keep moving, no matter how exhausted I feel. Better exhausted than dead.

Eighteen

Early morning rays beam over the horizon when I arrive at Claiborne Lighthouse. It looks just as I remember, tall and stately, black and white bands stark in the light of day. A beacon of hope in a world of darkness. "Lighthouses are for saving people," Maggie once said. Now, I can only pray she's right.

The most obvious place to begin my search is the cottage beside the lighthouse. It's still painted the same white with black trim that I remember, but approaching the home makes me uneasy. I lift the metal gate latch and slip inside the tidy picket fence, dread making my feet feel like lead as I mount the tall steps. When multiple knocks on the door produces the muffled sound of a man yelling, I back away and consider running. But I need to see this through.

The door swings wide and I freeze as the scent of alcohol wafts from a bleary-eyed man wearing only a white pair of underwear. His body is small and tan, his sagging skin peppered with white hair.

"Wha' da ya want?" he growls, stumbling a bit before grabbing the doorframe to steady himself.

"Hello," I say, proceeding with caution.

He grunts a reply, prompting me to cut to the chase.

"I'm looking for a man named Lir Delacroix, but he may go by Leo. I was hoping you could help me."

The old man's eyes narrow as he holds up an index finger. "You kids need to learn that I have a job. See that lighthouse? Well, it don't run itself. And I don't have time to fart around answering stupid questions. Sun up is my time to try and get some fuckin' sleep."

I swallow hard and push ahead. "I'm so sorry. I can assure you I won't bother you again, sir."

"Damn straight, you won't."

"But I have to find him," I press, unwilling to give up so easily.

He glares. "Never heard of him."

"What about the Claiborne family?"

The man's nostrils flare. "Don't know what a nice girl like you'd want with the likes of them."

"So you know them?"

"Wish I'd never met the sons-a-bitches." He jerks his head to the left. "Live on down the road there, but I'd be careful if I was you." He spits again and slams the door.

I look in the direction he pointed, wondering if I should attempt to make contact. If the Claibornes are as he insinuated, I'd rather not. But what choice do I have? I force my feet down the narrow road bordered with shallow ditches filled with tall reeds and murky, stagnant water. Eventually the road turns to a smaller winding trail bordered with barren lots overgrown with wild grass. The sun beats down on my head and shoulders, but I don't stop until a pasture fenced with thin strands of barbed wire appears on my left. The property holds a yellow clapboard farmhouse, built high off the ground with brick skirting around the base, with a large barn and chicken coop sitting behind the house.

When I get closer, I see Claiborne written on the mailbox and a black Dodge pickup parked in the yard. The truck is big and shiny with mud flaps and a Republic of Texas bumper sticker. I stop just short of the driveway, next to a tiny dirt trail that winds through the pasture to a small cemetery encased in decorative metal fencing. All the graves are above ground, encased in concrete tombs and mausoleums just like the kind I remember in New Orleans. By its size and proximity to the farmhouse, I assume it must be a private cemetery.

The sound of an air compressor makes me crane my neck toward the barn, where an old Ford Bronco sits with its hood open. I duck behind a clump of fragrant lantana, wanting to get a look at who I'm dealing with before making my presence known.

When the compressor kicks off, I hear the clanking of tools. The sound of voices. A skinny young man with dark hair steps out, and I strain to make out the conversation.

"Try it now," a man's voice calls from inside the barn.

The young man leans inside the Bronco and after a few tries, the motor roars to life. The second man steps out, sunlight glinting off his dark auburn hair as he wipes grease off his hands.

"Thanks, buddy. Sure couldn't have done it without you," the young man says. "You want a beer? Got some in my cooler."

"No thanks, man. It's still a little early for me."

The young man shrugs and jumps inside the truck, his elbow resting on the sill of the open window. "See you around."

When the Bronco rumbles out of sight, the other man disappears back inside the barn. Out of reasons to delay the meeting, I run a hand over my hair, trying to steady my nerves as I step into the barn. It takes my eyes a minute to adjust to the dimness and see the face of the man who stands staring a few feet away. It's hard to make out his exact features, but based on the outline of his body and cut of his jaw, he's very handsome.

"Uh, hi," I say, unsure of how to proceed. "Are you Mr. Claiborne?"

"What?" he says, taking a step forward, but the toe of his boot catches the edge of the compressor, causing him to stumble.

"Are you alright?" I say, rushing forward.

He winces and regains his footing. "Sure. Just clumsy." His face is pale, his laugh shaky. "Sorry ... I thought you were somebody else. I mean, you remind me of somebody." He shakes his head. "Uh, what did you say your name was again?" He sticks out his hand, composure returning.

"Max Fontaine," I say, enjoying the feel of his warm grasp. But the minute the words are out, I wish to take them back. To say my name is Mary or Betsy. Anything but Max. But our conversation isn't following the script I'd rehearsed in my head. I look down and realize he's still holding my hand.

He clears his throat and pulls away, heat creeping up his neck. "I'm Cash," he says, standing a little straighter. "What can I do for you?"

I lift my chin and try to sound confident as I spill about Lir. Or Leo. Or whatever he calls himself now.

Cash crosses his arms and tucks his chin. "Can't say I know him. Why're you looking?"

I clear my throat and try to keep my tone casual. "He's an old friend I haven't seen in a while." I wave a hand toward the road. "We used to hang out around the lighthouse. I was just wondering if maybe you've seen him around."

"What's he look like?"

"Tall. Dark hair. Blue eyes. Kinda thin."

"How old?"

"Twenty-two."

He studies me a moment, something flashing in his eyes. "Well, sorry I can't help you more, but I haven't seen anybody around here like that." I gulp down my disappointment and turn to leave, but he stops me, jutting his chin toward the road. "Hey, did you think to ask the lighthouse keeper? Name's Walter. Course I wouldn't try right now. But maybe six or seven tonight when he's up."

"Too late. Already made that mistake," I say with a grimace.

Cash's eyes widen and he whistles. "Damn, I'm surprised you're still alive."

"He wasn't that bad," I say, brushing it off. "But he certainly didn't have anything good to say about you," I can't help but add.

Cash closes his eyes and shakes his head. "I swear, he ain't never gonna let me live that down."

"What happened?" I say, unable to suppress my curiosity.

"It's a terrible story." He clears his throat and heat colors his neck. "I ... uh ... ran over his cat a few years ago."

"On purpose?" I blurt, unable to believe him capable of such an act. Cash may be a stranger, but there's a warmth to him that puts me at ease. Makes me feel like I've known him forever.

"No, nothing like that. It was a complete accident. But you'll never get Walter to believe it."

"So, maybe you should do something about it," I offer.

He frowns. "Like what?"

"Like get him a new cat," I say slowly.

Cash smiles and shakes a finger in my direction. "You know, you just might be on to something."

Returning his smile is easy, but by the time I leave the barn, my stomach is in knots. Finding Lir was a long shot, but at least it was some sort of plan. The weight of being completely alone and aimless is heavy as I trudge across the circle drive to the main road. My money will buy me a little more time, but I can't risk spending another night on the road. I need a safe place to sleep. Away from everyone. A place to recalibrate.

A rabbit jumps across the road, its fast, gray body scampering down the trail that leads to the cemetery I'd passed earlier. When it disappears into the safety of the tall grass near the iron fence, an idea forms and I duck behind a tree until

Cash steps back inside the barn. When the coast is clear, I crouch low, running along the trail after the rabbit and don't stop until I'm inside the fence, hidden behind the concrete mausoleum at its center. I touch the indented letters inscribed on the exterior plaque, the words giving me comfort.

In Loving Memory of
Owen Thomas Claiborne
1832 - 1915
Rose Margaret Claiborne
1837 - 1929
"The Lord is my light and my salvation;
whom shall I fear? The Lord is the strength of my life;
of whom shall I be afraid?"
Psalm 27:1

On either side of the structure, the tiny windows cut into the exterior walls give a glimpse of two tombs encased in concrete. When I lean inside, a bird abandons its nest in a panic and flies out the opposite window in a flash of dark blue.

There's a wooden door mounted at the front of the structure, but it's locked tight. I try to judge the approximate size of the windows and whether I'm small enough to squeeze inside. Starting with my head, arms, and shoulders, I balance my hips on the sill and grasp the nearest tomb to pull myself the rest of the way through.

Once inside, I'm able to stand up straight and survey my new home with the eye of a child practiced in the art of make believe. Except I'm not a child. And I don't have a real house to go home to when I tire of my game. This is it. Or it will be once I tidy it up a bit.

The walkway between the tombs is quite spacious, but the rest of the interior is dim and dusty with leaves and debris collected against the corners and layers of cobwebs along the low ceiling. I make a mental list of the supplies needed and how far it is back to the nearest store. It seems like I passed one before reaching the lighthouse. A small grocery called Johnson's or Jerald's or something.

With a plan in place, I sit on the nearest tomb and breathe a tentative sigh of relief. Surely, no one will find me way out here. And even if they were to visit one of the graves, I would hear them coming in time to hide. There are crawl spaces behind each of the tombs—one to hide behind and the other to store supplies.

The rumble of an engine signals Cash's truck pulling out of the driveway. I stick my head out the window and try to gauge the time of day. Around noon, I'd guess, which explains the ache in my stomach. I seize Cash's absence as the perfect time to get the supplies needed to set up house and hurry back.

Johnson's Market is a tall, wooden structure, painted in bright shades of pink, purple, and blue in keeping with the island feel. Built high off the ground with spacious windows to let in the breeze, the store is an open-air style market with a colorful selection of locally grown fresh fruit and vegetables. There's an elderly couple too involved in arguing over the ripeness of the avocados to notice my presence, so I loop a basket over my arm and hurry to drop in a few apples, oranges, and bananas before heading to the back of the store where nonperishables line the shelves. I try to think of things that don't require cooking. Peanut butter, jelly, bread, bottled water, nuts, cookies, chips. Granted, none of it is up to Eden's standards, but it'll keep me alive.

I pick up a bargain sized package of chicken-flavored Ramen, ever popular at the shelter for its savory cheapness and ability to feed the masses for pennies on the dollar. I remember Miss Janie telling us that Ramen was the only thing her son ever requested during his tour in Afghanistan. "They say it's so hot over there, all they have to do to cook it is set the bowl out in the sun for about thirty minutes," she loved to say. I think of the heat shimmering in waves off the black pavement outside and drop the package of Ramen into my basket. It doesn't get much hotter than a Texas summer.

The far wall of the grocery store has a variety of camping supplies gathering a thin layer of dust with ALL ITEMS 50% OFF scrawled in uneven handwriting across a notecard held to the wall by a yellow thumbtack. It doesn't take long to tabulate the cost of a sleeping bag, metal bowl, toilet paper, broom, dustpan, and disinfectant wipes. I may be living among the dead, but I refuse to live in filth.

Just as I'm about to leave the section, I spot a pair of binoculars with the words AS IS $10 scribbled on the box. Besides a broken cord, they seem okay. If I'm to keep a decent lookout, they may come in handy. So, I drop them into the basket with everything else.

Pleased with my selections, I carry the mountain of items over to the register where the middle-aged cashier sits smoking a cigarette with one hand and scribbling on a crossword puzzle with the other. Her name tag says Melinda. "Will this be all?" she asks in an unconcerned voice.

"Yes, please. And this," I say, placing a chocolate bar on the counter. It's been years since I've had such a treat, and my mouth waters at the idea. But as my items start to add up, I regret my impulsiveness. "Actually, no," I say, shoving the candy back into the box under the counter.

Melinda shrugs. "Your total comes to $74.38. Will that be cash or charge?"

"Cash," I say, trying to swallow the lump in my throat as I stare at the total. But remembering the fifty percent off sign, I decide to speak up. "Ma'am, can you check to make sure I got the discount for these things?" I point to the items I purchased from the back wall.

She glances at the receipt. "Sure did."

"Just seems like a lot," I say, handing over the bills.

"Well, life's a bitch and then you die." She takes another puff of her cigarette and leans across the counter to grab the bar of chocolate I replaced. "Here," she says, tossing it into my bag. "Go enjoy yourself."

When I try to thank her, she waves me away with the excuse of wanting to finish her puzzle. But before I walk away, the barest hint of a smile appears, and I know she's pleased with her generosity. I remind myself that a gift can be as much for the giver as the one who receives. So instead of feeling guilty, I decide to feel proud. Proud that I was there to receive her light. And that one day, I could pass that same light to someone else.

Nineteen

I stare at the bowl of noodles, swishing them around with my index finger and thumb. I'd forgotten to buy silverware, an oversight I've come to regret, especially concerning the peanut butter and jelly situation. Grabbing a clump of Ramen, I bring it to my mouth and try to chew and swallow quickly. But the taste turns my stomach in spite of my resolve. At first, I didn't mind the flavor, but after alternating Ramen with peanut butter and jelly sandwiches for the past six consecutive days, my appetite wanes when I think of either option.

With my ration of cookies, chips, and fruit depleted, I wish for something, anything, to break the monotony and remind myself to look for other options next time I venture to the store. But the thought of abandoning the relative safety of the cemetery puts me on edge. Granted, I could really use a bath. But at least I'm safe. I don't have to worry about Jude or anyone else. I mean, who would think of a mausoleum?

The first night turned out to be the hardest. Every sound made me jump and sweat. After a while, I settled onto my sleeping bag between the tombs and fell into a deep sleep, but my body was still lethargic when I woke late the next morning. The following days have been spent trying to come up with a realistic plan for my future. I need a job, but after days of scouring the businesses within walking distance, I've given up. Even the ones with help-wanted signs turned me away. It seems no one is anxious to hire a strange girl who's pregnant to boot. I spent the rest of my time on the beach, looking for shells to make jewelry to bring back to Sloane. But the tide was high and the pickings were slim.

Out of options, I retreated to the mausoleum where I've passed the hours behind my set of binoculars. Occasionally, I'll abandon my post to relieve myself behind a tall gravestone at the back of the yard. I made sure to bring along a plastic grocery bag to hold the paper, lest someone discover the mound of white tissue and suspect my presence. So far, I've been lucky.

I finish slurping up the last of the noodles and pop a prenatal vitamin into my mouth. The pills are huge and taste terrible, but I know I need them. The baby needs them. I shake the bottle and wonder how many are left. Not many, from the hollow rattle.

My remaining food rations line one of the crawl spaces. A package of Ramen, two heels of bread, and approximately three tablespoons of peanut butter and jelly. I was fortunate to discover a spigot inside the yard to refill my bottles with fresh water, but my other resources are painfully low.

I raise my arm and sniff. The odor makes me wish I'd bought some soap. My hair is caked with grease and dirt and goodness knows what else. I can't recall ever being this filthy in my life and the knowledge makes me itch with the need to feel clean again. I've tried bathing in the ocean at night, but without soap or shampoo the effort has been largely futile. With only ten dollars and sixty-two cents left to my name, toiletries are a luxury I can only dream about.

Holding the binoculars up to my face, I scan the yard around the homestead for movement. So far, Cash's daily life is the only thing of interest. I watch as he putters around the yard, mowing, weeding, tending to the chickens. Most evenings, he barbecues in the back, the breeze delivering the scent of charcoal, peppers, and steak. I see him propped up against the porch railing, sipping beer and listening to country music, and find myself expecting other people to show up. Friends, family, neighbors. But they don't. Once, a state trooper pulled into the drive, but she didn't stay long, and I couldn't make out their conversation.

And so the days have fallen away, one by one, with nothing to show for my efforts. The way I see it, I have two options. I can stay the course and run out of money and food, or I can take matters into my own hands. I've never been weak. That was my mother. I'm strong. I've proven that much. And I haven't overcome so many obstacles to stop now. If I want change, I have to make it happen. Not wait for it to fall from the sky.

By the sun, it's still early morning, which means Cash will

soon be heading to the gym. I can always tell by his black shorts and running shoes. He usually returns after an hour or so, giving me plenty of time—I hope.

Waiting until the sound of his motor quiets, I climb from the mausoleum and make my way to the house. I'm quick to retrieve the key from under a flower pot on the front steps, mentally shaking my head at the obvious hiding spot, and approach the door. I knock, waiting for sounds of barking to alert me of an animal or other human present, but after a few moments of silence, I insert the silver key, my hand shaking as I twist the lock. When the door gives way, I bounce inside with a burst of nervous adrenaline and remind myself I'm not here to cause any real harm, just make use of the facilities. If I want any shot at a job, my appearance has to change and this is the only way.

The house is quiet and dark, and the faint smell of breakfast lingers from a plate on the kitchen table. Though a bit cluttered, the interior is prettier than I imagined, with tasteful decor and well-chosen pops of color that remind me of Sloane's boutique. I tiptoe through each room, scanning for signs of anyone else present, but all I find are the usual signs of a man living alone. Dirty dishes in the sink. An unmade bed. A pair of cowboy boots in the corner. A copy of *Lonesome Dove* beside a pile of loose change on the bedside table. Clothes piled in a heap beside the washer. A spare bedroom that seems untouched. Beer cans in the trash.

I check the clock on the wall and pause at Cash's desk, a massive oak piece with papers and notes strewn across the top. I run my hand over the soft, dark wood, enjoying the feel of the polish until I come to the photograph of a pretty brunette with long hair. I pick up the frame and study her face, nails, the fabric of her jacket. I wonder who she is. A girlfriend, perhaps. I envy the curve of her mouth. The sparkle in her eye. Her place in Cash's heart.

The knowledge sinks in my stomach like a stone as I head to the spacious bathroom at the back of the house. With a large shower and claw-foot tub, the room represents everything I miss about a real home. Soft towels. Clean toilet. Toothpaste. All things I took for granted while living in the main house at Eden, but not enough to make me want to go back.

Before I know it, I'm standing in front of the shower, my clothes in a heap on the floor. I know what I'm doing isn't right. Isn't moral. But as long as I leave everything as I found it, and replace the products as soon as I can, who am I really hurting?

My inhibitions melt away as the stream of hot water runs over my body. I would love nothing more than to sit down right here and spend long minutes enjoying the sensation, but there's no time to waste. I grab a bottle of two-in-one shampoo and bodywash and set to work scrubbing every inch of my hair and skin. It has the heavy scent of men's cologne, but I don't care. Anything is better than stinking. When I'm done, I dry the droplets of water from the shower walls and hang my towel on the silver bar where I found it. Hopefully it'll dry out before Cash notices.

With the evidence of my shower erased, I slip on my clothes and search for a brush to untangle the knots in my wet hair. The drawers under the sink turn up a flimsy plastic comb that results in many painful minutes of trying to rake through the unruly mass. When I'm finished, I retrieve a pair of rubber gloves and a bottle of cleaner from under the sink and set to work wiping down the lavatory with a yellow sponge. But before I'm done, the faint rumble of an engine makes me stiffen. I run toward the kitchen as fast as my legs will carry me to try and get out the back door before Cash sees me. But as I round the corner of the hall, heavy footsteps thump across the porch. I freeze in terror, but running is pointless. I'm caught—my fate sealed with the simple twist of a knob.

Twenty

By the time Cash's green eyes lock with mine, my shaking legs struggle to remain in an upright position. I tell myself to breathe, but the action does nothing to calm the burn of dread in my throat as he shuts the door with a quiet click. I will myself to say something, anything, but he beats me to the punch.

"Sorry, thought I'd get back in time to let you in. But looks like you didn't have any trouble finding your way around." He motions to the rubber gloves covering my arms, sponge still in my hand. I stare at it in an effort to understand his meaning.

"I'll be heading back out in a few minutes," he continues, walking toward his desk. "Just need to grab my laptop and I'll be out of your hair."

Unsure how to respond, I remain rooted in place as he casually places his computer inside a leather messenger bag and slings it over his shoulder. Could he possibly be confusing me with someone else? But who? I've been watching this house for days and no one has entered, except him. Why is he acting as if I belong here?

Is he crazy?

Am I crazy?

I replay his first words. The gesture to the sponge in my hand. Cleaning. He thinks I'm cleaning. But why? Does he recognize me from the other day? And if so, am I forgetting the part where I offered to clean his house? I want to ask, but fear of him realizing his mistake keeps me silent. Whatever this weird little encounter is, the moment he walks out that door I vow to slip away and never return. If he were to find out who I am. What I'm really doing ... No, I can't think about that now. Positive thoughts. Just a few more steps and Cash will be out the door. Out of my nightmare.

I hold my breath as he steps over the threshold, the light from the door narrowing. But my relief is short lived. When it swings back open a second later, my mouth turns to cotton and time seems to slow as he leans inside the frame, a frown marring his handsome face. "Almost forgot to pay you," he says, waving his wallet in the air. But as he counts out the bills, he freezes and looks up as if in a daze. "Wait ... I've seen you before."

Sweat trickles down my spine as I press my back against the wall. "Oh?" I manage to say with the last bit of oxygen left in my lungs.

"Yeah, you're that girl from the other day, right?"

I smile and shrug in an effort to seem nonchalant about the coincidence, but my insides are churning so hard I think I might vomit.

He tilts his head and places a stack of bills on the table by the door. "Small world, huh? Okay, well that should cover the first week." I look at the money on the table, speechless at my good fortune.

He frowns. "Or do you want me to write you a check?"

"No, cash is fine," I manage to say.

"Good," he says, seeming relieved. "Sorry if I seem a little unorganized. I've never had a housekeeper before."

"Housekeeper?" I blurt before thinking.

"Yeah. You know, the job I'm paying you for?" But his grin slips off his face the next instant. "Sorry, that was my bad attempt at a joke ... You're probably ready to quit now, right?"

"No!" I say in a voice much too loud for the circumstances. "I mean, no. I definitely want the job."

"Okay then." He smiles in a way that seems genuinely happy with my response. "It's Max, right?"

I nod, pleased he remembered my name.

"Well, Max, I'll be back later on this evening. You know where the key is. Just be sure to lock up when you leave."

"Wait," I say before he gets away. "If it's not too much trouble, could you explain what you're needing me to do? I'm pretty new to this kind of work, and I don't want to leave anything out."

He shrugs. "I don't know. Just clean the place up. There's a few clothes I need washed if you don't mind. I'm not real picky. Think you can handle that?" When he winks, I feel my face heat up.

"Yeah, sure. No problem. And you want me to come every day?"

"Suits me to a T. Except weekends, of course."

When I hear his motor fade into the distance, tears of relief slip down my cheeks as I marvel at my stroke of good luck. I run to the table by the door and count the bills he left. One, two, three, four hundred dollars! Not only have I landed a steady paycheck, but I also have an excuse to use the facilities without anyone noticing.

With renewed hope, I float into the kitchen and set to work attempting to load the dishwasher. After a few tries, I get the door to shut properly but have to reopen it to put in the detergent. Luckily, I remember a little about housework from the forced chores of my childhood in New Orleans. So far, the school of hard knocks is paying off far more than I ever expected.

When I move from the kitchen to the laundry, a *thump, thump, thump* at the door makes me freeze. I look through the window to see a woman standing on the porch with the words Merry Maids written across her black ball cap.

"Hello?" I say, cracking the door enough to show my face.

"Yes, is this the Claiborne residence?"

"It is."

She extends her hand. "Hi, I'm Susan. Merry Maids sent me to fill the housekeeping position requested by Mr. Cash Claiborne. Is he at home?"

"Uh, no he's not," I say, hoping she can't detect the tremble in my voice. "And actually, I'm sorry to say the position has been filled."

"I don't understand. My manager spoke with him this morning and ..."

"I'm very sorry," I say, shutting the door before she can reply.

When her van pulls out of the driveway, I breathe a sigh of relief. But I can't shake the feeling that at any moment I may be found out. I think of the woman's clothes, sensible jeans and sneakers so different from my threadbare dress and flip-flops. If I'm to play the role of a modern working woman, I need to look the part. Surely with the right clothes and attitude, I can pull this off. What other choice do I have?

I find a piece of paper on Cash's desk and start a list to bring with me on my next trip into town. Several of the stores and boutiques looked promising.

With renewed hope, I start a load of clothes and pick up the clutter from each room, dusting and wiping down each surface as I go. When that's done, I search for a way to clean the floor. Luckily, the hall closet holds a mop, bucket, broom, and lightweight vacuum.

When the household chores are complete and every surface shines, a sense of pride in the accomplishment creates a lightness I've never experienced. To work hard and be paid accordingly may not be a luxury for most, but to me it's everything. It's the first real step in becoming the person I want to be. To having the life I've always dreamed of. Not one filled with riches or extravagance, just peace and security and the freedom to make my own choices. My own mistakes.

Before leaving, I decide to leave Cash a note. After several minutes of debating the appropriate structure and wording, I scratch out the words in what I hope is the proper format for a personal note.

Dear Mr. Claiborne,

If it's not an inconvenience, would you mind if I use the stove and refrigerator to make lunch for myself during the day? I'll make sure to be very careful and clean up everything before leaving.

Sincerely Yours,
Max Fontaine

I purposely leave out a request to use the shower or anything else in the house. How would I be able to explain it? But the smell of cooking is hard to hide and might be detectable. So, I reread the words of my note and hope it will do. All he can say is no, but the request still makes me nervous, and my hand shakes as I place the scrap of paper under a magnet on the refrigerator.

The next morning dawns bright and fresh as I set out on an early trip to the market before heading to work. Cash's truck is already gone, making it easy to escape the cemetery undetected. As I pass the lighthouse, I see Walter trudging the path to his cottage. A rambunctious Calico kitten darts back and forth behind him, making me smile and wave. He doesn't wave back, but his sour mood doesn't dampen the optimism surging through my veins like waves lapping the shore on a windy day. I turn my face to the breeze, breathing in the early morning energy of the ocean. On this day, the sun seems a little brighter, the colors more vibrant.

With my vision no longer clouded by perpetual worry, I'm free to notice the smaller details of Jamaica Beach. The quaintness of the shops along the sea wall offering ice cream, kites, and souvenirs. The smell of freshly ground coffee from the place on the corner. The cackle of laughter from a salon across the street. The tinkle of wind chimes in front of a clothing boutique.

I stop to look through the window at racks of clothes, purses, and shoes in styles I see on other people but can't imagine on myself. For as long as I can remember, besides nudity, sarongs and loose linen have been my only options.

"Max? Is that you?"

The window's reflection shows a woman behind me. I stiffen and hesitate to turn.

"It's me, Olivia. From the library."

"Oh, hi," I say, breathing a sigh of relief. "I didn't expect to see you again. I mean, outside the library."

"Me either. But I should've guessed we'd meet again. I live right down there ..." She points to a row of houses at the end of the block. She glances around and lowers her voice. "How's the search going?"

"Actually, better than expected."

"So, you found him?"

"Well, no ... But I got a job as a housekeeper for Mr. Claiborne."

She claps her hands together. "That's great. Tell me everything."

I glance back at the shop window. "I actually have a few things I need to buy before heading to work."

"Perfect. I'll help you shop." She grabs my hand and pulls me inside the boutique.

A bell jingles, announcing our arrival to a young woman in the back. She calls out a brief hello but heads out a side door.

Olivia grabs a pair of sunglasses and checks her reflection in the mirror. "No," she says, pulling them off her face. "I should stick to aviators."

I want to join her. To float around the store like I've done this a million times. But I stand by the door, reluctant to begin the daunting task of dressing myself in a world of endless variety.

Olivia notices and waves me forward. "So, of course I want all the details about how your search landed you a job. But first, I need to know what you're looking for in here."

I shake my head. "I don't have any idea. Just something different than what I'm wearing. But still comfortable."

"Like jeans?"

"Yeah, like that," I point to a mannequin wearing jeans and a top that's pretty but not overly ornate.

Olivia nods. "But what about?" Her eyes flick to my rounded stomach.

I look away, unable to meet her eye. "Oh, yeah. Probably not a good idea, huh?"

"No, it's fine. Come on, the maternity section is over here. I bet we can find something that works."

She walks to the back of the store and starts flicking

through the circular racks. "In shirts, I'm guessing you're a small. But what about pants?"

"I'm not sure. I haven't worn them much since I was a kid."

"What? Like ... for religious reasons or something?"

"You could say that."

"Well, do you know your measurements?"

"No."

She walks behind the counter and retrieves a soft tape measure.

"Are you supposed to do that?"

She shrugs. "It's not like Charity cares. Spends most of her time outside smoking. Don't worry, I'll let her know when you're ready to check out. Now, hold your arms out."

"Is Jamaica Beach always this relaxed?" I ask.

"Yeah, pretty much. No different than any other small town, I guess."

As she measures my chest, waist, and hips, I explain Cash's need for a housekeeper and my need for a job in the simplest terms possible. I'm careful to leave out the part about living in his cemetery and hijacking the position from the real housekeeper, but some things are best left unsaid.

She grabs a pen from the cup by the register and writes my measurements on the palm of my hand.

"What's that?"

"That's you. Chest, waist, hips. Nice numbers, considering you're expecting. Here," she says, shoving a pile of blouses into my arms. "Take those back there and I'll bring you some jeans in a few minutes."

I venture into the soft lighting of the dressing room and am overwhelmed by how something as simple as new clothes can make me feel so good. As I slip on a pair of comfortable jeans with an elastic panel to hug my tummy, I'm shocked by the transformation. When I settle on a mint top made of soft cotton to pair with the jeans, I pull back the curtain to show off my new outfit. "How do I look?"

Olivia's eyes widen. "Fantastic! But there is one thing." She waggles her fingers at my chest. "Where's your bra?"

"Oh," I say, covering my breasts with one arm. "I forgot about that."

"No worries. Be right back."

After several minutes of trying to determine my correct bra size, we move on to shoes and I select a pair of black Converse. I decide to buy enough clothing for three days, so I can sneak my things into the washer at the house on alternate days.

"Thank you so much for helping me with this. I couldn't have done it without you," I say, giving Olivia a quick hug.

"Absolutely." She checks her watch. "Listen, I gotta run but I'm sure we'll see each other around."

"Can I wear this out?" I ask as Charity bags up the purchases.

She gives me a look that says she couldn't care less what I do as long as I leave her alone. So I hurry back to the dressing room and reemerge feeling like a new person. A new Max.

Twenty-One

As I mount the steps to Johnson's Market, the change in my confidence is astounding. For the first time in my life, I feel like anything is possible. I can be whoever I choose, without anyone hovering. The freedom is almost too much. Like being deprived of water and then given too much wine. Euphoria takes over, threatening to drown out all the bad. How easy it would be to forget Eden ever happened. To get swept up in the joy of a fresh start without the pain of revisiting the past. But I need to remember. I want my son to know there is evil in the world waiting to swallow him whole if he isn't careful. It was a lesson Maggie never learned. But I did.

Taking the steps to the grocery store two at a time, I find myself gridlocked with someone on the other side of the door. I stop pushing and allow them to exit first.

"Sorry about that, I ..." The words die on my lips as I stare into the same green eyes I'd been terrified of yesterday morning.

But instead of feeling scared, I'm mesmerized by the tiny gold flecks in Cash's gaze I hadn't noticed before.

"Ma'am," he says, tipping the brim of his cowboy hat. In his Western boots, jeans, and snug white T-shirt, he cuts a nice figure.

"Thanks," I say, hating the way my stomach flutters at the scent of his cologne. The flex of his biceps as he holds the door.

"You're up and at 'em awful early, I see."

I nod and try to turn away, but he stops me with a light touch on the shoulder.

When I flinch, he seems embarrassed. "I just wanted to say I got your note and to feel free to make yourself at home. Use the stove. Keep stuff in the ice box. Whatever you need. Not like there's a whole lot in there, anyhow. I'm not much of a cook myself."

I glance up. "Are you sure it's not an inconvenience?"

He laughs, eyes sparkling. "Hell, after how great the place looked when I came in yesterday, the only inconvenience I can think of is if you were to quit on me."

"I don't think you're in danger of that happening, Mr. Claiborne."

His brows snap together. "Mr. Claiborne's my dad. Call me Cash."

"All right, Cash."

"That's better. Listen, when you get done in here, why don't you stop over at Mojo's across the way and have a cup of coffee with me?"

"Oh ... I really should be getting to work."

"Nonsense. The house still looks great from the job you did yesterday. I barely touched it. Promise."

I glance over to see Melinda watching our interaction with curiosity. "If I say yes, will you go on and let me finish my shopping? People are starting to stare," I say, darting my eyes toward the register.

His deep laughter catches me off guard. "Who, Melinda?" He turns to give her a wink. "You getting all this, baby doll?"

She smirks. "Oh, get the hell outta here and leave that poor girl alone, will ya?"

When he's gone, I chide myself for accepting the invitation. I was just being polite. Or was I? I can't deny the attraction I've felt since our first encounter. But I'm seven months pregnant. And I don't know the first thing about him. He could have a girlfriend, or a wife, for that matter. Just because I haven't seen her doesn't mean she doesn't exist. Or maybe I have seen her. The woman in the photo on his desk. Why else would he keep her picture there? I decide to skip coffee. The last thing I need is to become romantically involved with a man that's taken.

I hurry through the aisles, throwing things into the basket in hopes of making it back to Cash's house before he notices I blew him off.

Melinda lifts a brow. "In a rush?"

"No."

"Couldn't help overhearing you two a while ago. You working over there now?"

I lift my chin. "I'm the new housekeeper."

"Interesting."

"Why do you say that?"

She shrugs and scans a bag of potatoes. "No reason."

I lean forward and lower my voice. "Please tell me. Is there something I should be worried about?"

"Oh, no. Nothing like that. Just heard he hasn't had much company since he's been back."

"What do you mean?"

"Well, since his wife—" Her head snaps up at the sound of a customer entering the store. "Tell you later," she whispers.

As I walk the road back to the house, I wonder what Melinda was going to say. Why she was so hesitant to mention Cash's wife. From the looks of things, they're no longer married. But people get divorced all the time. Why the secrecy? Unless, he's the one to blame. Maybe he did something terrible to drive her away. Based on my experiences with men, integrity doesn't seem to be high on their list of attributes. Why should Cash be any different?

As I pass the lighthouse, the rumble of a truck cuts my thoughts short. I recognize the hum of the engine, the heavy tires crunching along the gravel behind me, but resist the urge to turn as the flash of black in my peripheral slows to a crawl.

Cash leans out the window. "What are you doing?"

"Walking," I say, keeping my eyes forward.

"Want a ride?"

"No, I'm fine."

"Come on, Max." He stops the truck and climbs out before I can protest. "Let me get these for you," he says, placing my bags in the back. He takes off his hat, squinting into the sun. "It's hotter'n hell out here. Why don't you let me give you a ride?"

Not wanting to seem difficult, especially after standing him up at the coffee shop, I climb inside and tell myself he would have done the same favor for anyone.

"I waited for you," he said, pulling forward.

"Yeah, well, coffee's not really my thing."

He drums his fingers on the steering wheel. "Fair enough. I actually wanted to talk to you about something."

My spine stiffens at his serious tone, and I wonder if I've done something wrong. Or worse, if he found my hiding spot in the graveyard. I swallow hard and berate myself for ever entertaining the idea he was interested in me. But every time I look at his handsome face, my common sense seems to go out the window.

I cut my eyes to the left. "What is it?"

He shifts in his seat, resting his wrist on the steering wheel. "I wanted to ask about the guy you were looking for the other day. Were you able to find him?"

"No. But it's not a big deal."

He clears his throat. "The reason I ask is I might be able to help, if it's something important. You said his name is Lir Delacroix, right?"

I'm amazed by Cash's memory for detail, but my search for Lir is no longer important. Contacting him was a last resort, but with my new job, I don't need his help. It would have been nice if he had at least taken an interest in his own child's future, but I refuse to run after a man who doesn't want either of us. He had his chance and he blew it.

"Thanks for the offer," I say, cutting my eyes to the left. "But it's not important anymore."

"Just thought I'd ask." He pulls into the driveway and kills the engine. "So, you say you don't like coffee, but how do you feel about hot chocolate?" When I give in to the urge to smile, he laughs. "See, I knew I'd figure out what you like."

"Honestly, I've never had coffee," I admit.

"What? Never had coffee? Well, that's just ... it's un-American, that's what!"

"Are you always this dramatic?" I tease.

He thumps his chest with his hand. "That hurt. But I'm willing to overlook it if you'll try a cup."

"I don't know ..."

"It's settled, then." He pulls to a stop in the yard and kills the motor, but instead of getting out, he turns and looks me in the eye. "You go on in and I'll bring the groceries."

"Are you sure it's okay to keep them here for a few hours? I'll bring most of them home with me when I leave."

He frowns. "Why wouldn't it be okay?"

His words put me at ease, but watching him carry in my things still feels strange. At Eden, everyone had set chores and routines. No job was pawned off on someone else. Even at the shelter, rules and regulations governed our time. Nothing was left to chance or played by ear. I remind myself that I'm in the real world now and need to adjust. To relax and go with the flow.

Cash drops the bags on the counter. "Now, about that coffee. Let's see ..." He pulls open one drawer and then another.

"I put it all in here," I say, opening a cabinet where the coffee filters, grounds, and creamers are organized.

A smile lights his face. "This is exactly why I need you here."

"It was a bit ... scattered," I agree, thinking of the haphazard state of the pantry when I arrived.

"I still can't believe how much you got accomplished yesterday. You're a real lifesaver, you know."

Uncomfortable with the praise, I make an excuse to retreat to the laundry room while the coffee percolates. But when he calls out that it's ready a few minutes later, I find myself eager to return to the kitchen. To him. His easygoing nature is like no one I've ever known. At least no man I've ever known. And as he fusses over the correct amount of cream and sugar to add to my cup, I can't help feeling jealous of the woman who held his heart. I glance at her smiling face on the desk. He's obviously still in love with her. Why else would he keep her photograph?

He hands me the cup, and I take a small sip.

"What do you think?" he asks.

I linger over the creamy liquid, enjoying the strong flavor. "It's delicious."

"See, I knew you'd like it." He takes a sip of his own. "Come on. Let's go sit on the back porch."

We settle into a pair of wooden rockers to enjoy our coffee as hummingbirds swarm a red feeder hanging above the railing.

Cash smiles as he watches them. "I've caught one before."

"A hummingbird? Really?"

"Flew into the house one day and was going crazy. I didn't want to scare it, so I waited for it to settle down then eased over and lowered my hands until I had it. I guess it was exhausted because it was perfectly still, just lying there in my hands. It's amazing to see one without their wings going a million miles an hour."

"What did you do with it?"

"Walked outside and let it go."

"I didn't know it was possible to catch one without hurting it."

"Guess you can call me the hummingbird whisperer."

"The what?"

"The hummingbird whisperer. You know, like the horse whisperer?"

I cut my eyes in his direction to see if he's joking. "I seriously have no idea what you're talking about."

He sits up, his mouth open in disbelief. "You're saying you've never seen *The Horse Whisperer*? Robert Redford?"

"It's a movie?"

"And a book. I'll loan you my copy if you like. Books are always better than movies. But I don't know, it doesn't get much better than Robert Redford, does it?"

I nod in agreement, hoping he doesn't pick up on my ignorance. I remember reading lots of books at school, more than Maggie deemed appropriate for sure, and watching a few movies on TV back in New Orleans. But after so many years in seclusion, many details of pop culture have been forgotten.

"I noticed Walter has a new kitten," I say, changing the subject. "That wouldn't have anything to do with you, would it?"

"You gave me some great advice," Cash admits, flushing a little. "Figured it couldn't hurt to at least try and patch things up."

"Did it work?"

"Who knows. The old man's still not what you would call

friendly." He gives me a conspiring grin. "But he hasn't flipped me the bird lately, so maybe we're making progress."

When I place our empty cups in the sink, Cash takes a seat at his desk.

"Aren't you going to the gym?"

He looks up from his computer. "What makes you say that?"

"Isn't that what you do every day?" At the look of confusion on his face, I realize the slip and scramble to come up with an excuse. "I mean, yesterday you had on gym clothes, so I thought maybe that's your routine."

He clears his throat. "Uh, yeah. Usually I do. But today I have some work to tend to."

When he mentions work, I realize that despite all my spying, I haven't figured out his profession. "What are you working on?" I say, my curiosity piqued.

"Just a new case I'm thinking about opening."

"So ... you're a lawyer?"

He shakes his head and points to a silver badge pinned to the jacket draped around his chair. "Texas Ranger."

I nod and keep wiping the counter, but my pulse pounds in my ears at this turn of events. From what I remember about Texas Rangers, they are kind of like cops but more powerful. Suddenly, his offer to help find Lir makes more sense. There was a time when I would have jumped at the chance to tell Cash my plight. To explain every sordid detail of my situation in an effort to expose Eden and bring Jude's world crashing down around his ears. But if the police don't believe me, why should Cash? And if he thinks I'm crazy, I could lose my job. My security. Everything my future depends on. I can't let that happen. So, I bite my tongue no matter how much it hurts.

Cash leans back in his office chair and smiles. "What about you? Where'd you work before this?"

I paste on a smile and try to round the truth into something believable. "I was a nursery worker at a daycare."

"Oh, really? Which one?"

I wave my hand in the air. "It's small. You probably haven't heard of it."

"Try me."

My stomach pitches. "It's uh ... it's called ... Eden," I blurt, unable to think of another name.

"Haven't heard of that one. It's nearby?"

"Kind of," I say, giving a noncommittal shrug. "So, what kind of case are you working on?" I ask, hoping to turn the subject away from myself.

He frowns. "Can't really say yet. Some things take time to figure out." He looks up, a smile spreading across his face. "Feels good to be home, though."

"You were away?"

"More like in and out over the last few years. Been up in Dallas a lot."

"Do you plan to stay long this time?" I twist my hands together, hoping the answer is yes. To be out of a job this nice after only a few weeks would be devastating.

He closes the lid of his laptop and pushes back his chair. "It's looking like it. That's part of the reason I hired you. Now that I'm back, without ... Well, let's just say I could use a little help to keep things going."

"It's a beautiful house. Didn't take any time for me to clean it yesterday."

When he gives me a sheepish grin, I realize how easily my statement could be taken as an insult. "I'm sorry. That came out wrong. I never meant to insinuate you're lazy or anything." I bite my lip, cringing at how fast I've managed to go from mildly rude to full on insulting. "No, that's not what I mean either ... I ..."

He laughs. "Max, calm down. I think I know what you're trying to say, and I agree. The housekeeping isn't that hard. Heck, I've been doing an alright job for the last couple of months. But if I'm being honest, I'm ..."

Cash doesn't strike me as the shy type, so his reluctance to finish the sentence is intriguing. "What is it?" I say, hoping to coax the answer from him.

He sighs and shakes his head. "It might sound silly, but I'm not the best at being alone."

"So, you hired me to keep you company?" I say, my muscles tensing at the admission.

He holds up a hand as alarm bells clang in my head. "Listen, I know how it sounds. But I promise it's not what you're thinking."

My hands clench into fists as I suppress the urge to run through the nearest door and never look back. "Then ... what is it?"

His ears turn red, and he covers his face with both hands. "Wow, this is really embarrassing. Let me see how I can explain. I guess as long as I can remember, there've been people around. First my parents, then my wife ..."

"The woman in the photo?" I say, unable to suppress my curiosity.

He nods and gives a heavy sigh. "Yeah. I mean, back in Dallas it wasn't something I really thought about. I had a couple of roommates to keep me company. But coming home this time was different. When I got here, the house was so empty. Lonely. I just missed somebody being around. Somebody to have a cup of coffee with. Guess that's a pretty stupid reason to get a housekeeper, huh?" He turns away, unable to meet my gaze as he shuffles the papers on his desk.

I lean back against the counter, letting his words soak in. But as I reflect on my own experience with loneliness, empathy bubbles inside like a volcano, forcing me to shake my head. "No, Cash. It doesn't make you stupid. It makes you human."

Twenty-Two

The next morning, I place Cash's copy of *The Horse Whisperer* on his desk.

He glances at the book and frowns. "You didn't like it?"

"Oh, no. I loved it."

His mouth falls open. "You mean ... you finished it?"

"Yeah."

"But you've only had it one day."

"It was a good book," I say, ducking my head as heat creeps up my neck. "I mean, the ending was a little unexpected, but it was still wonderful. Thanks for letting me borrow it."

"Hang on a minute," he says, walking out of the room. When he returns, he hands me copies of *Lonesome Dove* and *Outlander*. "Looks like you're ready for these now."

"Thank you," I breathe, caressing the worn covers.

"And this," he says, holding up *The Horse Whisperer* on DVD.

"Oh, I don't want to take your movie," I say, thinking how pointless it would be to borrow something I have no way of watching.

He inclines his head. "Why not? I don't mind, really."

I want to agree, but if I do, he'll expect me to watch it and may question me afterward. My stomach clenches as I try to come up with a believable excuse. "I, uh, don't really watch many movies because I ... fall asleep," I finish lamely.

Cash taps his chin. "Well, we can't have that. Listen, I have an idea. Why don't you watch it here? And I'll make sure to yell in your ear if I see your eyelids drooping," he jokes.

I suppress the urge to smile. "I don't think so. I still have work to do."

He shakes his head. "No, I don't mean right now. Maybe later tonight, if you aren't busy."

The suggestion makes me tense, but I have conflicting emotions. I want to agree. To see him smile. He's obviously lonely. I'm lonely too. "I don't know if I should," I admit, hating my indecision.

"Okay, you got me." He holds out his hands in mock surrender. "I'll throw in pizza too. You're a hard one to bargain with, you know?"

I can't help but smile. He has a way of smoothing away my worry, making me feel like everything's okay. What would it hurt? I mean, it's not like he's hitting on me. He just wants a friend. And this is what normal friends do. They hang out.

"Okay," I say. "That sounds good."

"Great. Does eight sound good?"

"Perfect."

When the pizza arrives later that night, Cash insists we have a picnic on the sofa.

"What if sauce gets on the fabric?" I worry, studying light linen covering the expensive-looking sectional.

He looks up from the slice he's devouring. "Don't worry about it. If it gets ruined, I'll get a new one." He flashes a mischievous grin. "Or ... I'll just make the housekeeper try to get the stain out."

Before I know what's happening, my body lurches forward to lightly punch him in the shoulder.

"Ouch!"

"Oh! I'm so sorry!" My breath catches in my throat at the faux pas. The uncalled-for familiarity. How could I have done that? Actually *punch* him? Granted, that's the kind of horse play Lir and I enjoyed as kids, but Cash is practically a stranger. And a grown man. And my *employer*. I close my eyes, my face burning with humiliation. "I shouldn't have done that. It was totally inappropriate."

"Max, look at me."

I open my eyes but can't bring myself to meet his gaze.

"Please?" he says in a quiet voice. "What just happened is totally fine. You didn't hurt me. You were just being yourself, and I like it. I like you, Max."

"Really?" I say, my eyes lifting to find his.

"Yeah. In fact, I'd like to know more about you."

"What do you want to know?"

"Anything."

"Why don't you go first?" I say, uncomfortable with the idea of talking about my past.

He tosses a half-eaten pizza crust into the box on the ottoman and leans back against the cushions. "Okay, what do you want to know?"

I tally up the check list in my mind, starting with the least invasive first. "So you grew up here, in Jamaica Beach?"

"Yep. My sister and I were raised right here in this house. I bought it from my parents when they retired. Just couldn't get used to the idea of it slipping out of the family."

"You have a sister? What's her name?"

"Gracie. She and her husband live up in Round Top. Run a cute little bed and breakfast."

"And your parents?"

"Oh, they come through every once in a while. But as soon as they sold this place, they bought a motor home and hit the road. They're somewhere up in Canada right now enjoying the nice weather."

"That sounds lovely."

"Yeah, can't say I inherited their adventurous streak. I get pretty antsy anytime I have to leave Texas."

"So, is that why you chose to be a Ranger?"

"Ha. Well, I do love Texas, but can't say that's why I'm a Ranger. Just always had a lot of respect for them, I guess. They're the oldest law enforcement agency in the United States. It's not easy to become one, but I like the sense of duty and honor. There're only about a hundred and sixty of us, so it kinda keeps the shady characters to a minimum."

"You mean bad cops?"

"Well, yeah. Seen enough of that when I was a state trooper. Don't get me wrong, there are plenty of good ones out there. But plenty of bad ones too. My wife used to tell me my heart was too good to wear a badge. I told her that's exactly why I need one."

I sit up straight. "Your wife?"

He bites his lip and nods. "Yeah, Sadie. You might've seen her picture. She was something else."

"Was?"

He looks away. "She died."

"Oh."

"Four years ago." When his voice cracks with emotion, I suppress the urge to reach for him. But he's not mine to hold.

"I'm sorry," I say, jumping to my feet. "I should go."

"What? Why?"

I stare at the floor. "I don't know. I just feel bad for bringing that up, I guess."

He lets out a breath. "The truth is, I like talking about her. Really. I know she's in a better place. Took me a long time to be okay with it, but you just gotta keep going. Keep living life. For her and ..." He shakes his head. "Well, it's over with now." He shifts in his seat. "Sorry ... I'm the one who shouldn't be bothering you with my problems."

"You're not bothering me," I say, reaching out to touch his arm. "It's good to talk."

His face breaks into a warm smile. "Well, you're easy to talk to."

My throat closes at the praise, and I have to turn away.

His eyes widen at the tears in mine. "Well, hell. Why are you crying? I'm the only one allowed to be sad, remember?"

I hide my face with my hands and laugh. "Sorry. I don't know what's wrong with me."

He grabs the remote and hits play. "Come on. If you want to cry, this movie should do the trick."

Twenty-Three

To Cash's amusement, I finish *Lonesome Dove* and *Outlander* within a few days and am left hungry for more. Following my passion down to the local bookstore, I become acquainted with the store's large selection of romance that continues to feed my addiction. But books aren't the only reason I look forward to my daily treks through Jamaica Beach. Just like my growing friendship with Cash, the community has become a sense of comfort. In this place, I'm not seen as the pitiful daughter of a New Orleans' stripper. A charity case to be both exploited and endured. Here, I'm able to start fresh without my past weighing me down. Here, I can envision a future for myself. For my son.

With its quiet expanse of beach, I spend most afternoons after work reading on the shore until the light fades, the breeze pushing at the pages of my novel as the sun glimmers off the expanse of water in the distance. Then, under the cover of darkness, I creep back to the mausoleum where I lie in the gloom, the words of fictional lovers crooning in my head.

I long for the type of closeness I find in those books. The electricity between Elizabeth and the prideful Mr. Darcy. The passion and commitment of Jamie and Claire. But maybe these are things that only exist in fiction. My brief encounter with Lir certainly doesn't qualify. Looking back, our lovemaking wasn't that at all. It was sex, plain and simple. Nothing more than an impulse of the moment. Something to look back on and ask myself why?

The skin of my enlarged stomach stretches tighter with every passing day, and I love to feel the baby move beneath my fingers, but a child changes everything. "Good men don't want a woman with baggage," Maggie used to say when R.J. would yell at me for being too loud. "They want their own kids. Not another man's brat. You remember that." But if that's the truth, my future looks bleak.

Gazing out toward the farmhouse, I wonder what Cash is doing. Wearing. Not wearing. I know I shouldn't, but I can't stop. The attraction is futile and yet it grows. Day by the day. Hour by hour. Minute by minute. And every small kindness, confession, conversation, cup of coffee just makes me want more. Sometimes I wonder what life would be like if I were more than just the housekeeper.

But that way lies madness.

It's not like Cash would ever feel the same. He doesn't even know me. The real me. Sometimes I itch to tell him the truth about my past. About Eden. About everything. I want to believe in the kind of heroic justice displayed in books. But I still haven't recovered from the last time I asked for help and the crushing disappointment that followed. I don't want the same thing to happen with Cash. I can't bear the idea of anything changing. I want to stay right where I am, living and working. Sharing a laugh. Watching the hummingbirds on the porch.

I toss and turn on my sleeping bag, unable to quiet my mind. And when the first rays of light streak across the sky, I'm glad for an excuse to leave the lumpy bed and head to work. But when I knock at the front door of the house, it's several minutes before Cash answers, puffy eyed and shirtless.

"Oh, hey. Is something wrong?" he says, squinting into the sunlight.

I tear my eyes away from his chiseled chest and try to answer coherently. "No. I'm sorry for waking you. I didn't mean to come so early ... I'll come back later."

He shakes his head. "No, don't go. Come in. I'll get us some coffee."

When he heads over to rinse out the pot, I excuse myself and hurry to brush my teeth and hair thoroughly in the luxury of a real bathroom rather than bent over the spigot in the graveyard. By the time I return, he's waiting for me on the porch.

"Did I put in enough sugar?" he says when I take a sip.

"It's perfect. Thank you."

He takes a contented breath, his gaze drifting over the early morning fog. "This is my favorite time of day. When everything is still fresh and new."

"Mine, too. I've always enjoyed mornings. But I feel bad for waking you so early. I've been up for a while."

"It's fine, really. Can't sleep?"

I touch the bulging reason for my discomfort and make a face.

He grins at my expression. "When're you due?"

"Middle of this month."

"You don't talk about it much," he says, nodding to my stomach. "I don't mind, you know. If you want to talk."

My heart does a flip at the simple offer. "It's a boy," I say, my face growing warm with pride.

He smiles. "Got a name picked out?"

I shake my head.

"Guess you could always name him after his old man. Call him Jr." His eyes bore into mine, the air heavy with unspoken questions. When I grimace, he stammers an apology. "Sorry ... I didn't mean anything by that."

"It's okay. The father's not in the picture," I say, miming the words I heard so many times growing up. It was Maggie's go-to statement regarding my own father's absence. And now it's mine.

Cash dips his head but doesn't look away. "You want to talk about it?"

"Not really," I say, avoiding his gaze.

"It doesn't have anything to do with that guy you were looking for, does it?" At my shocked expression, Cash's lips press into a tight line. "I've actually been waiting for the right time to bring this up, but I ran a search for him." When I start to protest, he holds up a hand. "I know you said to leave it alone, but let's just say I have my own reasons too."

"What did you find?" I say, my pulse pounding in my ears as I wait for his answer.

He hesitates, his hand flexing around his cup. "It ain't good."

———

When I enter the library, glimpses of Olivia's red hair flash through a shelf near the back.

"Hey there!" she calls with a bright smile as I near. "How've you been?"

"I'm okay," I say, lifting my hair off my neck. "Thought I'd get up early and beat the heat. Guess I was wrong."

Her eyes widen. "You walked here?" When I nod, she looks appalled. "Why don't you let me give you a ride back in a bit? I only work half a day on the weekends."

"I couldn't inconvenience you—"

"Oh, hush," she says with a flick of her wrist. "We're both headed to the same place." She grabs a few books and walks around the shelf. "Is there something I can help you find?"

I glance around to make sure no one is listening. "Actually, I came to talk to you ... if you have a few minutes."

"Sure." She studies my face. "Is something wrong?"

I step closer and lower my voice. "Kind of."

She glances at a young woman pushing a cart of books. "Come on," she says, taking my elbow to guide me to a far corner.

When we are out of earshot, I lean close. "You know the guy I was looking for a while back?"

"Yeah. Did you find him?"

"No, but Cash did. He said Lir was in jail recently."

She gasps. "What for?"

"Drugs and armed robbery, I think."

"Shit."

"But that's not all." I take a breath and try to decide how much to reveal. "Cash says someone bailed him out a few days ago. A guy I know. Someone really bad. I was hoping he would leave us both alone, but now I see that's not the case. He found Lir and if I don't do something to stop him, he'll find me too. I know it." I glance around, my nerves quivering with dread. "I'm sorry I can't tell you everything," I whisper. "But I need some advice."

She squeezes my hand. "Of course. What is it?"

"Like I said, this guy is dangerous. Deadly. I tried to tell the police a while back, but they weren't any help."

"But I thought you said Cash wants to help?" she interrupts. "He's a Ranger, right?"

I nod.

"So what's the problem?"

I shrug. "I don't know. I mean, the cops already dismissed my accusations. But they're so ..."

"Corrupt?"

My eyes round at the accusation. "I was going to say incompetent. But you think they're actually corrupt?"

She tilts her head to the side. "All I'm saying is I've lived here my whole life and as soon as Andrews was made chief about ten years ago, things went downhill."

"How so?"

"Let's just say, I have a cousin who's been a cop here for years and years, but never had anything to show for it. Always complained how hard it was to raise a family on that kind of salary. But when Andrews came in, my cousin went from barely making rent to buying a brand-new five-thousand-square-foot beach house right on the water. And few months later, he bought a new truck, new boat, and a pair of matching jet skis for him and his wife. He tries to say it's because she went to work over at the elementary school, but you can't tell me her little teacher salary made that big of a difference."

"So you suspect your cousin might be involved in illegal activities?"

"I hate to think so, but yeah."

I kid myself for not suspecting it all along. In the grand scheme of things, paying the cops to keep quiet would be one of Jude's lesser crimes.

Olivia shakes her head. "Honestly, I wouldn't trust anybody working for Andrews." She raises an eyebrow. "But I would trust a Texas Ranger."

"Why would they be any different?"

She waves me into her office. "Call me nosey, but after I ran into you the other day, I looked Cash up." She gives a mischievous smile. "You forgot to mention he's drop-dead gorgeous." My face turns red, making her laugh. "Look at you. You've totally noticed, so quit acting like you haven't."

I close my eyes and cover my face with my hands. "Okay, okay. I've noticed. Are you happy?"

She takes a seat at her computer and clicks on the screen. "Look what I found," she says, nudging me with her elbow. "I think this might help you make up your mind."

A video plays, showing Cash being interviewed by a Dallas news anchor concerning an operation he conducted leading to the exposure of over twenty officers who were involved in confiscating narcotics from criminals, only to turn around and sell the drugs for profit.

When it comes to an end, Olivia smiles. "If that isn't the opposite of corrupt, then I don't know what is. Can you believe he was able to do all that in his first year as a Ranger? And just look at the way that reporter is hanging on to his arm." She fans herself. "Damn, what I wouldn't give to throw a few questions at him myself. Something like ..." She pretends to hold a microphone up to her mouth. "Now, Mr. Claiborne, based on your impressive track record, I think it's safe to say you just might be the Lone Star State's most eligible bachelor. That is, if you're single? Oh, you are! Well, isn't that dandy!" She leans forward. "May I ask what qualities you're seeking in a partner? Red hair, green eyes, and a love of books? You don't say!"

I can't help laughing at her silliness.

"Seriously, though, he seems legit," she says. "You need to tell him what you know."

"What if he doesn't believe me?" My stomach churns at the thought. "What if he thinks I'm crazy and I lose my job? What if—"

Olivia holds up a hand. "Stop right there. You're working

yourself up for no reason. Of course he'll believe you. It's not like you're a stranger or something." She leans in and lifts an eyebrow. "Besides, what man can resist helping a damsel in distress?"

I make a face. "You make him sound like the hero from a romance novel."

She presses a hand to her heart. "He's a handsome Texas Ranger. That's close enough for me."

Twenty-Four

When Olivia pulls into Cash's driveway, he's walking toward his truck with a large, leather duffle bag in his hand.

"Is he going somewhere?" she asks, nodding in his direction.

"I don't know," I say, opening the car door. "Thanks for the ride, though."

When she drives away, I walk toward Cash with hesitant steps. No more secrecy. It's time to come clean and hope for the best.

"Hey," he says as I approach. "I'm glad you stopped by."

I lift my chin and look him in the eye. "Do you have a minute to talk?"

He glances toward his truck, then back at me. "Actually, I'm in a bit of a time crunch. Just got a lead on the case I'm looking at, so I'll be away for a few days. I was going to call and let you know, but you keep forgetting to leave me your number." He pulls out his phone. "Let me go ahead and punch it in while I'm thinking about it."

I paste a smile on my face, but my mind races for an excuse. I've given so many already, it's hard to keep them all straight. It seems everyone has a cell phone, but the idea of wasting money on such a luxury seems pointless.

"Listen, why don't you let me house sit while you're away? I can't keep an eye on the place and if you need me, all you'll have to do is call your landline."

He lifts an eyebrow and studies me a moment. "Yeah ... That actually sounds like a great idea. You sure you don't mind?"

"Not at all. I can sleep on the couch, and I'll be sure to get in some extra cleaning. Baseboards and stuff," I offer, hoping he won't change his mind.

He shakes his head. "Don't you dare. You're the one doing me a favor. Just make yourself at home. And that couch is uncomfortable as hell. Use my bed. I insist."

My face heats at the idea, and I drop my gaze to focus on the shiny silver star pinned to his chest. "How long will you be gone?"

"Not sure yet. Maybe a week. But I better get on the road. Can we talk when I get back?"

"Sure."

"Let me know if you need anything, okay?" His mouth opens like he wants to say more.

"Is something wrong?"

He runs a hand through his auburn hair and gives a shaky

laugh. "No. I mean, I don't know. Hell, I don't know what's wrong with me ..."

I touch his arm. "Tell me."

He looks down, focusing on my hand until I pull away, embarrassed by my impulsiveness but not as sorry as I should be.

"Used to look forward to getting called out," he admits. "But this time is different. Kinda hate to leave the place. To leave ..."

My mouth goes dry and my imagination begs to run wild. To finish his sentence. To let myself believe it ends with the word you.

When I get brave enough to meet his gaze, he clears his throat. "Anyhow, it's nice to know you'll be here when I get back."

I stand in the driveway until his truck is out of sight. Our talk will have to wait, and part of me is glad. For a little while longer, I can pretend to be a normal person. Pretend this house is my own. A place where I'm free to do as I like.

When dusk falls, I run a giant tub of hot water and indulge in the novelty of soaking until my hands and feet turn to prunes. Climbing from the tub, I study myself in the mirror. Despite my nearing due date, my arms and legs remain thin in contrast to my swelling belly and breasts. I turn to the side, noticing how much my stomach has dropped over the past couple of weeks. But according to my copy of *What to Expect When You're Expecting*, that's normal near the end.

The end.

Little words with a big meaning. I've seen women in labor

many times, but watching something and experiencing it are two different things.

Flashes of Maggie's final hours boil to the surface, making me doubt my strength to see it through. Maggie thought she would be fine. Kept insisting she had delivered me with no problem. How was she to know the next time would end her life?

I press a hand to my stomach, my son's tiny kicks like the ticking of a bomb with the power to decide whether I'll live or die.

In the bedroom, I cut out the lights and try to push the thought to the back of my mind as I snuggle into Cash's pillow and wish for sleep. But his spicy scent sends another kind of heat coursing through my veins. I bury my face farther into the pillow, but I'm wide awake. After sleeping on nothing more than a sheepskin at Eden—and my discount sleeping bag in the mausoleum—my body revolts against the squishy softness of a real mattress.

I throw back the coverlet and pad to the living room where I grab a blanket and settle on the couch in front of the television. Clicking through the local channels, a car commercial featuring an average-lookin bald guy in a suit and tie flashes on the screen. But his eyes are familiar enough to make me stand and walk closer to the set.

"You've already shopped the rest, so come on down and shop the best!" He waves a hand toward a sparkling line of pickups in the background. "I can guarantee you won't find a better deal or my name's not Buddy Babineaux!"

As a jingle plays urging customers to visit Buddy Chevrolet, I try to place where I've seen the man.

When the memory hits, it feels like a punch in the gut.

The man standing beside his wife, their happy faces washed in the glow of Claiming ceremony torches. Horror gripping my heart as they took my newborn sister in their arms, kissing her tiny face as if she was their own flesh and blood. As if her real mother hadn't just been buried like a stray cat in the backyard. As if I wasn't standing right there, resenting their happiness with every fiber of my being.

But how were they to know about the dark side of Eden? Maggie's death was just one of many hidden secrets. "Our clients' journeys must not be hindered by such tragedies," Jude would often say. "The past is gone. Let us live in the present."

But as I stare at the car salesman on the television eight years later, my anger feels as fresh as the day it happened.

"Well, hello there little lady. What can I help you with?"

The glossy floor of the dealership squeaks as I turn to see who's speaking.

A lanky man with a crew cut holds out his hand. "Frank Jones, Sales Manager," he says with a wide smile.

I shake his hand but scan my surroundings in an effort to spot the man from the commercial. "Is Mr. Babineaux here today?"

"He is. But he's out to lunch right now." Frank ushers me toward the side of the dealership where an abundance of cars and SUVs are parked with balloons tied to the antennas. "What did you say your name was again?"

"Max."

"Well, it sure is nice to meet you, Max. Why don't you let me show you around while we wait on him to get back?" He holds open the door leading to the parking lot, where plastic flags flap in the wind. "Is there a something in particular you're interested in?"

I look at the sparkling new vehicles parked in rows and realize I know nothing about them. What I like. What to ask for. I only came to get a look at Mr. Babineaux, but for the charade to work, I need to at least pretend to be interested in buying a car. So, I say the first thing that comes to mind. "I like red."

Frank's head bobs up and down. "We certainly have a few red ones. Are you wanting a car or something a bit roomier?" He nods to my stomach. "By the looks of things, I'm guessing something family friendly might be in order. Like this one right here." He leads me to a white SUV. "Now, the Tahoe has been a best seller for years, and if you like the looks of it, we could surely get it for you in red."

I touch the iridescent pearl paint. "Actually this color is nice too."

"Pearl is a best seller. With the heat and all, it's a great choice for this climate. And with these third-row seats, there's plenty of room for kids, dogs, you name it. If you need extra storage, the seats fold completely down. Perfect for groceries, camping trips, sports equipment. Whatever you're into."

His sales pitch makes me remember all the things Eden took

from me. Somehow I jumped from being a child to an adult with nothing in between. No first dates, no high school football games, and certainly no driving lessons.

When Frank opens the door of the Tahoe, a rush of heat brings the pleasant scent of new leather. "Go ahead, take a look."

I glance back at the dealership showroom. "If you don't mind, could we go see if Mr. Babineaux is back?"

Frank nods. "You bet. Oh, look. There's his truck pulling in right there."

I follow Frank and try to smile as he makes the introduction.

"Call me Buddy," Mr. Babineaux says, shaking my hand with a firm grip. "Is there something I can do for you?"

"A friend of mine referred me to your dealership and said I should ask for you," I say, rehearsing the line I prepared last night.

"Sure thing. I see Frank's been showing you around. If you found something you might be interested in, I'd be happy to run the numbers."

I point to the pearl Tahoe. "I like that one."

Buddy leads me to a spacious office where he settles behind a wooden desk and begins to punch information into his computer.

As he peppers me with questions, I stare at the family photos lining the walls. "Is that your little girl?" I ask, hoping to direct his attention away from my fabricated personal details and toward his own.

At the mention of his daughter, he beams a smile and flips

around a framed photo of her wearing a huge smile and pink cowboy boots. "That's my little Ava. Just turned eight, but she sure does love her horses," he says, indicating the big white quarter horse she's sitting on. "Took first place at the rodeo here in town last weekend," he says with obvious pride.

I gulp and stare at the face that looks so much like my own at that age. But the image is bittersweet. Based on the photographs, Ava has the loving family life I always wanted. The life Maggie tried to give, but couldn't accomplish.

"And here's one of her learning to ski up in Aspen last year," Buddy says, pointing to another photo. "She was scared at first, but it didn't take her long to get the hang of it, and pretty soon she was skiing better than her mama." He laughs and indicates the blond woman I remember seeing at Eden. "Boy, Susan was worried to death to let her off the bunny slopes."

I stare at Susan holding Ava's hand, their faces bright with joy, and my anger starts to dissipate. No matter how Ava came to be with Buddy and Susan, she's obviously better off. And I'm happy she has a good life. A good family. I hope she never faces the kind of hardships I had growing up. I want to hate them for taking her. Hate Jude for giving her away. But I can't. What Jude did wasn't necessarily good. Or moral. Or legal. But for Ava, it turned out to be right.

"Max, are you okay?" Buddy asks, his brows pinched together in concern. "Would you like me to get you a bottle of water or something?"

My head snaps up, and I have the sudden urge to flee. To get as far away from my conflicting feelings as possible. I don't know what I expected to find, but a fairy-tale ending wasn't on the list. It's not like I wanted Ava to be in a bad situation, but the perfection of the one I've found is unsettling to say the least. Almost as if Jude was right all along.

I shake my head and make a hasty excuse to leave the dealership, heading home as fast as my feet will carry me. I feel like running. If only I knew what from.

Twenty-Five

"As you can see on the map here, we are expecting thunderstorms to roll in from the Gulf over the next few hours," the weatherman says, indicating a patch of red hovering over Galveston. I grab the remote and turn up the volume. "This storm is expected to bring lots of heavy rain and winds up to fifty or even sixty miles per hour. So be sure to bring your pets inside tonight and limit your travel during this time, if possible."

I rub my stomach, trying to ease the mild cramping pains that have been sporadic over the past few days. Based on the description from my book, they are not real contractions, just Braxton Hicks. Just as I check the clock on the wall, the phone rings and Cash's voice is full of worry. "You all right?"

"Yeah, fine. Just about to bring in the plants from the porch."

"Okay, that's good. But try to stay in the house after that.

Looks like this storm might get pretty bad." He says something else, but the sound is muffled.

"Where are you?"

"Driving home," he says, his voice a little clearer now.

"No. They said it's not safe to be on the road. Pull over somewhere," I demand.

He laughs. "I'll be fine. Promise. Be there soon."

I run to the porch and look out at the darkened sky. Wind chimes clang in frantic anticipation as I rush to bring in the plants, and by the time I'm done, rain is blowing sideways, spattering my arms and stinging my face.

From here, the mausoleum is barely visible. Tucked into the crawl spaces behind the tombs, my bedding and other stuff are semi-protected from the rain. The only thing the water could potentially harm is the recorder. And if I don't go now, I may not get another chance.

With a burst of adrenaline, I hurry down the porch steps, water soaking me to the skin in a matter of seconds. But I can't let anything happen to the recording. If I ever want Cash to believe me, to help protect me from Jude, I have to present a convincing argument. And the recording is the best piece of evidence I have describing my time at Eden.

Just as I make it to the graveyard fence, another pain hits, much stronger than any I've felt before. I pause to catch my breath as the wind and rain push against me with a terrifying strength. When the pain subsides, I have to fight for each step through the blinding rain. But with the ground soaked and soggy, the going is slow. My foot catches on the edge of a gravestone, and I slip, falling hard and twisting my ankle. I cry out, but the sound is drowned by the sheets of falling rain.

Gathering my strength, I roll to my knees and crawl the rest of the way to the mausoleum. But just as I pull myself through the tiny window, I feel a rush of warm liquid down my legs and know it's not the rain. I lean against one of the tombs, my body trembling in shock. Stumbling to my hiding place, I grab the recorder and wrap it in a plastic bag. But when another pain hits, it clatters to the floor as I double over and cry out.

Waves of pain and panic crash as I fight to control my breathing for what feels like forever. Then a voice shouts over the storm, "Max! Max, can you hear me?" I fight back tears of relief when Cash appears at the window, his face a shadow of worry.

He disappears, his muffled voice yelling for me to get away from the door. I crawl to the far end of the mausoleum as the thick wood barrier shakes on its hinges and crashes to the floor with a bang.

"How'd you find me?" I say as he gathers me in his arms. Wild eyes search my face.

"I drove up and saw you running through the yard. What the hell are you thinking? You could've gotten hurt. Tell me you're not hurt," he demands, his voice shaking.

"No, I'm not hurt. But I think my water just broke," I say, gritting my teeth as another pain hits.

He curses and prepares to lift me from the floor.

"Wait," I say, reaching for the plastic bag with the recorder. With it safely clutched to my chest, I nod. "Okay, I'm ready."

We are across the yard in what feels like seconds, Cash's

steps steady despite the raging wind and streaks of lightning. As we bust into the house, my earlier panic fades. With Cash's help I can do this. I'm not alone.

He places me on the sofa, his breathing ragged. "Stay there. I'll call an ambulance."

I start to protest. To tell him I'll ruin the fabric, but the look on his face as he punches numbers into his phone stops me.

"Yes, this is Ranger Claiborne. I need an ambulance right away. Eighty-four Claiborne Road, Jamaica Beach."

I close my eyes as the contractions come closer together, taking my breath with their intensity. Pressure builds between my legs and the urge to push is strong.

"Just hang on," Cash says, kneeling beside me. "An ambulance is on the way."

I shake my head. "I can't wait. I have to get out of these." My hands struggle to tug at my soaked jeans.

He jumps to his feet and runs to the bedroom, returning with a plastic box of medical supplies. Scissors appear and my jeans make a ripping sound as they are cut from my body. I should be embarrassed, but I'm not. All I can think of is the overwhelming desire to push this child from my body.

"Can you see anything?" I ask, panting.

"I don't know," he says, hands shaking as he slides on a pair of gloves from the kit.

I try to process the idea of delivering this baby right here. Right now. But it's happening too fast. What if I can't do it? What if I'm destined to end up just like Maggie.

I grip Cash's arm, looking into his own fearful eyes. "I'm scared," I whisper.

He holds my gaze, his jaw set. "I'm not going anywhere. I've got you. I'd never let anything happen to you. Do you believe me?"

Peace washes over me when I realize the answer.

I open my eyes to the sound of a nurse's voice as she enters the room, pushing a bassinet. "Look who's been asking for you," she says with a smile as my son attempts to wiggle out of his swaddling.

When she places the baby in my arms, I marvel at his weight, his smell, the little dark curls covering his head.

Cash rises from a chair by the window and comes to stand at my side. "Cute little guy," he says, his voice barely above a whisper.

"Do you want to hold him?"

He shakes his head but doesn't move away.

"Here," I say, insisting he take him from my arms.

He yields, but a look of terror crosses his face as he cradles the baby with obvious unease.

"That's it, just keep his head supported," I say, enjoying the sight of the big man handling an infant with such care.

After a moment, his tension lessens, and he ducks his head to smell the baby's hair. He stays that way a long moment, and when he lifts his head, his eyes are bright. "Have you decided on a name?"

"Yes," I say, studying his face. "Aaron Cash Fontaine."

His mouth opens, but no sound comes out.

I grin, enjoying his reaction. "I think it's only fitting that he should be named after the man who helped bring him into this world."

Cash's face turns pink, and he blinks. "I'm ... honored. But I really didn't do anything much."

"Are you kidding? You did everything. By the time the ambulance came, it was all over. You were amazing."

"Well, little Aaron here didn't seem to want to wait." He ducks his head and clears his throat. "To tell you the truth, I was terrified."

"What? You? I thought tough Texas Rangers weren't afraid of anything," I kid.

Cash looks away, his expression unreadable. "We're afraid of plenty."

"What is it? Tell me."

He hesitates before taking a seat in the rocking chair by the bed. "The night Sadie died ... Well, I guess seeing you like that just felt like the same thing was happening all over again."

"You mean, she—"

"Yeah. Our baby girl too."

I stare at him, speechless. I never asked him how Sadie died. Don't know what I expected. But definitely not this.

"It's something I'll never forgive myself for," he continues, shaking his head as his eyes grow distant. "She insisted on having a home birth. I wasn't happy about the idea, but it was her choice so I went along with it. Everything seemed to be going fine, at first. Her contractions weren't too bad, and she was dilating like she was supposed to. But when it came time to push, we found out the baby was breech. I asked if we needed to go to the hospital, but the midwife kept saying no." Cash takes a deep breath. "I shouldn't have listened. Should've done what my gut told me and brought her anyways. When the baby finally came, she was purple." His lip trembles at the memory, and I ball my hands into fists to keep from reaching for him. "The midwife tried to revive her, but it was too late. After that, I ran outside and kind of lost it. Just had to get away." He wipes his eyes with the back of his hand. "I was so focused on the one I'd lost, I didn't think about Sadie still lying in there. Didn't think it could get any worse. I should've stayed. Should've at least been there to hold her hand."

"It's okay," I say, tears clouding my vision. "It's not your fault."

He closes his eyes and nods. "I know that now. Just took me a while."

I take a deep breath and search for the right words. "Cash, I know what you did for me was hard. And I want you to know I'll always be grateful."

"Do you remember the first day we met in the barn?" he says, his voice barely above a whisper. "You seemed to appear out of nowhere. Just a silhouette outlined by the sun. At first, it was all I could see, and you looked so much like her ... It was almost like, for a minute, she was back, and I was so happy." His voice cracks as he stares at Aaron. "I wanted so much for her to be back."

I fight to swallow the lump in my throat. "You must have been pretty disappointed, then," I say, unable to keep the sadness from my voice.

He looks up, his eyes full of pain. But before he can answer, there's a knock at the door.

A woman with curly blond hair peeks in. "Hi, I'm Laney, your breastfeeding coach. May I come in?"

When she enters the room, Cash excuses himself. I want to ask him to stay. To finish our conversation. But he doesn't come back until long after Aaron finishes nursing and returns to the nursery.

"Hey," Cash says, taking a few steps inside the room. "I've been meaning to ask if there's anyone you want me to call. Family or friends you want to notify."

I look away, unable to meet his gaze. "There's no one."

The bed dips as he takes a seat at the foot. "Look at me, Max."

When I turn, his face is serious, his eyes penetrating. "When I found you in the cemetery, there were other things in there. Your things, I'm guessing. What were you doing out there?" When I don't answer, he leans forward. "You can tell me anything, you know. You're safe. I just want the truth."

I take a steadying breath, the sincerity in his voice easing the way. "I was living there."

"How long?"

"Since the day we met."

He shakes his head. "Why didn't you tell me? Let me help you?"

I hold up a hand, the need to come clean stronger than ever. "There's more. So much more I need to say. But I couldn't at first. I had to make sure ..."

"Make sure what?"

"That I could trust you."

Hurt flashes in his eyes, making me regret the words.

"Surely you know you can," he says, his gaze unwavering.

"Yes. I do now."

"And you know you and Aaron will have a place to stay with me as long as you want. I can fix up the spare room. We'll get a crib and whatever else you need."

"No, I can't just barge in and disrupt your life like that. It wouldn't be right."

He gives me a rueful smile. "What life? Besides work, I have no life."

"That's not true. You can have any life you want."

"And I'm saying I want you in it."

Hope surges in my chest at the admission. "You want me?" I repeat, slowly.

"Yes. I mean, no." His head snaps back, and heat rises in his face. "That came out wrong. What I'm trying to say is I want you and Aaron to have a safe place. I have a spare room and you're already at the house every day. It just makes sense."

I smile, enjoying his attempt to cover the slip, but the last thing I want is to be seen as a charity case. "If we come, I insist on paying rent."

He tilts his head to the side. "How about you help me with dinner and we'll call it even?"

I extend my hand. "Deal."

When he takes it in his warm grasp, my voice catches at the electricity I feel. I wonder if he feels it too. But the moment is cut short when a nurse comes in holding a tray of food.

"I'm going to run to the house for a quick shower, but I'll

be back later," Cash says, releasing my hand and standing to his full height.

I glance at the tiny window seat that serves as a makeshift bed. "You really don't have to stay the night."

"I know I don't have to. I want to."

The nurse overhears and gives me a knowing wink.

Cash walks to the door and pauses. "Are you sure there's no one else you want me to call?"

I bite my lip and picture Olivia's face. "Actually, there is one person."

Twenty-Six

The shrill sound of Aaron's crying makes me bolt upright in bed. It's our first night home, and I still startle every time he wakes to nurse. So far, it's been every two hours, and I'm starting to feel like a bit of a zombie. I swing my legs to the side of the bed, but before I can stand, Cash's footsteps thump down the hall.

"I got him," he says, flying over to retrieve Aaron from his crib.

Feeling bad about waking him again, I shake my head. "You really don't have to get up with us every time."

He frowns. "I want to."

"But I'm sure you need sleep. You have work."

"My job's flexible. And I told them I'd be taking a few days off." He bounces Aaron gently in his arms and nods to the wooden crib and changing table. "It was really nice of your friend to get you all this."

"It was," I agree, smiling at the memory of Olivia's visit to the hospital. "But she made it clear the library workers all pitched in. I still can't believe it. I'm sure most of them don't even know who I am."

"That's the one thing I've always liked about the people around here. Hospitality just comes natural."

He hands Aaron to me and looks away as I unbutton my nightgown. I smile at the gentlemanly gesture, thinking how unnecessary it is. He delivered my child, for goodness sake. I have nothing left to hide. Nevertheless, he keeps his eyes averted, even after Aaron begins to nurse.

I laugh and reach for his arm. "You can look at me, you know. I'm not really the modest type, anyhow," I say, thinking of the free-spirited nudity back at Eden.

Cash clears his throat and glances my way. "Okay. Just didn't want to make you uncomfortable. Make you think I was trying to, uh ..."

"Hit on me?" I tease.

He lets out a breath. "Yeah, that."

I tilt my head to the side and study his handsome profile in the dim glow of the nightlight. "Don't worry," I say with a surge of boldness. "I'm smart enough to know you wouldn't be after a homeless housekeeper with a kid when you could have any woman in town."

His head snaps up. "Well, I'm smart enough to know you're selling yourself short." He grins. "But I would like to hear more about why you think I could have any woman in town."

I laugh and roll my eyes. "Make yourself useful and go get Aaron a diaper."

When he walks to the changing table, I notice a strange cardboard box sitting on the floor by the door.

"What's that?"

"Oh, just some stuff you left out in the cemetery. The storm ruined most of it, but I wanted you to look through it before I dumped it in the trash."

"Did you find a red Bible?" I ask, hoping he had.

"Yep." He bends to retrieve it from the box and lays it on the bed. "It's ruined too."

"No, it's okay. It's been like that for a while."

A line forms between his brows. "At the hospital you mentioned having things to tell me. What kind of things?"

I knew this moment was coming, but now that it's here, my insides quiver with dread at the idea of his reaction. But it has to be done sooner or later. There's no point delaying the inevitable.

I pat the bed beside me. "You should probably sit down. This may take a while to explain."

As I rock Aaron back to sleep, I bring Cash up to speed on the events of the past months. He manages to take it all in with a straight face, but I can tell my story affects him more than he would like me to know.

When I lay Aaron back in his crib, I find the recorder and hand it to Cash.

"That's why you went back for it during the storm," he says. As he turns it over in his hand, I can see pieces of the puzzle start to come together in his mind.

"It's the only proof I have of what I told the police. I also saved this." I hand him the letter from Charlie

Andrews. He reads over it with a look of disbelief on his face.

"This is bullshit," he says under his breath when he finishes. "Par for the course."

"What do you mean?"

"I'm not really supposed to tell you this, but I've been looking closely at Andrews' dealings here lately, and based on what you've told me about your experience, I have reason to believe he's not on the up and up."

"Is this the case you've been thinking of opening?"

"Yeah, but you can't tell a soul. And if you do, you'll be held legally accountable. Do you understand how serious this is?"

I nod. "Of course."

"I need you to answer something for me. Is this the same Jude Delacroix that bailed your friend out of jail a while back?"

"Yes. Lir is Jude's son."

A muscle in Cash's jaw flexes. "I knew there was something fishy about all that. When I called to ask, the department was hesitant to talk about it. I dismissed it, but now it's starting to make sense." He holds up the recorder. "You go back to bed. I'm going to go listen to this and make some notes. I'll close the door so you won't be bothered."

"Aren't you going to try to get some sleep?"

"I couldn't sleep right now if I tried."

"Want some?" Cash nods to the coffee maker on the counter. "Just made a fresh pot. Let me get you a cup."

Early morning rays streak through the kitchen windows as I take a seat at the table. "No, I probably shouldn't," I say with regret. "Whatever I have goes straight to Aaron, and I don't need him any more wired than he already is."

"He still asleep?"

"Thank goodness. Back at Eden I took care of dozens of newborns and never saw a kid that likes to eat as much as he does." I laugh, enjoying the freedom to talk about my past without having to monitor my words. It's as if a weight has been lifted off my chest.

Cash runs a hand through his hair and closes his computer. His eyes have dark smudges underneath, and he sags in his chair.

I nod to the recorder sitting on his desk. "Did you stay up all night listening to that?"

"Yeah, and I have to say your story is one of the wildest things I've ever heard. And the way Andrews handled it is even worse." He leans forward, his lips pressed into a tight line. "This is big, Max. Bigger than any case I've ever been a part of. If my suspicions are correct and the police are being paid off, it'll be national news."

My mouth falls open at the idea.

"I'm going to need your help, Max. You're the key to unlocking all of this."

"Like testifying?"

"That and more."

"Do you have a plan?"

He nods. "But before I tell you what it is, I need to know you're ready."

With Cash on my side, the dream of achieving justice no longer feels out of reach. I straighten my shoulders and look him in the eye. "Whatever it is, I'll do it."

"You won't get scared and change your mind halfway through?"

I frown. "I would never do that."

"I'm not trying to sound like an ass, I promise. I just want you to know what you're getting into isn't something you can back away from later. Once you're committed, that's it."

"I understand. Whatever it is, I promise I can handle it."

His eyes narrow as he leans across the desk. "Even if it means going back?"

Twenty-Seven

Slipping into a tub brimming with hot water, I sigh in relief at the early morning pleasure and lean back to stretch, enjoying the little bit of me time before Aaron wakes up. He's a good baby, but all infants are demanding. And with the extra job of nursing and pumping every few hours, it's taken longer than I thought to get used to the extra strain. As I rub the soapy washcloth over my skin, I'm pleased to see that besides enlarged breasts and a few stretch marks, my body has returned to normal. After almost eight weeks of motherhood, I finally feel like myself again.

As I rinse the suds from my skin, movement on the video monitor catches my eye. I lean over the tub to get a better look and see Aaron lying in his crib, sucking his fists and kicking his little legs. It's only a matter of time before he'll be howling for someone to rescue him. After considering my options, I decide to see if Cash minds getting him while I finish my bath. But when my call is met with silence, I yell his name again, much louder this time.

I frown at the sound of running feet but am not prepared for the sight of Cash bursting through the bathroom door. When he sees me on display in the tub, he blinks in surprise and his wild-eyed expression is replaced with a gaping open mouth.

"Fuck," he says, averting his eyes as heat rises in his face. "Sorry, I thought something was wrong. I didn't mean to—"

I laugh at his distress. "It's fine, really. You don't have to apologize. I just saw that Aaron is awake. Do you mind getting him out of his bed?"

Still looking away, Cash tugs at his collar and nods. "Uh, yeah sure thing." Clearly flustered, he heads out of the bathroom but has to return a few seconds later to close the door.

I sink back into the water and think about his reaction. The flash of lust in his eyes before he turned away. To know the sight of my body affected him, even a little bit, brings a satisfied smile to my face.

When I finish my bath and head to the kitchen, the low rumble of Cash singing slows my steps. I creep forward and peek around the corner to see him standing at the window facing the backyard. He has a pair of binoculars in one hand and Aaron in the other.

My heart swells at the sight. How easy it would be to envision Cash as a father. A husband. My vision blurs and the floodgate of emotion I've been burying hovers close to the surface. I want the fairy tale of a happy family. For myself. For Aaron. But

I'm smart enough to know things won't stay like this forever. One day, Cash will move on, whether I like it or not.

"What are you two doing in here?" I say in the brightest voice I can manage.

Cash lowers the binoculars and points to the window. "See those little brown dots at the far end of the pasture?"

I squint my eyes and try to make them out. "What are they?"

"Deer."

"So, you're teaching Aaron to be a hunter?"

"More of an observer." He winks. "We just like to watch them, don't we, little buddy? Might even go put out some corn for them later. Do some man stuff together."

"As long as it's not man stuff like drinking beer and chasing wild women," I tease.

Cash shakes his head, the corners of his eyes crinkling. "No, I'm saving that lesson for his first birthday."

I laugh and roll my eyes.

"And speaking of birthdays ..." Cash walks to his desk, pulls a small box from one of the drawers, and passes it to me.

The card on top has my name on it. "But ... how did you know?"

He grins. "Saw it on your hospital wristband."

"Thank you," I say, my hands tingling as I pull out two slips of paper, each labeled as gift certificates: one to Sloane's clothing boutique and the other to a salon here in Jamaica Beach.

"Didn't know what to get you, so Olivia helped me a little. Said you'd probably like to pick something out yourself." Cash runs his fingers through his hair. I can tell he's nervous, but his thoughtfulness makes my heart leap.

I shake my head in disbelief. "It's perfect. Just what I've been needing. I can't remember the last time someone remembered my birthday."

He nods to the box. "Open the other one."

When I lift the lid, the sight of red leather makes my vision blur. "Oh," I say, my finger tracing the gold letters of my name engraved across the bottom of the Bible.

Cash gives me a sheepish look. "Thought you might want a new one since the other one got ruined. Couldn't find the same size. Hope you don't mind that it's a little bigger."

"I absolutely love it!" I rush to throw my arms around him, squeezing tight. But when Aaron kicks his legs against my chest, I laugh. "I guess he wants to keep you all to himself."

Cash tickles him under his chin. "Well, looks like he's about to get his wish."

"What do you mean?"

"Go look outside."

I frown and walk to the window in time to see Olivia's car pull into the driveway. "What's going on? Tell me."

He nods toward my hand. "Since you got two gift certificates burning a hole in your pocket, I thought you might enjoy letting Olivia help you spend them." His mouth twitches at my shocked expression, and he waves a hand toward the door. "Go on, she's waiting for you."

"But what about Aaron? I still need to pack his things, and I—"

"I've got Aaron," Cash interrupts. "You just go have fun."

I wring my hands together. "But ... I've never left him and what if he needs me?"

"He'll be just fine. And before you say it, yes, I have plenty of diapers, wipes, and milk." He winks. "I already checked."

"But what about his—"

"Snuggle bear? Got it."

"But when he's hungry, you have to remember to—"

"Heat the bottle on the stove, not in the microwave."

"And if he won't go to sleep at nap time, you'll need to—"

"Take him out to the rocker on the back porch. I know."

I narrow my eyes at the smug satisfaction on his face, but can't help smiling at his thorough knowledge of Aaron's habits and needs. "Fine," I say with a sigh. "As long as you're totally sure. I can't believe you want to keep him all day."

He tilts his head to the side. "Last I checked, birthdays last all day and even into the night."

"What's that supposed to mean?"

"It means I'm taking you out tonight to celebrate. Anywhere you want to go. Just you and me. And before you ask, Olivia volunteered to watch Aaron while we're gone."

Heat rushes to my face at the idea of spending time alone with Cash, but I try not to read too much into the offer. He's a naturally thoughtful person; this is just his way of being a good friend. So, I decide to be gracious in return. "That sounds wonderful."

When I bend to slip on my shoes, he holds up his hand. "Oh, before I forget, I have a phone conference today with my lieutenant and two other Rangers to discuss moving forward on the case."

My pulse jumps at the thought. "Do they know about our plan?"

"That's what they want to talk about."

"Do you think they'll go for it?"

"I hope so. If not, we'll just have to come up with something else."

"But—"

"Listen, there's no sense worrying about anything until after the call. We'll talk more about it tonight. If it's meant to be, then everything will fall into place."

The hairstylist spins me around to face the mirror and runs her fingers over the length of my hair. "What kind of style are you thinking of, honey?"

I survey the dark hair hanging in unruly clumps over the shiny purple cape snapped around my neck. The sight of the long jagged ends falling well past my waist is frightening, even to myself. I have no idea where to begin. What to say I want. Part of me wants to tell her to chop it all off. If I'm being honest, the desire to do so probably has less to do with wanting short hair and more to do with Maggie never letting me have it. I pull the long strands away from my face and try to imagine myself with a French bob like the kind I begged for as a child. But tucking the ends under around my jaw to simulate the style isn't as pleasing as I'd once imagined.

The stylist shoves a few magazines in my hand. "Why don't you take a look at these."

"Help me," I say, passing one to Olivia, who sits in the vacant styling chair next to mine.

The pages are filled with dozens of images arranged in rows. Happy mugshots of cuts and colors in an endless variety. At least, that's what it seems like to me. I try to imagine myself wearing one of the styles, but they all look too fixed. Too done.

"Do you have anything more, I don't know ... free looking?"

The stylist points to a messy pixie. "Like that?"

I shake my head. "No, not that short."

Olivia stands to snatch a Victoria's Secret magazine off the rack. "Like this," she says, pointing to the brunette on the cover.

Though shorter than mine, the model's hair falls in long waves, the color melting from a rich brown at the base to warm honey on the ends.

"It's beautiful," I say, touching the glossy page. "Yes, just like that."

Olivia points to a cosmetic display in the corner. "Before we leave, we should get you some new makeup too."

"Are you trying to say I'm ugly?"

Her eyes round. "What? No!"

"I'm kidding," I say with a laugh. "You should see your face right now."

She purses her lips, but I can tell she wants to laugh too.

The stylist smiles and places her brush on the station in front of me. "I hate to interrupt, but I think you should know we will need to take about twelve inches off to get the look you want. You all right with that?"

A jolt of excitement makes me sit up straight. "Positive."

"There's enough here to donate, you know."

"Donate?"

"To Locks of Love. They make wigs for cancer patients."

"Oh, yes. That would be wonderful. How do I do that?"

She grabs a rubber band and a plastic ruler from a drawer. "I'll take care of it for you. Don't worry about a thing."

When she spins me around a few hours later, I stare at the woman in the mirror, barely recognizing the image as my own. I lift my hand, my fingers gliding over silky waves of chocolate and honey, and for the first time in my life I feel beautiful.

"You're gorgeous," Olivia says with a little squeal. "Now all you need is the perfect outfit for your date tonight."

"It's not a date."

She purses her lips together. "Sounds like a date to me. And in case you haven't noticed, I'm totally jealous."

"If you're so jealous, maybe you should ask him out yourself."

"Girl, if I thought he was interested, I'd be all over that in a heartbeat and you know it. But if you can't see that man follows you around like a lost puppy, then I don't know what to tell you."

I arch a brow at her theatrics. "A lost puppy? Really?"

"That's right." She crosses her arms, a smile playing on her lips. "And you know, puppies just want to be loved."

I shake my head at Olivia's imagination, but as we approach Sloane's boutique a little while later, I wonder if she could be right. If Cash just wanted to take me out as a friend, then why make arrangements for Aaron to stay behind? Just yesterday, we packed him up in his car seat and went to lunch at The Rainforest Cafe. Why would tonight be any different? Maybe Olivia is right. Maybe I am going on a date.

But what about Sadie? Based on Cash's words at the hospital, he's clearly still in love with her and isn't over the loss. Isn't ready to move on. No matter what I feel for him, I don't want to compete with a ghost.

TWENTY-EIGHT

Olivia opens the door with a whoosh and pulls me inside. "Come on. Quick. I made Cash and Aaron go to the back porch so they wouldn't see you."

"It's just a new hairstyle. It's not really that big of a deal," I say, embarrassed by the attention.

"That's bullshit and you know it," Olivia says, ushering me into my bedroom. "We can't have him seeing you until the whole look is complete."

I drop my bags on the bed. "Can't I just wear jeans or something?"

Her eyes bulge. "Absolutely not. I didn't just spend all day helping you for you to go out looking like a ragamuffin." She rummages through the bags until she finds my new cosmetics. "Come sit down and I'll do your makeup."

I glance toward the door. "Would you mind checking on Aaron first? And ask Cash what time he wants to leave?"

When she walks out of the room, I tear into the bags with my new clothes, shoes, and jewelry. I hang the black mini dress in the closet and try to imagine Cash's reaction. With its form-fitting design, it's much skimpier than anything he's used to seeing on me and my heart lurches at the idea he won't like it.

"Aaron is perfectly fine," Olivia says, stepping back into the room. "He's sleeping like an angel in his swing. Cash says he's ready whenever you are."

When I emerge from my room, the sky has turned gray and the house is lit with a warm glow. I try to steel my nerves, but my pulse pounds and my legs feel like Jell-O as I clip down the hall in new red heels that match my lipstick. I still can't believe the transformation. Long dark lashes glossy with mascara. Lids shadowed with soft brown and lined with black. My skin, radiant and flawless thanks to Olivia's expert skills. Staring into the mirror, I've never felt more like a movie star. But my hands still shake as I touch my silver earrings one last time to make sure they are in place.

"Go on. You look perfect, I promise. Cash is going to be speechless," Olivia whispers, giving me a nudge.

I take a breath and nod. "If you say so."

When I round the corner, Cash is nowhere in sight. I turn to Olivia with a questioning look, but her expression tells me she's as confused as I am.

"He was here a minute ago," she says, waving toward the sofa.

"Be right there," he calls back from the direction of his bedroom. "Sorry, had to grab my wallet," he says, rounding the corner into the living room. "Took it out when I changed clothes but forgot to—" He stops walking and stares at me, the words dying on his lips.

"Told you," Olivia mumbles.

"You ready?" I say in an attempt to cover my embarrassment at his reaction.

He clears his throat. "Uh, yeah ... I just need to uh, grab my wallet." He gives a nervous laugh and runs his fingers through his hair. "Wait. No, I just did that." He takes a breath and clasps his hands together. "I'm sorry. What I mean to say is that you look great. Beautiful, actually."

My stomach does a flip at the heat in his gaze. "Thanks. You look great too."

Olivia ushers me toward the door. "You two get going. Aaron and I have important business to tend to. The *Gilmore Girls* marathon isn't going to watch itself, you know."

As we walk to the truck, awkwardness hovers between us. Part of me wishes I wouldn't have dressed up and changed my hair. I want Cash to be himself. To be comfortable, not sweating and stumbling over his words. Sure, I'm flattered. But I'm also uneasy.

I settle into the passenger seat and tug at the hem of my dress. "Are you sure I look okay? Maybe I should go change."

"Why do you say that?"

My heart pounds in my chest at the idea of pointing out the elephant in the room. "I don't know. You're just acting kind of strange."

He glances my way and chews his bottom lip. "I'm sorry, Max. I didn't mean to make you uncomfortable. I just wasn't ready for you to look so—"

"Overdone?"

"Sexy."

My brain sputters to a stop. "You think I'm sexy?"

"Well ... yeah." He grins and puts the truck in gear, but his eyes flash with an intensity that makes my mouth go dry. "Where to?"

I lean forward, fiddling with the air-conditioning until it's blasting cold air directly at my face. "You pick."

He wags a finger. "Oh, no, little missy. This is your birthday, not mine."

I sit back and picture bright twirling lights. The laughter and hum of the boardwalk at night. But I keep silent, fearing Cash will think it's too juvenile.

He reaches over to nudge my knee. "Come on. Speak up."

I glance at him from the corner of my eye. "There is one place, I guess. But you're going to laugh."

"Try me."

"Pleasure Pier."

"Why would I laugh at that?"

I lift a shoulder. "Because it's childish."

"Well, then you'll have to call me a kid because Pleasure Pier is one of my favorite places."

My eyes widen. "You're kidding."

"I swear." His eyes crinkle. "What's better than roller coasters, cotton candy, and losing forty bucks trying to win a stuffed tiger that's only worth ten?"

"I've only been to a carnival once, back when I was a kid, but I don't remember much."

"Well, I'll make sure you remember tonight."

When we park beside the seawall, he insists I stay in my seat as he comes around to open my door. Shivers travel my spine as I take his hand, the breeze from the ocean soft on my face. As I step onto the sidewalk, something shifts and it take a moment to register the change in myself. No longer am I the scared, homeless girl running for my life. And I have Cash to thank. For the first time, I feel strong and in charge of my future.

Cash nods toward the sun setting at the far end of the ocean. "Hard to believe there's a hurricane out there somewhere."

The local news has talked of nothing else for days. Hurricane Ike this. Hurricane Ike that. I guess living on the Gulf my entire life has made me a bit jaded. And the anchor's breathless excitement as they detail the doom feels more like theatrics than reality.

Cash's warm hand hovers at the small of my back as he escorts me toward the pier. "Bubba Gump's has pretty good food if that sounds alright for dinner," he suggests, gesturing to the massive restaurant positioned at the entrance to the pier.

When I agree, we turn to mount the steps, but a glimpse of yellow in the distant water makes me freeze.

"What's wrong?" Cash says, following my gaze as I study the cigar boat slicing through the waves.

My throat closes, making it hard to breathe. I tell myself it's unlikely to be Jude, but it's not until I catch sight of a woman driving that I know for sure.

I let go of Cash's arm and try to breathe normally. "Sorry. Jude has the same kind of boat. I thought it might be him, but it's not."

Cash studies me with narrowed eyes. "You know you're safe with me, right? I'd never let anything happen to you. Ever."

"I know. I just can't shake the feeling that he could be anywhere. Watching. Waiting to get his revenge. And if he found out about Aaron—his own grandchild—I don't want to think about what he might do."

Cash reaches into his pocket for his phone. "Hey, Olivia. Yeah we just got to the restaurant, but Max wanted to check on Aaron. He is? Oh, that's great." He gives me a wink. "See? Aaron's just fine."

I give him a wobbly smile.

"Oh, really? Just now?" he says into the phone. "Damn, okay thanks for the heads up."

"I thought you said Aaron was fine."

"He is. Come on, let's get you inside," he says, leading me to a table overlooking the water. "Great view, huh?"

"Tell me what's wrong," I say, unable to wait a moment longer.

He shakes his head. "Olivia just said the city manager came on the news issuing a mandatory evacuation of the west end of the island. Seems like they're predicting Ike will hit us pretty hard down there."

"So, we have to leave?"

"Not technically. Mandatory just means that if you stay, you're on your own." Cash rubs a hand over his face. "Damn, this shit is really gonna screw up our plans."

"Plans?"

"For Eden."

I sit up straight. "That's right. You were supposed to talk with the other Rangers today. What did they say? Did they like our idea?"

"They loved it. Even agreed to go undercover, posing as the adoptive couple. Our goal is to catch Jude in the act. Wire him the money and be handed a child in return. The Rangers are ready to make the move this weekend."

"But that doesn't give us much time. What if there are no infants available? Or there's a waiting list?"

"I thought of that. I didn't want you to worry, but I've been in contact with Jude via email for several weeks."

"What? How?"

Cash holds up a hand. "It took some work, but I was able to locate him on the dark web. Based on the information posted by other clients on there, I was advised to simply send a message stating my name and a Bible verse, of all things. Apparently, that's how he's been able to distinguish real clients from the authorities."

I sit up straight. "Was it Genesis 1:28? The one about being fruitful and multiplying?"

"Yeah. How did you know?"

"It's the same one we had to recite to be admitted to Eden back when I was a kid."

Cash leans forward. "You're right. I remember you saying that on the recording. I can't believe I didn't put it together."

"What name did you give him?"

"Well, I couldn't give him a fake name since I'm sure he does background checks on his clients. So, after a bit of scrambling, I was able to come up with an alias that looks legit."

"Wait. If there are people talking about Eden on the dark web, why haven't they been caught already?"

"They never use their real name in the forums or refer to Eden as anything other than 'the island,' and since almost everything on the dark web is untraceable, their true identities remain a mystery."

"Did Jude reply to your email?"

"Yeah. Sent me back a message with a date and time, price and the letter M with a number one beside it. I'm guessing that means they have one male child for sale, but I can't be sure. If he would have said anything more specific about what kind of deal we are making, I would be able to use the email as evidence. But as it stands, nothing can be proven ... yet. It all depends on this weekend. Saturday, to be exact."

"But that's when they're saying Ike will make landfall, right? Isn't that going to screw everything up?"

"That's the million dollar question." Cash closes his eyes. "Jude has been asking a lot of questions himself, and I just get the feeling that if we call it off, he won't bite again so easily. If we want to catch him, now's our chance. We need to get in, make the deal, retrieve as much other evidence as possible, and get out."

"I agree. Personally, I don't want to evacuate. This is more important than running from some storm. The hurricane may not turn out to be anything, but I know Jude. His mood can change at the drop of a hat. And with me gone, he's bound to be more paranoid than ever."

"I think you're right. Do you still think Jude's mother will be cooperative?"

"I hope so. Hazel is a good person, and she knows what Jude's doing is wrong. But at the end of the day, he's her son ... so I can't be completely sure."

Cash shrugs. "Best case scenario, she'll be willing to help. Worst case, I'll have to detain her in her home until it's over. Hopefully, she'll be willing to listen to reason."

"What if something goes wrong during the deal? I've seen Jude turn people away for the slightest thing."

"That's why I need you there with me. While the Rangers keep Jude and the others busy at the Claiming ceremony, we'll sneak into his office and try to get our hands on some documented proof of past adoptions. He'd most likely keep all his files and things there, right?"

I shake my head. "I honestly don't know. He was always so secretive about everything. I've only been in there a handful of times with Lir. I know where the boat keys are kept, but that's about it."

Cash chews his bottom lip. "Damn, I wish we could bring in reinforcements on this."

"Why can't you?"

"Because in compound-type situations like this, the worst thing law enforcement can do is run in with guns blazing. If history has taught us anything, it's that a big show of force only serves to scare people into a standoff, or worse. No matter what, it never ends well. We've got to be smarter than that. I want to get in and get out without being seen. We don't want another Waco on our hands."

Twenty-Nine

When we step onto Pleasure Pier, night has fallen, forming the perfect backdrop for the flash of colorful lights as they spin and twirl, dip and turn, to the screams of passengers. This side of the island is still business as usual, even as the threat of chaos brews across an ocean away.

"One please," Cash says to a woman swirling a stick inside a vat of cotton candy. He turns to me. "Blue or pink?"

"You really don't have to—"

"We'll take pink," he tells the woman, ignoring my protest.

I put my hands on my hips and grin. "What if I wanted blue?"

He turns back to the woman. "Make that blue."

I slap him on the arm. "You're impossible."

"You had your chance."

The woman passes me the cotton candy and leans across the

counter. "Just to let you know, they're about to shut down the Ferris wheel for the night. So, if you want a ride, I suggest you head in that direction."

"Thanks for the tip," Cash says, grabbing my hand and setting off toward the end of the pier. The air is electric with music and laughter, the smell of roasting peanuts, and the whoosh of airbrakes mingling with game hawkers' cries.

"Hold your horses," I say, tugging on his arm as I struggle to keep up. "I'm in heels, remember."

He slows his pace but doesn't let go of my hand. My stomach flutters at the contact, and I marvel at how good it feels to walk beside him, his grip steady and confident. How perfectly natural it would be to believe he wants me. To believe he's mine. But I can't give in to the temptation to dream. I have to put a stop to whatever this is before I fall too far.

As we approach the Ferris wheel, I pull out of his grasp and do my best to ignore the disappointment flashing across his face. I tell myself I'm doing the right thing, but the sinking feeling in the pit of my stomach makes me wonder.

When we are about to board, the sound of a familiar voice makes me turn. "Well, I knew you were going on a date, but I didn't think we'd run into you here," Sloane teases. I open my mouth in surprise as she bats me on the shoulder.

"Sloane Richards," she says, extending her hand to Cash.

"Cash Claiborne. Nice to meet you, ma'am."

She waves to a tall man with dark hair and a short beard covering his face. "This is my husband, Blake. And this little wildcat is our daughter, Everly," she says, nodding to the little girl perched on his shoulders.

Everly's auburn curls dance in the breeze coming off the ocean as she gives us an endearing snaggletooth smile.

"Are you excited about going on the Ferris wheel?" I say.

Her blue eyes sparkle as she looks up at the ride. "Yes, ma'am. It's my first time."

Sloane smiles and takes her hand. "She's been a little too afraid to try it in the past."

"Well, don't tell anyone, but it's my first time too," I whisper, enjoying the little girl's wide-eyed reaction to the news.

"I was just telling Blake how good it was to see you again today and how anxious I am to get my hands on more of your creations. I could keep you busy full time, if you wanted."

"Oh, thank you. I'd love that. I'll be in touch. Promise."

"I look forward to it." She inclines her head and gives me a wink. "You look great by the way."

"Well, if I do, it's because you dressed me."

She laughs and waves off the compliment.

"You ready?" Cash says, indicating we are next in line.

I hurry to follow him into the gondola, but when the bar is locked in place and we ascend into the night sky, Cash's nearness reminds me that we are alone.

"I remember you telling me that Sloane bought a necklace from you. But you didn't mention she wants you to do it full time," he says, his forehead wrinkling.

"Would you mind?" I say, curious to see his reaction.

"I can't say I like the idea of someone stealing you away from me," he teases. "No, you know I want you to do whatever makes you happy. And if that means working for Sloane. So be it."

"So, you're saying I should take the job?"

"If that's what you want, sure."

His encouragement to pursue my talents sends fresh energy through my veins. "You know, since the housework only takes a few hours, I bet I could do both."

Cash surprises me my taking my hand and bringing it to his lips. "It's good to see you smile," he says, brushing a soft kiss across my knuckles.

Intimidated by the attention, I pull away and scoot to the far edge of the gondola where I pretend to be extremely interested in the scenery below. But Cash slides close, the scent of his cologne making me shiver with anticipation.

"You cold?" he says, his arm circling my shoulders. "I'd give you my jacket, but I didn't bring one. If you want to come closer, I don't mind."

I dig my nails into my palms in an effort to resist the temptation of his embrace. "I'm fine," I say, staying in my spot.

Needing a distraction, I tear into the bag of cotton candy and busy myself with letting the sugary treat melt in my mouth and stick to my fingers. "Want some?" I say, shoving the open bag toward Cash.

He leans forward, his green eyes glowing. "Sure," he says, taking hold of my wrist. My skin prickles with electricity as his head dips, his breath tickling the back of my hand. And when he takes the tip of my finger into his mouth, I suppress the urge to moan with desire at the feel of his tongue flicking over a leftover bit of cotton candy.

"What are you doing?" I whisper, afraid to break the spell. Afraid I'll wake up and come crashing back to reality.

He smiles and licks his lips. "Having some cotton candy."

The clanking of the gondola door makes me jump and jerk my hand away. I clutch the bag of cotton candy to my chest and stumble onto the platform, eager to escape the feelings clanking around in my head.

"Wait up," he says, jogging to catch up as my heels click down the boardwalk.

"I was thinking maybe we should head back," I say, keeping my eyes straight ahead. "Aaron may need me."

"Here, let's call and check," Cash says, taking out his phone. "Hey, Olivia? Yeah we just wanted to check on Aaron. Oh, he is? That's great." He laughs. "Okay, I'll be sure to tell her. Bye."

I stop walking and arch a brow. "Tell me what?"

"Olivia said Aaron finished off his evening bottle a little while ago and went right to sleep in his swing. She also said to tell you we have to stay gone for at least another couple of hours so she can finish the *Gilmore Girls* marathon." He inclines his head and gives me a playful grin. "So, we could either stay here. Or ..."

I cut my eyes in his direction. "Or what?"

"We could grab the bottle of wine out of my backseat and go have a little picnic down on the beach. I even brought a blanket. What do you say?"

"You packed wine?"

"Of course. It's your birthday." He wiggles his eyebrows and pokes me in the ribs, making me giggle despite my resolve to stop flirting.

I cross my arms and jut my chin in the air, prepared to tell him no. But just as I open my mouth, an idea forms that is sure to wipe that flirtatious grin right off his face. "You're on."

We walk to a spot near the steep incline of the seawall, and Cash's face beams with satisfaction as he spreads a blanket over the soft sand. "There we go," he says, settling onto the blanket and uncorking the wine. "Damn, knew I forgot something. Looks like we'll just have to drink straight from the bottle. That okay with you?"

"Perfectly," I say, taking the bottle and tilting it up for a longer-than-necessary drink. I start to hand it back but decide to take another long swig just for good measure before implementing my plan.

I wait until he's in the middle of a sip to lean close, the corners of my mouth twitching. "It's too bad I'm only twenty, not twenty-one."

Cash's eye bulge, and he chokes. I lean back on my elbows, satisfied with the results of my little joke as he coughs and sputters and tries to recover.

"So, what do you have to say for yourself, Mr. Texas Ranger?" I wag a finger in the air and tsk my disapproval. "Maybe you should have taken me home, like I asked."

He shakes his head. "Damn, how'd I get that wrong? Guess you just seem older."

I cross my arms over my chest. "And just what is that supposed to mean?"

He closes his eyes and shakes his head. "I'm not saying you seem old. Shit. You know what I mean."

"Are you trying to say you're sorry?"

He sighs. "Yes, that's exactly what I'm saying."

"Apology accepted," I say, grinning and reaching for the bottle.

"Oh no you don't," he scolds, jerking it out of my grasp. "I see what you're trying to do, you little vixen."

I lean back with a huff. "Aw, you're no fun."

"Hey you're the one who decided to remind me you're under age."

I roll my eyes. "Barely. I swear, I'll never understand this country's laws. It's okay to let eighteen-year-olds go off to war, but heaven forbid they have one sip of alcohol."

He leans close and ducks his head toward my shoulder. "Don't tell anybody, but I agree."

"Good," I say, taking the opportunity to lunge for the wine hidden behind his back.

But he's too fast and catches me around the waist, hauling me against his body. "Oh, so now you're gonna trick me, eh?"

I squeal and fight as he tickles my ribs. "Uncle! Uncle!" I say, batting his hands away and trying to catch my breath.

His hands still, but he doesn't release me. "You're so beautiful," he says in a low voice as his fingers trace patterns on the exposed skin of my shoulders. I lean into the touch, wanting more yet knowing I shouldn't. When his thumb sweeps across my collarbone, I shiver as his mouth follows the trail, hot and dangerous in its effect on my senses. "I'm sorry, Max. I just can't seem to stop myself. I've wanted you for so long," he whispers.

I pull back, my spine stiffening.

"What's wrong?" he says, hurt flashing in his eyes.

"Nothing." I take a shaky breath. "Everything is perfect, actually. So perfect it makes me scared."

He tightens his hold, pulling me against his hard chest. "Tell me why you're scared."

I lift my chin to look into his eyes. "I'm scared you see someone else when you look at me."

"Who do you think I see?"

"Sadie."

His body goes rigid. "Why would you say that? I don't understand."

"At the hospital you mentioned her. Said I reminded you of her the first time you saw me."

He nods. "That's true. I did see her in you that day, but it was just a fraction of a second. A moment."

"So, you're not still in love with her?"

His head drops. "I'll always *love* her. But I'm *in love* with someone else."

I stiffen, not able to completely believe the implication of his words. I've been disappointed so many times by so many people, I can't let it happen again. Can't let myself fall prey to another illusion. But the truth is, I've already fallen. Whether I like it or not, Cash took my heart little by little, day by day, bit by bit, and there's nothing I can do about it.

Hope pounds in my chest as his mouth inches toward my own, rough hands grazing the skin of my thigh and making me squirm with need. I stop breathing, thinking I know what to expect. But when his lips fuse with mine, I'm unprepared for the spark of blinding lust that sweeps through my veins at the gentle touch. I cling to his shoulders, massaging the thick cords of muscle as he shifts to roll me onto my back. My fingers find the back of his neck, and I pull him in to deepen the kiss, hungry for all the things I thought could never be. He moans and massages my breasts, his thumbs circling my nipples through the thin fabric of my dress.

"Are you sure about this?" he pants, breaking the kiss and lowering his hips so I can feel the evidence of his desire. "If we keep on at this rate, I won't be able to stop."

Thirty

A flash of blinding light in my eyes forces me to freeze as a deep voice floats out of the darkness to inform us the fine for indecent exposure on a public beach is three hundred and nineteen dollars. I pull my dress down and scramble to my feet, cringing at the idea of being caught making out in public. Luckily, Cash and I are still fully clothed, but if the officer would have shown up any later, that may not have been the case.

Cash holds his palms up. "I'm sorry officer. We got a little carried away. Let us grab our stuff and we'll be out of here."

"Why didn't you tell him you're a Ranger," I whisper as we hurry back to the truck.

Cash laughs and shakes his head. "Breaking the law is breaking the law, no matter if you're a Ranger or not. But I gotta say, breaking the law with you felt pretty damn good."

Heat rises on my neck at the memory. "We should probably get back anyhow."

Cash nods and puts the truck in gear, but I can tell he's disappointed our night ended so soon. I'm disappointed too.

He holds my hand on the ride home, but by the time we pull into the driveway, doubt has time to seep in and make me second-guess ever letting Cash get so close. What if that cop hadn't showed up and I'd given myself over to the passion of the moment? I've made that mistake before and don't want to make it again. So, after telling Olivia goodnight, I mumble something about going to check on Aaron and tiptoe into my room. But once the door is shut, I turn the lock with no intention of opening it again until morning, no matter how good it felt to lie in Cash's arms.

As I slip off my dress and pull on a soft T-shirt, the light under the door turns dark. When Cash softly calls my name, it takes every bit of strength I have not to go to him. And when he finally walks away, I sigh in relief even as a lump forms in my throat at the thought of his disappointment.

I try to push away the cold feeling in the pit of my stomach, but the longer I wait, the larger it grows until I'm twisting in the sheets, desperate for relief.

It's easy to pretend a night with Cash would end the same as it had with Lir, but deep down I know that's a lie. Cash is different. Sincere. Loving. Unselfish. And above all, honest. So, if he tells me he loves me, I have no reason not to believe him.

But he didn't say he loves *me*. Just that he loves *someone*. I shake my head. At this point in my life, I need blunt honesty, not vague innuendos. Sure, Cash wants my body, that much is clear. But what about the rest of me?

I stand to my feet, grab the baby monitor, and glance at Aaron one last time. The house is dark and still as my bare feet pad down the hall, but judging by the light visible under Cash's door, I know he's still awake. At my knock, he calls for me to come in, his eyes searching mine as I shut the door behind me. He's sitting on the bed wearing a pair of boxers, the light from the lamp glinting off his perfectly formed chest.

"What're you doing?" he says, his voice husky as his eyes inch lower.

Wearing only a thin shirt that barely covers my ass, I should feel embarrassed, but all I feel is indignation. I stand up straight and put my hands on my hips. "I just want to get a couple of things straight," I say, my voice quivering despite my resolve to hold my emotions in check.

He pats the bed beside him. "Why don't you come sit down and we'll talk?"

"I don't want to sit down. I want answers."

His eyes widen at the ferocity of my tone. "What's wrong?"

I throw my hands up in the air. "I'm just tired, Cash. Tired of thinking I know someone, when really I don't know them at all."

A line forms between his eyes. "Are you saying you don't know me?"

"I'm saying I'd like to think I know you, but what was all that on the beach, huh? Before you say anything, all I ask is you give it to me straight. I may be younger than you, but I've been through more shit than people twice my age. And I don't have the time or the patience to get my hopes up for something that's never going to be real." Cash stands and takes a step toward me, but I hold up my hand. "I mean it. If what you want is purely physical, I promise I won't hold it against you for telling me the truth."

"But it's not just physical. I thought I explained that. Surely you know how I feel."

I bite the inside of my lip to keep from screaming. "No, Cash. You didn't explain. You said you loved *someone*. As in *anyone*. Yeah, I guess it could've been me you were referring to, but it could've also been any one of the other seven billion people on this planet." I close my eyes and lower my voice. "I'm sorry. I'm not here to give you a lecture. Or seem like some kind of obsessive bitch. But I'll be damned if I waste another second of my life trying to read smoke signals from a dying fire."

I spin on my heel and am half way to the door when Cash grabs my hand. He turns me slightly, but my adrenaline pumps too hard to meet his gaze. With my frustrations off my chest, all that's left is to lock myself in my room until morning and pretend it was all just a bad dream.

But when Cash squeezes my hand, his voice is calm. "I understand how you feel. And if I could go back and change the things I said, how I said them, I would. I want you to know it is *you* that I love. I was just ... afraid."

I search his face to see if he's being sincere. "Afraid of what?"

"Scaring you away. Can't you tell I'm crazy about you?"

My shoulders drop, the tension leaving my body in a whoosh as I close the space between us. "No," I say, running my fingertips along the light stubble of his strong jaw. "But you can show me."

His lips part as he sizes me up. "Well, aren't you the little temptress."

"Earlier you called me a vixen." I bat my lashes. "So, which is it? Am I a temptress or a vixen?"

"Both," he says, hoisting me in his arms and tossing me onto the bed. When I shriek, he takes the baby monitor from my hand and presses a finger to my lips. But his eyes go wide when I take the opportunity to run my tongue from base to tip. "Fuck," he whispers.

"Well, that is kinda what I have in mind ..." I lift an eyebrow and let my oversized shirt slip down to reveal a bare shoulder and swell of my breast.

His chest heaves as he stares at the bit of naked flesh. When he licks his lips and runs his hand up my thigh, I bite the inside of my cheek, suddenly nervous at my lack of experience. I want to seem confident and sexy, but my encounter with Lir has left me with doubts about my abilities in the bedroom.

Cash seems to sense my mood and his hand stills. "What's the matter?"

"Nothing," I say, trying to keep my voice bright.

"Tell me."

"No, it's embarrassing."

"What if I promise not to laugh?"

I look away and shrug. "I just feel unsure of myself ... I haven't had very much experience in this department, and I guess I just don't want to make a mistake."

Cash sits back, a frown marring his handsome face. "But

what about ..." He glances toward the screen of the baby monitor where Aaron peacefully sleeps.

"That was only one time," I rush to explain.

Cash's eyebrows go up. "By only one time, do you mean to say that it was your only time, ever?"

"Yeah," I say, ducking my head to hide the shame coloring my face.

"Look at me," he says, cupping my chin. When I glance up, his face is full of understanding that irritates more than encourages.

"You feel sorry for me," I accuse.

"No, you ... intrigue me."

My stomach does a flip as I recognize the desire in his eyes.

He tilts his head. "You want to know what I find the sexiest?"

I nod, my insides quivering with anticipation.

"A woman who's not afraid to ask for what she wants." He bends to nuzzle at my neck, sending shivers of pleasure shooting down the length of my body. "Tell me what you want, baby."

"I don't know what I want," I say, arching as his hands find my hips, rough fingers tugging at the red lace of my panties.

"You may not, but I think I do," he says, settling between my legs with a wicked grin.

His head disappears, making me gasp and writhe at the new sensation and it doesn't take long before I want more.

When I voice my request, Cash looks up and gives me a wink. "I love it when you tell me what to do."

I tug my shirt over my head and his eyes widen. "You're so

perfect," he says, pausing to nip at my breasts as his fingers lightly trace the long scars on my back.

I push my hips up against his hardness. "I want to feel you inside me," I beg, unable to wait any longer.

"Okay, give me a second," he says, hopping up to grab a condom from a drawer in the bedside table.

My breath catches as I take in the sight. The light bathes his skin in a soft glow. But when he crawls back in bed, I can't help tensing at the intrusion I know is coming.

He kisses my neck, his hand finding my center. "You're so wet," he whispers, his voice hoarse.

"I need you. Now." I clutch his shoulders, my nails digging into his flesh.

Despite my impatience, Cash takes his time, prompting me to reassure him he's not hurting me.

"Harder," I demand, enjoying the weight and feel of his body in mine.

He picks up the pace, but his face takes on a pained expression, making me ask if he's okay.

"It's too good," he pants, closing his eyes. "Don't know how much longer I can last."

His admission only makes me climb higher, my craving for him soaring until I fear I may never get enough.

Suddenly I'm there, standing at the edge of the cliff, ready to jump. All it takes is the feel of him shuddering against me to push me over the edge. Stars flash across my vision, and for a moment I wonder if I'm about to faint.

Cash's breath comes in shallow gasps as he rolls away and gathers me close. "You okay? Did I hurt you?"

I laugh. "I was just about to ask you the same thing."

He brushes his lips across my cheek as we linger over the exquisite feel of lying in each other's arms. I want to stay here forever, but the ever-present glow of Aaron's monitor reminds me of my first obligation.

"I better go back to my room," I say, swinging my legs over the side of the bed.

Cash catches my hand. "No. Please don't. I want you to stay. Forever if you want."

I start to laugh ... but the seriousness of his expression stops me, and I give him a questioning look.

"I mean it," he says, sitting up. "And if you want Aaron in here with us, I'll move his crib first thing in the morning. I don't know about you, but I meant what I said. I love you, and I want this to work. For the first time in a long time, I can see what kind of future I want. And you and Aaron are both in it."

Thirty-One

Cash's truck rumbles into the driveway as I step onto the porch. "Take your shoes off before you come inside. I just mopped," I call, not leaving the safety of my pristine floor to chance.

"Okay, boss," he says with a wink. "Hey, would you look at that?" A swirling mass of seagulls fills the sky, dipping and crying as they come in from the ocean. "Never seen so many all together before."

"Nice try, but you're still not coming in until you take those off," I say, pointing to his dirty boots as he stomps up the steps.

He lifts an eyebrow but bends to do as I say. "You don't have to go through all this trouble, you know. Parker and Sarah are both old friends."

I walk to the sofa and begin fluffing pillows. "I thought you'd want everything to look nice."

His eyes rove over the spotless house. Candles glimmering

on the mantle above the fireplace. Freshly baked cookies in a tray on the table. Aaron wearing his best outfit as he naps in his swing.

"I do, baby. I just don't understand what all the fuss is about," he says, grabbing me by the waist when I pass.

"We never have company. I guess it's kind of special."

"You've been working all day. Isn't it time for a break?" He bends to kiss the side of my neck, his tongue tickling and teasing until I squirm and push away.

"Stop trying to distract me," I say with a laugh.

"Not so fast." His hands circle my waist to untie my apron strings. "The house looks great. You look great. Aaron looks great." He grins and ushers me into the kitchen. "These cookies look especially great." He snatches one off the tray and shoves it into his mouth before I can object.

"No more until they get here. I mean it."

"Okay ... just one more," he says, snatching another and holding it high in the air as I screech and tug on his arm. "What? I'm just testing them. Don't you want to make sure they're okay before our company arrives?"

A knock at the door saves him from my wrath.

"You got lucky this time," I hiss.

His chin dips, green eyes smoldering with wickedness. "I kind of like it when you're angry. Keep that up and you might just be the one getting lucky."

When he winks, memories of last night make me blush. "Hush, they'll hear you," I say, walking to answer the door.

His deep laughter follows me as I open the door to greet our guests.

An attractive blonde extends her hand. "Oh, you must be Max. I'm Sarah and this is my husband, Parker." She indicates a tall man with brown eyes and a close-cropped beard.

My anxiety diminishes as we all shake hands, and I welcome them into the house.

"Oh, this must be the little Aaron we've heard so much about," Sarah says, bending over his swing. "Isn't he just a doll. All our boys are grown, but what I wouldn't give to have them back at this age again."

Cash offers them a seat at the table where we enjoy cookies and small talk for a while, but I can tell they're anxious to dive into the real reason for the visit.

When Cash spreads a map of Eden across the table, Sarah leans forward, her eyes sharp as she studies the details.

Parker glances at the map but holds up a hand. "Before we get started, I think we should discuss the timing." He points to the television where a news station tracks Hurricane Ike as it gains strength. "Is everyone still on board to proceed with the plan as usual?"

I glance at Cash and nod. "I don't know about everyone else, but I am."

"What about Aaron?" Sarah says.

"My friend Olivia is bringing him to Cash's sister's house where they'll be safe."

Cash nods. "And I've made special arrangements for the four of us to take shelter in the lighthouse. It's the best place around to ride out a storm."

Parker's eyes tighten. "I just think if we had more time, we could—"

"But that's just it. We don't have more time." The muscles in Cash's jaw flex. "Jude Delacroix is highly unpredictable. If you two don't show up for your appointment tomorrow, he's likely to call the whole thing off. And starting from scratch this late in the game could jeopardize everything."

Sarah and Parker give each other a knowing look. When Sarah nods, Parker turns back to Cash. "I see your point. Given the situation, it's probably best not to miss this chance." He nods to me. "Sarah and I spent yesterday listening to your testimony, Max, and we just want to tell you what a brave thing it is you're doing."

I thank them both, heat rushing to my face at the praise.

"We mean it," Sarah says, offering a warm smile. "There are not a lot of victims willing to stand up the way you have."

I twist my hands in my lap. "I just want to help. This has gone on too long. I don't want anyone else to get hurt by what they're doing."

"That's very admirable." She motions to the map on the table. "Now, why don't you tell us about this. I see the main compound labeled here, but what is this other structure on the opposite side of the island?"

Cash points to the east side. "Most of Eden's inhabitants live here, with the exception of Jude's mother, Hazel Delacroix, who lives over here on the west side of the island. Her home will be our point of contact while you two arrive on the other side as planned."

Parker taps the drawing of the boathouse. "So, the plan is to leave our boat in a slip and walk this path up to the main house?"

Cash nods. "Max says you'll likely encounter Jude's son, Lir. He's the one Jude bailed out of jail a while back. We can't be certain that he'll be on the island, but given the circumstances it's the most likely the place to find him."

Sarah and Parker ask questions about the normal procedures surrounding Eden adoptions, and I do my best to answer with as many details as I can remember.

"Above all, Jude likes to be obeyed," I say, my heart pounding at the memory of his unpredictable moods. "His spiritual theologies are always evolving and can change based on whatever he's been studying. So, if by chance he asks you to do something I haven't mentioned, just go with it. Because if you don't, he'll consider you uncooperative and unworthy of the gift Eden is bestowing. If that happens, it's very likely he'll call the whole thing off and demand that you leave immediately."

Sarah taps her chin, a line forming between her brows. "But if Jude's only desire is to make a profit, why waste time with ceremonies and rituals? Why not just make the exchange clean and quick?"

"Because if he were to do that, it would go against everything he has taught the Sisters about their calling. Their divine purpose."

"So, the ceremonies just serve as tools to further indoctrinate the Sisters?"

"Exactly. As far as they know, the transaction has more to do with their spiritual journey than the quest for money. They know Jude receives payment, but they're taught to consider the money as a tithe to help sustain the community and further the ministry."

Parker drums his fingers on the table. "Does Jude also believe the doctrine he teaches?"

I lift a shoulder. "I honestly don't know. I think part of him wants to believe it. To feel like some kind of hero rather than what he really is."

Sarah turns to Parker with raised brows. "This could definitely get ugly."

Cash clears his throat. "Are you having second thoughts?"

She lifts her chin. "No. We're prepared to do whatever it takes to take this guy down."

"That's right," Parker says, his jaw set. "We need to get these people behind bars as quickly as possible."

I frown. "After you arrest Jude, what will happen to all the others?"

Cash leans back in his seat and sighs. "From what you've told us, Jude isn't the only one profiting from the adoptions. Freyja, Dr. Chen, and Lir have all been accomplices to the crimes."

My throat constricts. "What about the Sisters? What about me?"

Cash nods to Sarah and Parker. "I think we can all agree that since you were brought to Eden as a child, you'll be granted complete amnesty."

"But how can you be certain?"

"Your testimony has been very powerful in getting us this far. I'm positive the court will grant a pardon for any involvement you may have had."

"And the Sisters?"

Sarah glances at Cash. "Since the Sisters arrived at Eden of their own free will, it may be difficult to prove their innocence."

My mouth falls open. "But they've been brainwashed. They're victims."

Cash takes my hand and squeezes. "They may be brainwashed, but they had the chance to say no to Jude before they were ever brought to the island. They knew what they were getting into, yet they did it anyway. And while I feel sorry for them and wish them no harm, they knowingly committed crimes. Many, many crimes. Since this is a special circumstance, the court may be lenient. But we are talking about human trafficking here. Do you understand how serious this is, Max?"

My chest tightens and my ears grow hot. "I completely understand how serious this is ... but you weren't there. You don't understand the kind of control Jude has over everyone."

Parker sits up straight. "I have a feeling that in this case, the Sisters will probably be offered amnesty in exchange for their testimony against Jude and the others."

My chest lightens a little, and I breathe a sigh of relief at the thought that the Sisters will have a way out. But new questions surface when my eyes go to the red *x* marking Jude's office on the map. I lean over the table, pointing to it. "If we are able to get into the office and get our hands on the files containing records of past adoptions, what will happen to the families who are listed there? Will they face jail time?"

Sarah bites her lip. "It's very likely."

I shake my head. "What about the kids?"

"Foster care is the usual course of action."

A chill descends at the thought of all those children being

ripped from the arms of the only parents they've ever known. Good parents. From what I've witnessed, Eden's clients simply wanted families of their own without the hassle of traditional adoption or the burden of taking on a child with special needs. Sure, some might call them lazy or shallow, but the children shouldn't be punished for the poor judgement of their parents.

"Is there any way the children could remain in the homes? Could the parents make a deal with the authorities, just like the Sisters?"

Cash shifts in his seat. "It's a possibility, but highly unlikely."

"That's right," Parker agrees. "When juries look at cases like this, all they see is another example of rich people who think they don't have to play by the rules. The kind who have enough money to buy anything they want. Even a child."

I turn to Cash. "I understand that they've committed a crime, but why would these people be held more accountable than the Sisters?"

Cash looks into my eyes, his own brimming with empathy. "Because the parents can't claim they were brainwashed."

Thirty-Two

I grip the handrail, knuckles turning white as salt spray cools my face and arms. The wind is strong, the water choppy—no doubt from the hurricane that is out there somewhere, plowing across the Gulf. Olivia and Aaron were able to leave early enough to miss most of the evacuation panic. The interstates continue to fill with long lines of cars, but Cash says the memory of the horrendous traffic situation before Hurricane Rita has made many people hesitant to leave this go-around. With the interstates gridlocked in the sweltering Texas heat, evacuating for Rita proved almost as dangerous as the actual storm.

I think back to the ones I experienced at Eden. No matter how bad the predictions, the idea of leaving was never an option. To Jude, the risk of death came second to the risk of losing control. In truth, I never really minded. It was as if some part of me craved the danger, the thrill of my destiny hanging in the balance. But as I look across the water to the island that's still just a dark blotch on the horizon, the danger that awaits feels anything but thrilling. I say a prayer for Sarah and Parker, myself and Cash, that we'll somehow be able to accomplish our task without harm. I want to say I know what we are doing is right. That my resolve is unwavering. But that would be a lie. I want those guilty to pay for their treachery. But my stomach lurches at the uncertain fate of the families and children involved.

"Max, you should come inside," Cash calls from the flybridge.

I hurry to the room where Sarah and Parker are taking turns checking the hidden cameras affixed to their shirts. While on the island, their movements and interactions can be monitored from Cash's laptop or phone at any given time. As they put the final touches on their outfits, it's amazing to me how easily this no-nonsense Texas Ranger pair has transformed into wealthy suburbanites in search of the American dream. They have the house, the car, the career ... but not the child and are prepared to go to any lengths to make their dream come true. It may not be legal or ethical, but they console themselves by rationalizing that if they don't take this opportunity—this child—someone else will. Like buying an expensive puppy from a breeder, one with papers and pedigrees; there are other puppies out there, free puppies in need of good homes. But is one puppy's life more important, more worthy of love and affection? At the end of the day, they are both the same. One is just easier to get. So, they pull out their wallet in the name of convenience and fall prey to a game that blurs the line between right and wrong in the most emotional way possible.

"Is that it?" Parker asks, pointing to Hazel's house as he turns the boat toward the shore.

Cash hoists our bags onto his shoulders. "Yeah, just leave us at the dock, and we'll see you back here after the Claiming ceremony."

Sarah's eyes dart back to Parker. "What if they want us to stay the night? What happens then?"

I shake my head. "From everything I've seen, all they really care about is that you stay for the Claiming ceremony. Once that's finished, they shouldn't have a problem with you leaving."

Sarah nods but her mouth presses into a tight line.

"You'll be fine," Cash encourages. "You two are some of the best Rangers I know. You got this."

Sarah's face relaxes, and Parker gives us a wave before they troll away from the dock. I turn toward Hazel's house and frown.

"What's the matter?" Cash asks, seeing the look.

"She would have seen us drive up," I say, my palms slick with sweat. "She would have seen me and come outside. Something's wrong."

I run down the dock and up the overgrown path, my feet slowing to tread through the soft sand. When I near the cottage, I see the front door hanging open to reveal a house full of dust and debris, rotting vegetables and a loaf of bread covered with mold. I call for Hazel but the silence is deafening as daylight fades.

My vision blurs as Cash enters behind me. "They took her. I know it. I have to go find her," I say, heading for the door.

Cash catches me by the arm, his eyes hard. "No, Max. Not yet. We have to stick to the plan."

"But she could be in danger. We have to find her."

"We will." He pulls me to him. "I promise we will do everything we can to find her when the time is right. But right now, we have to stick to the plan or risk putting Sarah and Parker in danger too."

I swallow hard, my heart pounding as I try to relax.

Cash places his laptop on the table and asks me to close the windows and doors while he pulls up the split screen showing the Rangers' movements.

The bright light from the computer shines like a magical beacon of hope in the darkness as I lean over Cash's shoulder, watching in anticipation as the pair make their way toward the dock at Eden.

I point to the screen. "These are from the cameras on their shirts, right?"

"Yeah. Amazing, isn't it?" Cash clicks on the screen, turning up the volume so we can hear the Rangers' conversations.

With a scruffy beard covering his hollowed cheeks and dark bags under his eyes, I barely recognize Lir as he flags them into the slip. The handsome young man I used to know has been replaced with a stranger wearing a blank expression as he bends to tie off the boat. I used to be angry. Angry that he left me. Angry that he let his life get so out of control that Jude had to bail him out of one prison just to put him in another. But now all I feel is pity. Pity for his selfishness. His missed potential. His missed life.

When Aditi appears behind him, my chest squeezes even harder at the sight of her smiling face as she presses her lips to the Rangers' palms. "Welcome. Blessings to you both."

Parker and Sarah murmur their appreciation and hasten to follow her up the winding path to the main house as the evening sun dips low in the background.

Wearing a green silk sarong, Jude waits to greet them on the open veranda. He presses his hands together and bows. "Please have a seat. Make yourselves comfortable," he says, indicating a pair of woven cushions. When they are settled, he leans forward. "I'm so honored your journey has brought you to Eden." His arm sweeps toward the tables surrounding the altar on the beach. "Soon, the sky will darken and the Claiming torches will be lit, honoring this very important and spiritual occasion where we will call on the Anahata Chakra to bless our ceremony." He offers his hands to the Rangers, his face glowing as they accept his grasp. "Let us breathe together for a moment," he says, inhaling deeply. "We will take this opportunity to invite life-giving energy and push out negativity."

After a few long breaths, Jude sits back. "You are not here by chance. You did not choose Eden. Eden chose you."

Freyja appears behind Jude, and the Rangers are summoned into a room where green silk robes hang on wooden pegs. "You will now change into the ceremonial robes. Wear nothing but the robes. No shoes. No hats. Nothing underneath. Nothing on top," she instructs.

Cash turns to me with wide eyes. "Why didn't you mention this?"

I wring my hands together. "I've never seen those robes before. They must be something new."

"Shit," Cash says, staring at the screen as Freyja leaves the room and the Rangers do her bidding. "Shit. Shit. Shit."

"Sorry, man," Parker whispers as he takes off his shirt and the camera goes dark.

When Sarah's camera follows suit, I wipe my hands down the sides of my jeans and my insides quiver with dread. "If they don't have the cameras with them, will our plan still work?"

Cash slams the lid of the laptop, his nostrils flaring. "As long as they leave with a baby." He bends to check the laces of his boots then waves for me to follow. "Come on. It's time for us to go."

Dressed in all black, dark paint covering our faces, we make our way across the dunes and through the woods to the other side of the island where Eden's dark buildings stand like inky blobs against the night sky. Cash follows close behind as I lead him down the trail to the main house, but my pulse pounds with dread at the fear of being caught. As we pass through the fragrant gardens surrounding the compound, I can see the distant flicker of torches burning around the altar on the beach. The eerily familiar sound of beating drums and Sisters chanting floats over the breeze as a grim reminder that I'm back in Jude's lair, where his rule is law. The hair pricks on the back of my neck, and for a moment, I fear I may be sick.

"You okay?" Cash whispers when I stumble over a rock.

I nod, thankful to have him with me. And even more thankful for the pistol strapped to his side.

He points to the fork in the path ahead and holds up his hands.

I wave him to the left, but we freeze at the sight of a woman carrying an infant up the path toward the beach. We look at each other, and I sigh in relief. Sarah and Parker's cooperation has paid off. Despite the loss of our camera feed, the Claiming ceremony is going as planned. Even if our search for files of past adoptions produces nothing, Jude and Freyja will still be charged with a third-degree felony for human trafficking, an offense that could easily land them ten years in prison according to Cash. And if he can prove they've bribed the local police to keep quiet, their sentences could be even longer.

But my relief doesn't last long. As the woman carrying the infant comes closer, my stomach drops.

"Oh no," I whisper, staring at her thin shoulders, stooped posture, gaunt face. "It's Hazel," I say, squeezing Cash's hand. "I have to—"

"No, Max," he says, holding me in place. "I need your help getting into Jude's office. We shouldn't be separated right now."

"If not now, then when? You promised."

Cash's head drops, the moonlight glinting off his hair. "Help me get into the office and when we're done, I'll help you with Hazel."

As she walks down the path and fades out of sight, fresh rage fills my veins at the sight of her malnourished frame. Starvation is one of Jude's favorite punishments, but there's something especially sick about the idea that he would impose it on his own mother.

"Are you okay?" Cash whispers, sensing my distress.

I square my shoulders. "I just look forward to the day I can watch that motherfucker pay for all the shit he's done."

Cash gives me a pat on the back. "I'll make sure of it."

With fresh resolve, we creep toward the main house where the lights have been extinguished. Jude's office is near the back, and it only takes a moment for Cash to pick the lock. Once inside, we take out our small flashlights and set to work searching the desk and file cabinets for any piece of information that might be useful.

"There's nothing here. Not even a computer," I say, at a loss for where else to look.

Cash walks to the large black safe at the back of the room. "Do you know anything about this? What the code might be? These kinds are usually four to six digits."

Cold sweat trickles down my spine as I wrack my brain for an answer. "I don't know."

"Birthdays, anniversaries, anything?" He shifts his flashlight to the other hand.

I shake my head. "Jude and Freyja are life partners, so there's no anniversary ... I think Lir was born in November, but I'm not sure. We never celebrated birthdays or anything."

Cash's head jerks up. "Hey, what's the number of that Bible verse? The one I sent in the email to Jude."

"Genesis 1:28?"

His fingers hover over the keypad on the safe. "Let's see. First book, first chapter, twenty-eighth verse."

I hold my breath as he twists the knob and watch in amazement as the door swings open to reveal a giant chasm filled with rifles and ammunition.

"I can't believe you did it," I say, squeezing my palms together.

Cash hands me the light, and I try to hold it steady while he searches the floor of the safe for paperwork.

After a few minutes, he rocks back on his heels and swears under his breath. "I don't understand. There's got to be more here than this."

"Wait," I say, my light catching a small black square secured to the ceiling of the safe with tape.

Cash reaches in and peels it away from the thick felt lining. "It's a memory stick," he says, his voice trembling with excitement.

"Do you think there's anything on it?"

He slips it into his pocket and bolts the door of the safe. "Don't know, but it's better than nothing. I don't think Jude would've bothered to put it in there if it wasn't important."

"Can we go now?" I say, anxious to find Hazel.

"Yeah, I'm ready to get out of here." He sniffs the air. "Smells like sweat and incense." His flashlight falls on a particularly grotesque Venus of Willendorf statue sitting by the door, and he shudders. "This place is fucking creepy."

Once outside, I motion for him to follow me down a rarely used side garden that wraps around the main house. Bending low, we maneuver down the trail on light feet, pausing every few moments to look around and make sure we haven't been spotted. The last thing we want is a confrontation with Jude.

When we get to a spot where part of the ceremony is visible, we crouch low and position ourselves near the main path, hoping to catch Hazel's attention on her way back to the nursery later. I want to go farther, to dart across the path and up to where I can see her standing with the child, but I know it's too dangerous. So we settle in and wait, our ears alerted to every snapping twig, every shift of the crowd as they feast on tables laden with fruit and fish and roasted meats.

From our vantage point, the sight of Jude seated next to Sarah and Parker makes me tremble with a mixture of rage and fear. Seated in front of the altar, they seem at ease as they partake of the feast. My chest swells with pride at their bravery, but my stomach drops when Aditi sets two small cups of dark liquid in front of them and encourages them to drink. They look at each other, clearly debating whether it's a good idea. Jude sees the look and raises his glass to make a toast, leaving them no choice if they want to avoid his wrath and risk failing the mission.

"Oh no," I say as they lift the cups. It isn't very long before Parker clutches his stomach, his eyes bulging as he stumbles from the table to retch onto the sand. When his stomach is empty, he returns to the table where Sisters hover with apologies while he gulps a glass of water.

"What the hell was in that?" Cash whispers, his voice rigid.

"It's called kava. Works kind of like alcohol, but stronger."

After a few minutes, Sarah laughs loudly and sways to the side.

"This isn't good," Cash says, cursing under his breath.

My mouth turns dry as I stare at her glazed expression. "It'll be over soon. See that?" I point to the sacred bath being filled with warm water. "As soon as that's done being filled, the ceremony will start."

When the drums settle and the sacred bath is brought forward, Hazel makes her way around the altar, cradling the baby boy in her arms.

"Are you sure Hazel won't stay for the whole thing?"

"Yes, after the baptism, she should be released to head back to the nursery."

I watch with bated breath as incense is lit and Hazel passes the child to Jude. He sprinkles the baby with water while imparting the ancient wisdom of the Anahata Chakra. When he places the child in Parker's and Sarah's arms, the group begins a chanting ritual that is accompanied by the echoing of singing bowls in the key of F sharp.

When the ceremony comes to a finish and everyone takes a seat, Hazel slips away and hurries down the path toward us. I breathe a sigh of relief even as my muscles tense in anticipation. As soon as she passes, Cash darts out and pulls her into the bushes, his hand over her mouth.

She struggles at first, her eyes wide until she realizes it's me. "But Jude said you were dead," she says, her voice shaking. "Told everyone you tried to run away. That your boat capsized. He said he jumped into the water to try and save you, but it was too late."

I grab onto her bony hand and hold it tight. "No, that's not what happened, at all. I'm fine. And you will be too. But you need to come with us. Everything's going be all right."

"I can't," she says, pushing me away.

"Hazel, listen to me. Now is your chance to get out of here and never look back. I know you're scared, but I told you I'd come back for you."

"I knew you would if you could," she says, her voice barely above a whisper. "But I can't leave. Not without Lir."

"Why not?" I say, a bit angry that she would sacrifice her own freedom for someone like him, even if he is her grandson.

She shakes her head. "I know you and Lir didn't part on the best terms, but lately he's really been trying to turn over a new leaf. After that trouble he got in a while back, he's been trying to get his life straight. And I have to help him. I'm the only one he has who truly cares. Truly loves him and wants him to make something of his life. I may not have done the best job with Jude, but I plan to make it up with Lir. I've gotta stay for him."

"I understand you just want to help him, but you can't help him unless you take this opportunity to help yourself."

Her thin shoulders sag and she bows her head. "Sometimes love makes you do stuff you never dreamed of. Stuff that don't make sense. But you do it anyway. Because not doing it would be like sticking a knife in your own heart."

When she turns to the moonlight, my throat constricts at the sight of her haggard face and watery eyes brimming with tears.

"Sounds like she's made up her mind," Cash says, stepping forward.

"But—"

"Leave it, Max. We don't have time to argue about this right now." He bends his head to my ear. "I promise we'll get her out of here one way or another. But right now, we can't afford to cause a scene. Trust me."

Disappointment tightens my chest, but I press my lips together, suppressing the urge to argue.

"You two better get out of here," Hazel says, glancing back toward the ceremony. "Don't worry about me. I've lived long enough to know what I want."

Thirty-Three

With adrenaline urging us on, we manage to make the trek back to the other side of the island in record time. Bursting into the dusty house, Cash hurries to position his laptop on the kitchen table and jams the memory stick in the side. My heart pounds in my ears as we wait for the program to open. He clicks a few times and, like magic, dozens of folders appear in a list on the screen.

"Is it ..." I'm unable to finish the sentence.

Cash scans the information in one of the folders and releases a breath. "Has to be. Look." He zooms in and points to the screen. "It's all here. Buyer's names, addresses, children's birthdays, weight, sex, hair color, blood type. Even the birth mothers' information." He scrolls down the screen, his face glowing. "There are hundreds of them. I can't believe we actually did it."

When I look at the excitement on his face, I want to feel

happy too, but my throat closes and cold sweat trickles down my sides when I think of the damage this information will do to the names flowing down the screen.

"Damn. Something's wrong," Cash says, frowning at his phone. "Sarah's and Parkers' cameras are back on, but the audio isn't coming through. I'm gonna go out and see if I can get a better signal," he says, rushing through the door.

When he steps out, I take the opportunity to scan the names lining the computer screen in alphabetical order and my stomach churns when I spot Ava's listing:

Byron "Buddy" and Susan Babineaux
1211 Jamaica Beach Rd. Jamaica Beach, Texas 77554
Baby Girl Born August 23rd, 2000 to Rhea
6 lbs. 14 oz.
Brown Hair
Blood Type O Positive
Departed Eden September 2nd, 2000

My body trembles as I stare at the listing. Sure, Buddy and Susan made a mistake. Participated in an illegal adoption. But I'll never believe they are on the same level as Jude. I've tried to see it that way, but I simply can't. And I certainly can't rationalize ripping Ava from their arms. From the only home she's ever known. A loving place full of all the things I never had. And for what? Vindication? To make us all feel like we've done our job thoroughly and made everyone pay? Well, in this case, the price is too high. I may want justice, but not this kind.

When my eyes fall to the name just below Babineaux, I do a double take.

Phillip and Landry Baron
413 Coliseum Street New Orleans, Louisiana 70130
Baby Boy Born March 9th, 2008 to Qetesh
7 lbs. 10 oz.
Blond Hair
Blood Type A Negative
Departed Eden April 26th, 2008

April 26th was the day I was admitted to the hospital in Galveston. Could this be the couple that rescued me? My mind races to piece together the events after I was pulled from the ocean. The letter B embroidered on the pillows and towels. The empty bassinet beside the bed. Pile of new baby clothes on the dresser. It all makes sense.

I go back to the woman's name and conjure her image. Blond hair, tan skin, red lips. The sweet scent of her perfume. Sound of her voice calling me sugar bee. Could this Landry be the cousin I remember?

My hand trembles as I scroll farther down to see if I recognize anyone else. Sure enough, my heart sinks as I read a name near the end of the list.

Blake and Sloane Richards
1608 Seaside Dr. Galveston, Texas 77550
Baby Girl Born July 6th, 2004 to Hathor
8lbs. 2 oz.

Auburn Hair
Blood Type A Positive
Departed Eden August 21st, 2004

I shake my head, willing the nightmare to end. I knew Sloane seemed familiar. But the reason makes me sick to my stomach. They don't deserve what's about to happen. If only there was a way to protect them from the hell I know is coming.

When Cash returns from outside, I decide to broach the subject. But as soon as I voice my concern, his arms cross and his expression hardens.

"You said it yourself," I say, trying to make him see reason. "Jude and Freyja will get what's coming to them even without this information. They could go to prison for ten years. Or even longer."

"That's not long enough," Cash says, his eyes flashing. "They deserve to be locked away forever."

"But at what cost?"

His eyes narrow. "What are you trying to say?"

I bite my lip and try to calm my voice. "The same thing I tried to say the other day."

"Listen, Max, I know this is hard, and I know you don't want to see the kids taken from their families, but there's no way around it. These people are every bit as guilty as Jude and Freyja."

"No, they're not. They made a mistake. But it's not the same. You know it's not the same."

Cash's hands scrub over his face, and when he looks up, his

eyes are tired. "I'm sorry you're upset. But I'm done discussing this. What's right is right."

My jaw clenches and it takes all my strength not to yell at him. Tell him he's wrong. And heartless. And completely missing the point. But he's a Texas Ranger. And Rangers have an ingrained sense of duty to follow the law to the letter, no matter their personal preferences. It's a trait I used to admire.

My muscles tighten when I realize what I have to do.

"You're right, Cash. What's right is right," I say, jerking the memory stick out of the laptop and making a quick dash for the door. It takes Cash a moment to realize my intention, his footsteps echoing across the floor as he runs after me, calling my name. Begging me to stop.

But I don't listen as my feet fly over the sand and into the dark waves. I raise my arm high and, without hesitation, pitch the memory stick into the inky blackness to be silenced forever in a watery grave.

My lungs seize as I release the breath I've been holding, waiting for the other shoe to drop, preventing me from accomplishing my task. I turn slowly, my heart sinking as I see the look of agony on Cash's face. He falls to his knees in the wet sand, the waves washing over his legs as his mouth opens in silent torment. Then I'm by his side, wrapping my arms around him. Desperately wanting him to tell me it's okay. That he understands why I had to do it.

"Say something," I beg, holding him tighter.

But the silence is deafening as he pushes me away.

"Please," I say, a sob catching in my throat. "I know you will never forgive me, but part of you has to understand why I did it."

The moon cuts harsh shadows across his features as his head dips. "No, I don't understand. It's like ... it's like I don't even know you."

When he walks away, I wrap my arms around myself and turn to face the sea, the salt of the spray joining with my tears until I can't tell them apart. I want the darkness to lift. To go home and pretend like I never returned to this cursed place.

But the darkest hour is just before dawn, evidenced by the sight of the Rangers' boat pulling up to the dock. I square my shoulders with the knowledge I did the right thing. Surely when Cash has time to cool off and see the silver lining, he'll realize I'm right. The child on that boat paired with my testimony is the only evidence we really need to lock Jude away for a very long time.

Cash is quick to board the vessel, but I follow at a slower pace, praying his heart will soften enough to forgive me. As I enter the flybridge, Sarah slouched in the corner with her head in her hands paired with Cash's wild-eyed pacing makes me quiver with dread.

"What's wrong?" I say, wondering if I'm to blame for the mood in the room.

Cash stops to give me a piercing glare. "They didn't get the baby."

Thirty-Four

I press my back against the cold wall of the boat as we sway with the rise and dip of a sea turning rougher by the minute. Staring at a naked bit of floor beside my shoe, I wish I could sink into it. Vanish into the polished boards and pretend the past hours haven't happened.

But as I watch Cash continually pace the floor in front of me, firing questions at Parker and Sarah, it seems I won't get my wish.

"I don't understand how this could've happened," he bellows, scrubbing his hands over his face. "Hazel brought you the baby. You had him in your hands. We saw it."

Sarah rubs her bloodshot eyes. "It's all my fault. I should've been more careful."

Cash stops pacing. "What do you mean?"

Her head dips, lips trembling. "Before the ceremony, they gave us some kind of bitter drink. I didn't think too much about it at the time. Thought it was some kind of health food thing. But when Parker threw his up, I started to feel really weird. Like I was drunk. But I couldn't figure out why because we hadn't had any alcohol. And by the time they brought the baby out, I was a little gone. I ..." Her voice breaks and tears roll down her face. She slams her fist against the wall. "I'm just so mad at myself."

"It's not your fault, Sarah," Parker says, his face contorting with empathy. "It was a simple mistake. Could've happened to anybody."

"What happened, Sarah? What did you tell them?" Cash asks, his voice quieter as he searches her face for answers.

"I was just holding that little boy, saying how handsome and strong he was. How good it felt to hold a sweet boy in my arms again. And how much he made me wish our three grown boys were that little again. I didn't even realize what I'd said until Jude walked over and jerked the baby away. And when he started questioning us, I wasn't ready for it. Wasn't thinking straight enough to come up with a good cover."

The agony written on Sarah's face as she recounts the event is painful to watch. I want to go to her, tell her I understand how she feels and that no one is immune to the effects of kava. But given Cash's mood and my own transgressions, I don't feel up to the task.

"It's okay," Cash says, putting an arm around Sarah shoulders as she sobs. "We know you didn't mean to say it. You'd never purposely compromise an assignment."

As he says the last sentence, his eyes lock with mine, and I shiver at the judgement evident in the depths of green. No matter my reasons, to him, I'm a traitor. While Sarah made an unconscious mistake, I destroyed evidence on purpose. Evidence that could have saved the mission.

Sarah wipes her eyes with the back of her hand and stands up straight. "Thank you for saying that, Cash. I needed to hear it."

Parker scratches his chin. "You say there was nothing in Jude's office?"

Cash's head jerks around, and he clears his throat before answering. "It was clean."

"Just seems odd. You sure you checked everywhere? You know, we might be able to come back and—"

Cash stiffens. "I said it was clean."

When he spins on his heel and heads for the deck, Parker's eyes widen. "All right, man. I didn't mean anything by it." Parker looks at me. "Is he okay?"

"I'll go check on him," I say, jumping to my feet.

When I make it onto the deck, Cash is leaning over the railing with his head in his hands. "Go away," he says when I approach.

"No, I won't go away. I want to know why you told them that."

"Told them what?"

"That we didn't find anything in Jude's office. If you're so set on following all the rules, why didn't you just tell them the truth?" My fists clench at the injustice of it all.

He lifts his head, staring into the darkness. "Yeah, I try to follow the rules and I tell the truth. But I'd be careful what you wish for, Max. Because what you probably don't know is that destroying evidence isn't just wrong, it's a third-degree felony." He lets out a harsh laugh. "But, hey, if you want me to march right back in there and point the finger at you, I'll be happy to oblige. It's your call."

The threat of jail time feels like a kick in the stomach. But as I ponder his words, another feeling takes over and spreads like fire through my veins. I take a step closer and lower my voice. "I know you're trying to protect me and I appreciate it. But how am I any different than all those people listed on that memory stick? How is my crime any more justifiable than theirs?" I clench my fists, trembling with rage. "It's not. So, if you want to turn me in for what I did, get after it. I'm done trying to play a game that I'll never win."

His face is stoic as he stares straight ahead. "I'm not turning you in, Max."

I throw my hands up in the air. "Why the hell not?"

His nostrils flare. "Because it isn't fair to Aaron. I could never do that to him. Never."

I incline my head. "Wait. So, let me get this straight. You're saying you'd never compromise Aaron's future based on one mistake I made. Is that what I'm hearing?" I let out a mirthless laugh. "But you're more than willing to do the same damn thing to hundreds of other kids in the name of justice. But hey, that's okay because you don't know those kids. Love those kids." I shake my head, sickened. "You may be a Ranger, and you may be a good man. A caring man. But right now, you're nothing but a fucking hypocrite."

As we approach the marina at Jamaica Beach, my silent standoff with Cash smolders with things left unsaid. Neither of us are ready to make peace. It's all too fresh. Too raw. And no matter how I try to think about tonight's events, I come up feeling like a failure. I know I did the right thing, and I rest easy in the knowledge that my little sister and countless other children won't be ripped from the arms of their adoptive parents as a consequence of my vengeance. But my decision also cost us the mission. Jude is still out there, free as a bird. And there's nothing we can do about it.

In the close confines of the boat, the tension is palpable, the conversation sparse. Random splatters of rain on the roof break the remaining silence. But I can tell by Sarah's empty stare that she assumes Cash's sullen mood is all her fault.

I nudge her knee with my own. "It's not about you," I whisper, inclining my head in his direction. "We had a really bad argument. He's mad at me, not you."

Her jaw clenches, but she nods.

"There's nothing you could have done," I continue. "If anything, I'm to blame. I should've thought to warn you about the kava. I've seen it knock people on their asses plenty of times. I can't believe it didn't cross my mind to tell you."

She breathes a heavy sigh. "What's done is done. It just wasn't meant to be. Not today, anyhow. But there'll be other days. Other opportunities. That's the one thing this job has taught me. Hardly anyone gets away forever."

I glance back at Cash's sour expression and wish we could go a little faster. I'm ready to be off this boat and back home. Back where I feel safe and secure and loved. But part of me is scared. Scared the place I've learned to call home will never be the same. I desperately want to recapture the fleeting sweetness Cash and I had in our grasp, but I don't know how. What to say. What to do to make it right. Every time I look at him, my throat aches at the lack of forgiveness radiating from his soul, and I fall a little further into a place where there is no light.

———

By the time we pull into the driveway, the swaying porch lights are barely visible through the water pouring from the sky.

Inside, I kick off my wet sneakers and hurry to grab our overnight bags of blankets and supplies as Cash pours himself into a chair at the kitchen table. When he doesn't move, I glance at Sarah and Parker. "Shouldn't we be heading over to the lighthouse?" I grab our overnight bags of blankets and supplies. "I can start bringing things to the—"

But Cash cuts me off. "Why don't you let us worry about that, Max. You've helped enough for one night, don't you think?"

Sarah glances at Cash and gives me an apologetic smile. "I think you're right, Max. Here, I'll help," she says, taking one of the bags.

I glare at Cash, but he refuses to make eye contact.

"Forget it," I say, spinning on my heel.

By the time I make it to the bedroom, my body trembles with indignation and I grip the edge of Aaron's crib to steady myself. Cash may be angry, but that doesn't give him the right to talk over me as if I'm not there. As if I'm a dumb child who should be ignored while the grown-ups are speaking. Sure, he's mad our mission failed, but he forgets that without me, without my testimony and firsthand knowledge of Eden, he wouldn't have a case at all.

"You okay?" Sarah whispers from the doorway.

I try to take a steadying breath. "Yeah. Just mad."

"Love amplifies everything, doesn't it?" she says with a sad smile. "It has a way of making the good times feel like Heaven and bad times feel like absolute Hell. But I promise you two will get through whatever it is that's standing between you."

I bite my lip until it hurts. "And if we don't?"

She shrugs. "Then you cross that bridge when you get to it."

A loud knock at the front door grabs our attention, and we round the corner in time to see Cash swing the door wide. "You got a minute, Claiborne?" says the short silhouette of a man.

"Sure thing, Walter. Come on in," Cash says, waving the surly lighthouse keeper inside. "Everything okay?"

Walter juts his chin in the air. "Hell no, it ain't okay. There's a damn hurricane headed straight for us. Unless you plan to ride it out in this matchbox, I suggest you get your asses down to the lighthouse while I'm still feeling generous."

Sarah crosses her arms and smirks. "I believe that's exactly what Max was just suggesting," she says, looking Cash up and down.

A flush creeps across Cash's cheeks.

Walter lifts his chin. "Damn straight. The Claiborne Lighthouse has been standing since 1872 and it ain't give in to a hurricane yet. Not even the one in 1900."

When he scurries out the door, Sarah frowns. "I know that was a bad storm, but I don't remember exactly what happened."

Parker speaks up. "I've read it made landfall right here at Jamaica Beach and covered the whole island with about ten feet of water. Killed like eight thousand people. Is still considered the deadliest natural disaster in U.S. history."

Thirty-Five

As we travel the road to the lighthouse, I try to focus on something besides Cash's arrogant indifference. The drive is short, but my pulse echoes the frantic rhythm of the windshield wipers as they work to keep up with the sheets of water pouring from the sky. Through the bursts of clarity visible through the glass, our headlights flash over palms bending in the wind and waves rushing the shore. There was a time when I would have thrilled at such power, but those days vanished the moment I laid eyes on Aaron. For the first time in my life, I have something more important than myself to live for.

As lightning rips through the sky in frantic bursts, the talk around me becomes laced with nervous energy. The old me would have joined in, vocalizing my worry like the others, but the fire flowing through my veins smolders too hot for conversation.

I stare at the back of Cash's head and wonder what he's thinking. Feeling. Are his emotions in the same jumbled mess as mine? Or is he too focused on our failed mission to care? Part of me longs to return to the fold of his embrace where everything seemed so right. So predestined. But I refuse to make apologies just to gain his favor. In that regard, Maggie taught me all I needed to know about what not to do. What not to be. My love for her never blinded me to her faults. And I refuse to follow in her footsteps when it comes to my own romantic relationships. Or anything, come to think of it. If Cash wants to reconcile, then he will have to come to me. When this ordeal is over, I'll take the job Sloane offered and move out as soon as possible.

I sit up straight and square my shoulders. This is not the ending I wanted, but life doesn't always give you what you want. And if I'm going to be any kind of an example for Aaron, I have to start now, no matter how much it hurts. I want him to grow up knowing I am strong and smart and no one's doormat.

When our headlights flash over the familiar black and white stripes of the lighthouse, it's no surprise that Cash takes charge. "Let's get all the bags and blankets inside, then we'll come back for the other supplies."

We jump out of the truck, but as soon as our feet hit the ground, cold water fills our shoes, slowing the progress as we fight our way through the wall of wind and rain that seems to come from all directions. After what feels like forever, we cram into the gloomy tower, wet and exhausted from the effort. Through the dim glow of ancient-looking bulbs, frightened silhouettes line the circular stairwell ascending into the sky. Seated in pairs, people murmur and shift and stare at their phones, faces etched with dread as they prepare for the inevitable. I recognize Melinda from Johnson's Market, and she nods in silent greeting as we pass, our wet shoes squelching on the gritty iron steps as we follow Walter up to a spot a few feet below the main gallery.

Parker and Cash stay behind to recruit volunteers to help unload the water and other supplies from the truck. But only when the final crate has been brought in and the door secured against the turmoil of the wind do I relax, my shoulders slumping against the rough brick lining the inside of the curved wall. I attempt to take a deep breath, but the thick air is musty with the scent of damp bodies converging with a century's worth of mildew and the metallic sharpness of iron. But I'm grateful to be granted a place of refuge while so many others do without. The shelter of the lighthouse is a rare blessing and one I don't take for granted. I place my hand against the ancient brick and the solidness grounds me in a sense of calm. The Claiborne Lighthouse has stood the test of time. People may come and go, but it has endured as a beacon for seafarers and now a shelter of refuge.

I turn to Walter. "I'm so glad you thought of opening the lighthouse as a shelter."

Walter shakes his head. "Oh this isn't the first time it's been used during a hurricane."

"Really?"

"Why don't you tell us about it," Sarah offers. "We could all use a distraction."

Walter repositions himself on the step above us, stretching his legs in front of him. "Well, it was first built back in the eighteen hundreds. Sixty-five feet tall, solid iron and painted red. But then the civil war came along and it was destroyed. Most of the southern lighthouses were darkened to prevent union ships from using them as navigational aids, and this one was completely dismantled. Most people say the pieces were used as armor plating for ships or melted down to produce military armaments for the confederacy. But no one knows for sure. Then, after the war ended, a temporary wooden tower was put up out here until a new one could be constructed. The Lighthouse Board eventually decided on a pattern based on Louisiana's Pass a l'Outre lighthouse, which is about one hundred and seventeen feet tall. It took them a couple of years to finish building this new lighthouse painted with the same black and white bands that it has today. And of course that's when Owen Claiborne was brought over from Louisiana to light the lamp."

I shift onto my hip and lean forward. "So, he was the first official keeper?"

"That's right. Owen and his wife, Rose, raised three boys in a little house where my cottage is now."

"What happened to the house?"

"The hurricane of 1900 took it out. During that storm, the Claiborne family opened this lighthouse as a shelter and one hundred and twenty-five people were saved because of it."

I look at the people lining the stairs and feel thankful to be counted as one of them. "You know, the first time I saw this place as a kid, I remember Maggie telling me lighthouses are for saving people." I smile at the bittersweet memory. "I just never thought it would be me."

"What was your mother like?" Sarah surprises me with the question.

"Not much to say, I guess."

"I doubt that's true."

"You're right. There's plenty to say. Just none of it worth saying."

"So you didn't get along with your mom?"

"You know, I don't remember ever having a real argument with her," I say, my mind drifting back. "But there was so much I held inside. So much animosity for the decisions she made."

"Like bringing you to Eden?"

I nod. "The ironic part is, she truly believed moving there would give us a better life ... and who's to say it didn't? Even with all the shit that went on, at least Maggie wasn't getting beat up every day. And we had food to eat and a dependable place to sleep."

Sarah's brow furrows. "So, that's how Jude did it. He made it seem like she didn't have anything to lose, right?"

"He could talk anybody into anything. And our life was so shitty in New Orleans that when he came along promising something better, Maggie just fell for it, hook, line, and sinker. She thought it was a step up. Looking back, I don't see how she could have been so blind not to see that it was just the same old thing in a better-looking package."

She pats my knee. "Mothers will put up with a lot if they think they're doing it for their children. Just like Aaron. I'd be willing to bet that you'd do anything to make sure he's taken care of. Even if it hurts."

It's true. I would do absolutely anything for him. And that's exactly why I have to distance myself from Cash.

When he trudges up the stairs a few minutes later, soaked and panting, I swallow hard to keep from staring at the way his wet hair falls over his handsome face. I itch to go to him. To pretend like nothing ever happened and force him to do the same. But that's exactly what I shouldn't do. What I won't do. I want Cash to love me enough to bend. Love me enough to forgive and move on.

But as he chats with the others about what to expect from the storm, I find my throat closing as tears well in my eyes. In this moment, I've never felt so alone. So left out. I want to run away, but there's nowhere to go.

I jump to my feet and climb the few remaining steps to the main gallery where Walter stands on the far side, gazing out the window. With his kitten in his arms, he watches the sky as it fades from black to gray.

"Is it okay if I join you?" I say, hoping he won't mind the intrusion into his private quarters.

The gallery resembles a small home, complete with comfy-looking leather chairs situated around a tiny wood heater, a desk with a computer, and a small makeshift kitchenette with a coffee pot.

He turns and his eyebrows go up. "Sure. Sure. Come on in. I was just about to go down and tell everybody they can take turns coming up here to stretch their legs."

I glance out the window. "What'll happen when the storm makes landfall?" I ask, not sure I really want to know.

Walter scratches his chin. "Well, we might get some water

down at the bottom. The most that's ever come in from a surge was five feet, I think. But that was back before Galveston had a seawall to stop any of it."

As the rain intensifies on the roof, I shiver at the thought of being trapped in the lighthouse with five feet of water rushing in. After Walter scurries back down the stairs, I settle into a well-worn leather recliner and fight to keep my own eyes open. After being up for almost twenty hours straight, my body begs for rest as the splattering of rain against the windows lulls me into a place where dreams replace troubles.

Thirty-Six

The murmuring of voices penetrates the fog of my brain, and I open my eyes to see the gallery filled with people peering out the windows. A loud crack of bright lightning makes me grip the arms of the recliner to steady myself.

"What's happening?" I say, shaking my head in an attempt to clear the cobwebs.

Walter takes a sip from the mug in his hand and juts his chin toward the windows. "Go have a look for yourself. Getting pretty bad."

I walk to where Cash stands and wince at the sight of water filling the streets, pushing cars into buildings and ripping shingles off roofs. Streetlights cast enough light to see the air littered with flying debris as stop signs twist in the wind and billboards rip apart. When a transformer explodes before my eyes, my heart jumps into my throat.

"Maybe we should go downstairs," I say, fearful that the top of the lighthouse may snap off at any moment.

"Walter's keeping up with the wind speed. He'll tell us what we need to do when the time comes," Cash says without emotion.

The sound of someone sobbing makes me glance at the couple beside me. "Just look at my car," the woman moans, pointing to the roof of a black BMW that's sandwiched between two other vehicles.

The man puts his arms around her shoulders. "It's okay, honey. We have good insurance. Everything we own can be replaced. The important thing is that we're safe." She nods and dabs at her eyes, but doesn't seem convinced.

Melinda walks over and nudges me with her elbow. Holding a can of Natural Light in one hand and a cigarette in the other, she observes the scene with indifference. "You won't see me crying over my Nissan, that's for damn sure." She motions to a ragged-out truck with chipped yellow paint parked in front of Johnson's Grocery. "That one's worth more dead than alive," she says with a wry grin.

When Melinda strolls away, Sarah stares at the can of beer in her hand. "Damn, I could sure use one of those right about now," she says licking her lips. "I swear that lady is the only one of us who's thinking ahead. Nobody should have to die sober."

I laugh. "Come on, you know we'll be just fine."

She gives me a lopsided grin and holds up her hands. "You're probably right. Just can't shake the feeling that—"

"Oh my goodness!" I say, cutting her off as I squint at the

window. Down below a lone figure marches along the sidewalk, head held high, silver batons flashing.

"Wait!" Sarah calls as I rush down the stairs. But it's too late. I've made up my mind. I can't let the twirler man die without at least trying to help.

I'm almost to the door when Cash's strong grip catches my arm. "What're you doing?" he bellows.

"Let me go."

"Like hell I will."

I throw my hands in the air. "Come on, Cash. You know as well as I do that it's over between us. So, you can quit pretending to care."

His mouth gapes. "What on earth are you talking about? We had a fight ... but we didn't break up," he says with a pained expression. "That's what people do. They fight and then they make up."

I shake my head and pull away. "Well, I seemed to have missed the second half of what you just described."

Cash tries to take my hand. "Please, Max. I don't want to fight. Ever. It's just, what you did took me by surprise and whether it was right or wrong, it made me feel ... betrayed. I'd be lying if I said I'm not disappointed in how things turned out. But I am sorry about how I reacted. It wasn't fair. You made a call based on your own convictions, and I should have respected that. No matter what my feelings are about it."

A pain shoots through my chest at his admission, but I've seen this song and dance before. Too many times. Maggie was the queen of forgive and forget, taking them back as soon as they told her what she wanted to hear. I'm not her and never will be. And I'll be damned if I subject Aaron to that kind of atmosphere. I'd rather be alone. For the rest of my life, if that's what it takes.

"Say something," Cash says, his eyes intent on my face.

"There's nothing left to say."

Since I was a child, I was the one who had to think ahead. Be the adult in the room. I had no choice. If I wanted to survive, it was up to me and me alone. And for one brief moment I let myself slip. Let myself believe that with Cash, I was finally able to breathe. To give up my iron grip and know he had my back. To rest in the knowledge that we were a team with our own unique abilities and talents to bring to the table. And regardless of what the future held, we could revel in the knowledge that we had each other. That we weren't plowing through life alone.

Now I see past that illusion. The truth is, fairy tales are just that. A fairy tale. There's a reason they always end with a wedding. Because shit gets real after the honeymoon is over and people get hurt. Well, our honeymoon is over, and I can mope around and let it get me down, or I can do what I do best and overcome. I'm a fighter. And nothing is going to stand in my way.

I grip the door handle and fling it open before he can respond.

The wind swirls in like demons at play, the deafening roar like the tortured souls of old men dying in an agony that is so painful I feel the hurt to my marrow. Cash's screams are drowned by the velocity of the wind as it rips the door from it from its hinges.

Too stunned to react, I watch in horror as the gaping hole in the wall acts as a vacuum, pulling on everyone inside. I attempt to make it to the group huddled around the stairs, but I have to fight for every step. Every inch. Then, my feet are swept out from under me, and I'm gone in an instant. Lost in a swirling gray vortex that sucks all the air from my lungs as I'm hurled across the sky. Sharp debris claws at my body, tearing my clothes and cutting my flesh. But I don't feel the pain. Only the shock of knowing that I'm going to die. Just before everything goes dark, I picture Aaron's face. Then Cash's.

Thirty-Seven

I'm jolted awake by the beeping of monitors. Combined with the cool crispness of cotton sheets and the feel of something taped to my left arm, I assume I'm in a hospital, and the realization that I'm not dead is overwhelming. Not because of what I overcame, but because of what I didn't lose. I will get to see Aaron again. Hold him. Love him. Watch him grow up. But what if I wasn't the only one sucked out of the lighthouse?

Tears spring to my eyes as I try to open them. But it's not until I hear footsteps followed by Olivia's voice that I'm able to accomplish the feat.

"Max, can you hear me?" she says, her words laced with worry.

I swallow and try to say yes, but my mouth feels like cotton and my throat aches, making the word sound more like a groan.

"I'll call for the nurse," she says, fumbling with something on the side of the bed.

I try again, determined to be heard. "Where's Cash?" I croak, my voice barely above a whisper.

"He's fine. Just fine," she assures.

"And Aaron?"

"He's right here," she says, lifting him from his carrier. "Everyone's fine. You were the only one who got hurt."

A sob rips through me at the sight of my baby's precious face, and I close my eyes in relief.

"I was so worried you wouldn't wake up," Olivia says, leaning forward to take my hand. "They said it might take a while. But I never thought it would be this long."

"How long?"

"Four days. They just took you off the ventilator yesterday. You were in really bad shape," she says, helping me take a sip of water from a cup on the bedside tray.

The liquid soothes my throat, making the words come easier. "Tell me what happened. I remember the wind picking me up, but not much after that."

The events that followed are more like flashes than true memories. Snippets of time I can't decipher. Fighting for oxygen. Wind and water and debris. Darkness.

Olivia takes a seat at the foot of the bed and repositions Aaron on her lap. "Cash says they didn't know where you were for a long time. If you were dead. Nothing." Her eyes well with tears, but she takes a breath, blinking them back. "And everywhere they looked, it was just a nightmare. The whole island. Even Crystal Beach. There's like one beach house left down there. They said six thousand people got killed." She shakes her head. "You should see Pleasure Pier. It looks like something out of a carnival-themed horror movie. The Ferris wheel broke completely in half. It's amazing it didn't fall on you."

"What?" I say, not comprehending how my rescue could have had anything to do with the Ferris wheel.

Her brows knit together. "That's where he found you."

"He?"

"The twirler man. He found you in one of the gondolas dangling out over the water at the end of the pier."

"So he's okay?" I say, relieved.

Her head bobs up and down. "It was nothing short of a miracle. You were even on the news. I swear, you've got to be one of the luckiest people I've ever met."

I blink, trying to comprehend the events she describes. "So, if I've been in the hospital for four days, have you been here the whole time?"

"Not all of it. I've been taking turns with Cash."

"Oh ..."

"Were you expecting someone else?"

I take a breath and stare at my feet, not sure how to answer. "No. It's just, the day of the storm, we weren't exactly on the best terms."

"And?"

"Well, I guess I just didn't know what to expect as far as our relationship is concerned. The day of the storm, I'd decided to leave him and start fresh. Just me and Aaron, somewhere."

Her mouth falls open. "Please tell me you've changed your

mind. That guy would do anything for you. He's been worried sick. Can't you see how much he loves you?"

I press my lips together. "I love him too, but I also know that I don't want to raise Aaron in the kind of environment where the man rules the roost and it's his way or the highway. I refuse to turn into my mother."

Her mouth twitches. "I know you don't want to be like your mom. You want to make smarter decisions. I get it. But if you can't see the difference between Cash and the men your mom used to drag up, then you're not as smart as you think."

My chest tightens and I look away, convicted by the truth in her words.

"Besides," she says in an ominous tone. "There's something important he needs to tell you about. Something bad."

Before I can respond, a knock at the door makes my heart jump into my throat.

When Cash enters the room, he stops in his tracks and his eyes go wide. "You're awake." In two steps he's beside me, his arms folding me in a tight hug. "How do you feel? The doctors said your injuries have all healed, but they couldn't promise when you'd wake up. They said maybe never." His voice cracks. "They told me to prepare for the worst, but I couldn't ... I just couldn't." The tears welling in his eyes causes my own vision to blur as he takes my hand. "You and Aaron are the most important things in my life. Period. And I don't ever want to be without you. I know you might still be mad at me and that's okay. You can be mad for the rest of my life, if you want." He laughs, his green eyes shimmering. "All I ask is that you love me too."

"I'm sorry, I was just ... afraid."

"Of what?"

I twist my hands in my lap and try to think of how to explain. "I was scared of losing my independence. My whole life I've done what other people wanted. What they said. I didn't have a choice. But now I do. I have the chance to be my own person. Have my own life."

He frowns. "I want you to know that you can always say no to me. I may not agree, but that doesn't mean you have to give in. Give up your power. With me you'll always have a voice. No matter what. I want us to be a team."

"And there's no I in team," Olivia says, walking forward with a knowing smirk.

I reach for her hand. "Thank you for being here. For taking care of Aaron. For everything."

She smiles and squeezes my hand, but when she glances at Cash her expression grows solemn. "I think it's time to tell Max what else has happened."

Cash gives me a wary look. "Maybe now's not the best time. Maybe we should—"

"No," I say. "Whatever it is, I want to know."

His chin drops and he runs a hand through his hair. "I hate to be the one to tell you this, but we found out that Hazel's dead."

A pain shoots through my chest making it hard to breathe. "What did they do to her? I knew we should have forced her to come with us. I knew—"

Cash holds up a hand. "No, that's not it."

I bite my tongue to stop the flow of questions and force myself to listen.

"Jude didn't kill her," he says, his mouth turning down. "The storm did. Eden's gone."

"What do you mean?" I say, shaking with a burst of adrenaline.

"The hurricane brought a seventeen-foot storm surge with it. The seawall protected Galveston from some of it, but it hit Eden full force, demolishing all of their buildings and wiping everything away. A news chopper circling the island was the first one to notice it the day after the storm. Since then, the National Guard sent in rescue teams to search the area for survivors. But none were found."

Long before the first rays of dawn streak over the bedroom floor, I'm wide awake listening to the steady rhythm of Cash's soft snore. I glance toward Aaron's crib, but it's empty, as usual. Every night I place him there, but every morning he appears in our bed, cuddled up on Cash's chest. I've warned him about spoiling Aaron to such things, but he never listens. And part of me never expects him to. I delight in the little ways Cash shows his love, strengthening the bond they share.

I slip out of bed and pad through the dark house on soft feet, readying myself for the walk to the lighthouse. The air is fresh and energizing with the slight crispness of a southern fall. I sip from my mug of hot coffee and breathe in the hint of salt floating across the breeze from the shore. It's become a ritual to travel the path every morning before the fog burns away, while the dawn is still fresh and unsullied.

But this morning I make a detour for the cemetery, the familiar creak of the iron gate conjuring memories of my days spent living in the company of the dead. I smile now when I look at the mausoleum and marvel at how far I've come. It's been a long and winding road, full of obstacles, joy, and sorrow. I have mixed emotions about Eden's tragic fate. Part of me feels like the end was fitting, but there is no joy. Only a deep sadness at the lives lost and wasted and the innocents harmed in the process. I used to think Eden was my fight to win. That alone I could conquer the darkness that lives in some men's hearts. But now I know better.

I am neither hero nor failure. I am simply human, just as I was created to be. God has a way of taking care of things in his own time. His own way. Even situations that seem hopeless. Even Eden.

In the dim light, my eyes rove over the names and dates etched on the gravestones, pausing at the two newest monuments in the center of the yard. The first is dedicated to Maggie, the other to Hazel. And though I mourn their memory, I rest in the assurance that death is not the end. God knew each of their hearts, no matter their earthly failings, and this knowledge gives me strength.

With a prayer of thanksgiving, I leave the cemetery behind and continue on my journey to the lighthouse. To where it all began. Gone are the days of lost souls waiting at the base of the ancient tower, readying themselves for the trip over the waves in Lir's wooden boat. But the vision is forever etched in my memory. A reminder of where I've been and where I'm going.

When I left the hospital, I asked Cash to take me back to Eden. I needed to see it for myself. To come to terms with everything that had happened. But as we walked through what was left of the gardens, it took a moment to register the change. To acknowledge that it was the same place I once knew. Only the stone altar remained, tipped on its side and shoved up into the trees. Other than that, it was as if Eden had never existed. Had never caused so much pain.

Cash asked if I wanted to go farther. To see Hazel's house. But I couldn't. So, we walked along the beach, not talking until we came upon a familiar piece of driftwood buried deep in the sand near the tree line. In all the months leading up to that moment, I hadn't thought once about the secrets inside my driftwood diary. Hadn't considered the importance of the information written on the stones.

I sank to my knees before it, the wind gone from my lungs.

"What's wrong? Tell me," Cash demanded, searching my face.

But I was already shoveling sand out of the hollow, both desperate and terrified of what would come next. I never once regretted destroying that memory stick. But it was my choice, alone. And even though Cash said he came to terms with the way things played out, I still wondered if it was true. Would he do the same, if given the choice?

So, when my fingers brushed against the first stone, what I had to do was clear.

"Here," I said, placing it in his hand.

"Is this—"

"Yes." I pulled out more, dropping them on the sand. "Eight years' worth of information."

Cash fell to his knees beside me, his breath coming in shallow gasps. "I don't understand."

I stood up and put a hand on his shoulder. "I think you do."

Cash touched each stone gently, rolling them over in his calloused hands for so long, I almost couldn't bear it. Then he stood and dropped them, one by one, back into the log. With a deep sigh, he dusted the sand from his palms. "We're done here. Let's go home."

Now I cast my eyes over the horizon, the sun glowing red as it rises from the sea. The two become one, a seamless beacon of fiery crimson as red as the blood that once stained my memories. But just like the changing tide, revenge gives way to redemption. Bitterness to peace. Darkness to light.

Also by Kate Boudreaux

CLICK HERE TO BUY NOW

"Written with sensitivity and grace, this book will stick with you. I'm just sick that I wasn't born in East Texas."

— Sean Dietrich

bestselling author, columnist, and podcast host known as Sean of the South

Acknowledgments

What a blessing it is to make art for a living. I'd like to thank God for His favor, my family for their unwavering support, and my friends for being my biggest fans. I love you all so much.

About the Author

Author of *Backwater*, Kate Boudreaux is a native Texan who specializes in authentic Southern storytelling across genres. Her work has been optioned for film and praised by some of the South's most exciting voices. *Driftwood Diary* is her second novel.

www.ingramcontent.com/pod-product-compliance
Lightning Source LLC
Chambersburg PA
CBHW020458310726
48979CB00016B/2702/J